CW00428234

to Kaye

OUT OF
YOUR HEAD

By Rose McClelland

love Rose x

Table of Contents

CHAPTER ONE

Mia

I REMEMBER PRESSING the doorbell that day. One simple act that set off a chain of events, leading to people dying and criminal charges.

The rain was lashing. I had an umbrella up and I just wanted to get inside the bar. He opened the door. That's the first time I set eyes on Liam Fitzpatrick.

"I'm here for the interview." I must've sounded like *Baby* in *Dirty Dancing*. *I carried a watermelon*.

"Come in," he said, holding the door open. He let me squeeze past close to him. I closed the umbrella behind me and shook it on the floor.

"Can I leave this here?" I pointed to a spot on the ceramic tiles.

"Of course," he smiled. "Let me take your coat." He was looking at me in amusement, as though I was a little puppy coming in out of the cold.

"Thanks." I shrugged off the wet garment and handed it over. His footsteps clacked confidently on the tiles as he walked across the room and slung it over a wall hanger. He picked up a clipboard from the edge of the bar and squinted at a list.

"You must be Mia Matthews?" he looked up at me again.

"Yup, that's me," I chirped, running a hand through my hair to simulate some sort of composure. He continued to look me up and down, taking in my pencil skirt, tight-fitting blouse and high heeled shoes. *At least I hoped he did.*

"Great, I'm Liam," he smiled, holding out his hand. "I'm sure we're going to get along."

With those words, I already sensed the chemistry starting to fizz. I felt it that early in the game.

"Coffee?" he threw it out of the blue.

"Sure", I beamed coyly. This was the most relaxed start to an interview I'd ever had. It didn't feel like an interrogation of any kind. Looking back, it was more of a friendly chat.

"Grab a seat," he pointed to a bar stool.

I perched on top of the stool and watched his movements. He glided along the bar with all the ease of an experienced barista. He juggled cups and coffee pods under the frothing machine effortlessly while he kept the conversation going. I couldn't help but notice the same eyes gazing past my open blouse to my cleavage.

"So, you're looking for bar work at the moment?" It was almost a castaway remark but I liked the charismatic way in which he introduced the subject. He made me feel like he was truly interested.

"I am yeah," I panned around the premises knowing that I was probably taking in my new work surroundings. It seemed strange being in a bar at that time of the morning. It felt empty and echoey and unloved, as though it needed the atmosphere of drunk people and loud music to bring it to life.

"It's a nice bar," he said, as if reading my thoughts. "Great vibe, friendly staff, and we get a nice crowd. Office types come in after work, then the usual weekend crowd. We have a good team here; everyone mucks in and gets on."

"Sounds fab," I smiled.

"Any experience?" There was a hint of flirtation in the raised eyebrow as he slid a cup and saucer in my direction.

"Yeah," I felt a tiny bit flustered. The way the question implied sexual experience. Was that just my dirty mind? *Or wishful thinking?*

I cleared my throat. "Worked in *Bar Ten* for a year. Before it closed. Sadly."

He glanced up again. "Yeah, shame the management shut them down." He picked up my CV and eyeballed it for a moment. "Well, you obviously have plenty of experience. And the references look good as well. Can I get in touch with these people?" He stared over again enquiringly. *Why did I feel he wouldn't bother checking with anybody?*

"Of course," I replied, wondering why I felt so self-conscious around him. Was it the smouldering gaze or the way he was paying me so much attention? Or maybe it was just because I found him attractive?

"Great!" he took a sip of his coffee. "What were the staff like in *Bar Ten*?"

"We all got on really well. Worked hard but

had lots of fun too."

He smiled. I guessed I'd come out with the right answer. Something told me there'd be lots of laughs with this guy.

I guessed right. Liam was the most laid-back manager I ever knew. There were loads of nights when he would call for a nightcap after closing. And of course, we all took advantage. He'd pour our chosen drinks and we'd sit around chatting and letting off steam about things that happened on that particular shift.

Early on, I sussed that Liam had a significant other. In zero time I picked up mention of his daughter Emma not once, but on numerous occasions. The name *Zoe* dropped into the conversation now and then but I knew he wasn't truly happy. Call it a sixth sense or a psychic vibe but I zone in on people's moods very quickly. By the way he actually mouthed the word *Zoe*, I was sure he wasn't in love with her. Not in the sense I feared. She seemed to have morphed into a mother figure for him. Someone always there in the background. Reliable, dependable, secure. But was he really still *in love*? Something in my bones said *No*.

More to the point, was he starting to fall in love with me? *I hoped so.*

It got off the ground with a bit of light flirtation. When we bumped into each other behind the bar, he would playfully grab a tea-towel and swipe it in my direction. There were times when he sat down to do the rota each week; my name always magically appeared next to his. When we worked shifts together, we wove in and around each other with the skill and dexterity of professional dancers. We just fitted together. We gelled.

One of the other staff picked up on it. During a staff drinking session, Vicky nudged me and whispered: "Check you two flirting all night."

My eyes widened. "You think?" I played it cool. I tried to keep a delighted grin from spreading all over my face.

"Of course," she teased, rolling her eyes playfully. "It's so obvious. The chemistry between you is ridiculous."

We giggled and I looked over in Liam's direction. He had spotted the two of us laughing and gossiping. He peered at us with amusement.

"What's so funny you two?" he called over, a smile tugging at his lips.

"Nothing," Vicky announced. "Just girl talk."

"That's not fair," another bar staff member called out. "Spill!"

"Truth or dare," Liam winked at me mischievously. "Tell us what you're whispering about or we'll give you a dare." His eyes smouldered and I started to melt. My insides were somersaulting with excitement.

"Dare," my eyes teased as I replied defiantly.

"You have to snog the boss!" someone cheekily called out. Everyone cheered in unison. The drunken devil-may-care attitude was infectious. There was a mixture of mildly drunken tiredness and the joviality of a finished shift.

His eyes bored into mine, provoking me, daring me to do it.

"He won't mind," someone else chirped in.

"Okay then," I said, defiantly. The tequila shots Liam had dished out earlier were giving me a boost of confidence. I stood up and walked right over to him. There was a look of burning anticipation in his eyes.

I sat on his knee, leaned towards him and we kissed. Long, hard and with probing tongues. Cheers erupted around us but I didn't care. My lips creased into a coy smile. When I pulled away, he grinned at me like the cat who got the cream.

I returned to my seat next to Vicky. She was laughing. "Told ya," she exclaimed, digging her elbow into me.

But when I went into work for my next shift, he acted as though nothing had happened. A cold exterior had crashed down like shutters outside a shop. He was back to being Liam the manager. The boss. Asking me to clear up empty pint glasses and mop dirty floors.

I was confused. What was that kiss about? The start of something new? A blossoming relationship? Or just a silly drunken moment?

Liam's moods became a push-pull cycle that I couldn't fathom. During the day he was professional, distant, straight. But when the booze kicked in, he was charismatic, flirtatious, sexy.

Like the time I was there after everyone else had gone home. It was a Tuesday night. It had been a quiet shift that evening. Only a couple of staff stayed behind for the drinks. I went off to the *Ladies*. When I came back, everyone else had disappeared. It was just me and Liam.

"Jeez, was I that long peeing? Where is every-body?" I quizzed.

He was lifting the empties and carting them towards the glasswasher.

"Here, I'll give you a hand," I lifted a couple of tumblers and followed him. I threw him a flirtatious look. "Who is your hardest worker in here? And who is your favourite?"

He stopped and leaned against the bar. Then he gave me that look; the one that travelled to my lips.

"I suppose you're the most attractive employee on the premises." His lips moved into a smile and he moved closer to me.

"Most attractive?" I repeated teasingly. "I guess I'll take that." I leaned in towards him as his hands reached up and firmly pressed on my back. I edged in closer still. Suddenly our mouths were all over each other. It was as good as I remem-bered. His tongue was softly pushing my lips apart. I was breathless.

He took my hand and led me into the staff room. We crashed down onto the sofa and he pulled me over him. I sat astride his body, kissing with ferocity and passion. His hands reached for my top and pulled it off.

That was the first night we had sex. His hands started exploring every part of me. It was explo-sive, powerful, ecstatic. I was hooked.

"God!" I gasped. It was all over and we were lying next to each other on the sofa. He looked at me intensely and flicked a lock of hair away from my brow.

I closed my eyes momentarily and allowed a deep feeling of relaxation to engulf me. I could have easily fallen asleep in his arms right there. Drifted into a sea of relaxed unconsciousness. Then I would have woken up the next morning and allowed him to rustle up *eggs' benedict* or something posh like that. I would have grinned smugly when the other staff arrived for work. Sat there territorially. Showed them he was mine now.

But it didn't happen like that.

He stood up, zipped his jeans, and said, "I better lock up babe."

Just like that. A metaphorical slap in the face.

I better lock up and you better go.

So, this guy thought he could turn me on and off like a switch. He had no idea of the type of woman he was dealing with. *I knew that love was like a game but I always had to win.*

CHAPTER TWO

Kerry

"**S**ERIOUS ROAD TRAFFIC incident on the Ravenhill. Looks like two fatalities. One's a child. It's a possible hit and run." The call comes through from the Incident desk. "Uniform and paramedics are there now. They want a DS to secure the scene for forensics."

"Okay, got it. I'm on my way."

I pull my car up to the edge of a sea of blue flashing lights and assorted glinting vehicles. I'm directed to the main witness.

"Abigail Jones?" I ask. "Detective Sergeant Kerry Lawlor. Can you tell me what happened?"

"I heard the crash before I saw it. An awful squealing of tyres, then a massive thud. It was so loud." Abigail is trembling, her face a mixture of shock and panic.

"Go on Abigail." I say gently.

"I ran around the corner. I saw a car crashed against a wall. A red car driving off. I walked up to the wrecked car and had a look at the damage." She hesitates. "Oh God, I saw the little girl in the passenger seat; her eyes closed. She was covered in blood. Is she dead?"

"We don't know yet, Abigail," I say soothingly. "The paramedics are over there dealing with it." I point towards the scene. "What else did you see? Try to think clearly."

"There was a man behind the wheel, slumped over, unmoving. Blood was splattered up along his window. I dialled 999. The woman asked for the nearest house number. I ran over there." She points to one of the houses. "Four one eight I told her. The wall next to four one eight."

"Yes, I understand that was the way it happened. You said there was another car. Tell me about that."

"Yeah" she answers. "There was another car. It just drove off."

I look around again. Paramedics are struggling to disentangle the two victims from the clump of wreckage.

Abigail resumes. "I think the other car was in front or it drove out in front. Or maybe crashed into them. I didn't actually catch the moment."

"It was terrible for you." I say gently.

"Hello?" A concerned neighbour has just arrived. "What on earth?" The neighbour appear kind and looks hugely sympathetic. She places a hand on Abigail's back.

I walk back to the crash area. I tip-toe around the medics and look at the guy slumped over the wheel. Beside him, the little girl is saturated in her own blood.

I stand there, taking in the scene. It's too quiet. An eerie silence. I do not need the ambulance crew to tell me it would be better somehow if the casualties are actually squealing in pain.

More neighbours arrive. A small crowd gathers. Most are wearing dressing gowns and slippers. Concerned members of the public who want to help but also can't suppress a morbid curiosity.

"Please stand back," I interject. "This is a crime scene. We're in the process of setting up a cordon." I wave to one of the uniformed patrol officers. He dashes towards me. "It's getting a bit out of hand. Forensics are due any minute. Cordon the area. Cover the point on the road where the car first swerved. The guys in white overalls will want to look that over." I make my way back to the witness.

I arrive back to Abigail as the neighbour is offering her a cup of tea. "For the shock," she says, scurrying off inside her home to switch on the kettle.

Tea and sympathy? *The two in the car need a lot more than tea and sympathy.*

The good Samaritan returns quickly with a cup of tea and a chair for Abigail. "Here, sit down," she orders kindly.

I make a mental note that the only witness we have didn't actually see the impact or even the lead-up. Out of the corner of my eye, I see the two bodies being stretchered to the waiting ambulances. Doors bang shut. The screeching of sirens starts up and cuts through the silence. The flashing lights recede into the distance as they depart for the hospital.

An unmarked vehicle pulls over and the forensic guys jump out. I recognise Mike, a crash technician, who I have worked with on several cases. "Okay to go look-see?" he asks. The group around him start pulling on the white Soco suits.

"Of course. Sorry we disturbed the site before you got here. It's life and death for two victims. Medics had to move them to Intensive Care. Just get started and we'll catch up later."

I stand back momentarily to take stock. I watch them launch into action. Photographing, picking out debris and dusting off the car uphol-stery. A fine drizzle of rain starts to fall. It's time to phone my boss. I hit the station number and someone immediately picks up.

"Detective Chief Inspector Simon Peters, please. Tell him it's DS Lawlor calling."

"Oh, hi Kerry. Simon's on his way to the scene as we speak."

I call the uniformed officers into a circle and instruct: "Keep the scene secure. Ask around if anyone saw a red car and check if there's any CCTV in the vicinity. We're outside the city camera zone but who knows? There may be private equipment on one of these houses."

Abigail is still sitting in the chair, nursing her tea. A blanket has been placed around her. "That'll keep you warm, dear," the neighbour says. Such kindness. A cup of tea, a chair and a blanket. Such everyday things whereas twenty minutes earlier, someone had crashed a car leaving a little girl dead or dying. Another car fled the scene. Or at least, it seems that way.

"Excuse me," I go back to the witness and stoop down in front of her. "I'm sorry Abigail, I know it's awful but I have to ask you a few more questions."

She quivers. "Of course."

"Try to be clear in your mind about the other car. You thought it was red?"

She furrows her brow, trying desperately to remember.

"Yes, a red car I think." She hesitates. She is the one witness and perhaps she has no idea. "My husband Paul used to always joke with me about my knowledge of cars. *Poor Abigail. She hasn't a clue. She only describes a car by its colour. She doesn't notice the type.* He found it endearing."

I don't find it endearing right now.

"Don't worry," I assure her calmly. "It's hard to notice these things in the midst of the shock of an accident. Were there two impacts or one? From the noise you heard, I mean?"

"I don't know," she says, her bottom lip trembling. "I don't know!"

✧   ✧   ✧

"A POSSIBLE HIT and run and a red car, that's all we've got." I say to Simon when he turns up. "There's a lot of questions arising."

"Like what? Give me a rundown."

"It certainly looks like a hit and run. Possibly a red car fled the scene, but there's a few things don't add up. The tread marks where the car swerved don't look like an accident. Forensics said something about layers of rubber on the road. Could be the driver accelerated into the wall. That's just a possibility."

"You mean deliberately? A suicide? With his own kid in the car?" Simon looks extremely perplexed.

"It's just another thing we have to clear up. Also, I didn't notice any impact grazing on the side of the subject matter car."

"So, the red car didn't actually crash into the casualties? It just drove on. Our car swerved on purpose? What did our witness say on that issue?"

"That's the problem Simon." I frown. "She didn't see the point of impact. She only heard one crash. The car hitting the wall. There's no evidence of a prior impact but we can't rule it out."

"Anything else?" Simon probes.

"Yeah, forensics handed me a cell-phone that was lying on the driver's seat. What do you think?"

"We need time to run it through the computer centre. We might find he was using it at the moment of impact."

"Mike and the Soco boys uncovered a driving licence belonging to a Liam Fitzpatrick. I phoned base and they gave me details of the next of kin. It's a Zoe Waller. She's the mother of the child. And I guess he's the father."

He nods. "You got her address?"

"Yeah, Ormeau Road. I've got the number here."

"Jeez. They were nearly home then."

"Yep." I replied. This is gonna be a fun call to make at one in the morning."

Having to tell another woman that her loved ones are lying in hospital. *Maybe dead already.*

CHAPTER THREE

Zoe

IT'S AROUND ONE when the door-bell rings.

"About bloody time", I mumble, as I pull back my blanket and get up off the sofa.

I'd told Liam to make sure he brought Emma home straight away. The one night I ask him to look after her and he fucks it up. I had been pacing back and forth the last two hours wondering where they are and why they aren't home yet. Of course, Liam isn't answering his mobile. I rush to the door, ready to fling it open and give him a piece of my mind.

And that's when I see two Police officers. Plain clothes and showing their ID. Standing looking at me, their faces sombre. Before they open their mouths, I know something terrible has happened.

"Oh no! What is it? Where are they?" The words fall out of my mouth as my hand dashes to my face.

"Ms Waller?" the male officer asks. "I'm DCI Simon Peters and this is Detective Sergeant Lawlor."

"Call me Kerry. May we come inside to talk to you?"

I push the door back to give them space to enter. My knees feel weak. People often say about their knees feeling like jelly. Mine are about to collapse under me at any moment. "Come through," I hear myself say as I push the front door closed and walk into the lounge.

"Please, sit," I point to the sofa. I drop into the armchair facing them. I can't breathe. I'm looking at them expectantly, waiting for them to say those awful words. *They're dead Zoe. They've passed away.*

"There's been an accident," Detective Lawlor took over. She looks apprehensive and apologetic.

"A serious accident," DCI Peters intervenes. "Mr Fitzpatrick and your daughter Emma were in a car that swerved into a wall."

I close my eyes. The image is too vivid in my head. A car. Crashed into a wall? No…

"They've been taken to the Royal Victoria Hospital and we're getting constant updates on how they're doing," the female officer advises gently.

"Hospital? What?" My brain feels frazzled. Like someone has dragged it through a mangle. "They're alive?" I ask with trepidation, scared of the answer yet hopeful.

"They're alive," she soothes. "But they're both in a critical condition, in intensive care."

I feel bile rising in my throat. "I'm going to be sick!" I bawl as I get up and run to the bathroom.

"It's okay. Take your time." Kerry calls after me.

I hurl myself at the toilet bowl, the contents of my stomach ricocheting off the white porcelain. A violent rejection of this news. Not Emma, not my poor baby…

I return to the living room. Kerry hands a glass of water to me, her lips creasing gently into a sympathetic smile, her eyes softening. There's a silence as I sit down, sip the water and try to digest the news. The two officers sit quietly; they watch me with sympathy.

"Can I go see them now?" I ask.

"Of course," Kerry says. "We'll drive you there."

I nod frantically. Somehow my head goes into planning mode. I have to put on my shoes and find my coat. Where's my bag? How am I managing to think of these things when my brain is so severely scrambled? At last, I get myself together. Finally, we're leaving the house. I'm locking the door behind me. I'm following Kerry and Simon to the car. I'm numb. I sit in the back of the police car, watching houses whizz by, thinking about my baby.

Why did I let her out of my sight? Why did I let him look after her? Why did I bother going to that stupid hen party? Why didn't I just say no? It was a favour for my cousin Una. I wanted to weasel out, but she was having none of it.

"Come on Zoe," Una had said on the phone me that day. "It's not every day your cousin gets married. Please come! It'll be such a laugh. We're going on one of those bar-on-a-bike things. We'll be cycling around town having a drink and a sing-along. It'll be brilliant!"

It sounded like my idea of hell. Peddling through town on what would probably be a wet afternoon. Singing off-key. Passers-by looking down on us like we're lower than pond-life.

"Zoe, we all know you haven't been out for ages. When's the last time you hit the town?"

I stalled. I tried to find an answer to that one. She was right. It had been months.

"Ever since you and Liam broke up again, you haven't gone out."

That was true. Liam and I were breaking up and making up all the time. The recent split hit harder than the ones before. I had a feeling this was definitely the end. He wasn't gonna come running back this time. I just felt it in my bones.

"You know what you need to do?" Una chirped. Her voice was laced with mischief. "You need to get yourself dolled up, look like a million dollars and then ask Liam to babysit. He'll notice how fantastic you look. Of course, you'll be drop dead gorgeous! He'll see what he's missing and come back."

The idea slowly percolated through my mind. Perhaps she had a point.

When Una starts, she can't stop. She was on a roll. "Even better, you could pull some fella and bring him back for the night. Liam will see red. He's the sort of guy that won't be able to hack it. You getting into a new relationship. The thought that some other bloke would be Emma's new daddy? That would kill him!"

It was a rather conniving plan but my mood lifted. It did sound fun.

"Okay, you're on," I agreed reluctantly. A slow smile spread across my face.

"Brilliant!" Una gushed. Before she clicked off, she added quickly: "By the way I need a cash deposit for the bike and the dinner. It's also a tenner cover charge for the club. Cheers, bye!"

The phone went dead just as I was starting to tot up how much this would set me back. A new outfit and a hair-do. Not to mention a present for Una. My earlier excitement about the cunning plan was now a source of financial pressure. Emma needed new shoes for next term and her satchel already had a tear in it. I would have to beg the bank for an increased overdraft. Again.

Picking up the phone, I had dialled Liam's number. Surprise, surprise. It went straight to voicemail. He never answers. But he somehow got round to phoning back half an hour later. That's lightning fast for him.

"You were looking for me?" he said hurriedly.

I remember when his voice sounded different. He used to have a caring, loving tone. This time he sounded like he was talking to an irritating child rather than a life partner. Okay, ex-partner. He seemed distracted. Like he had something on his mind or was with someone.

"How are you?" I spoke softly, trying to garner his full attention. The comfort of some humdrum niceties.

"Bit busy at work. Nipped outside to return your call. Is Emma okay?"

That would be his only reason for getting back to me. To check on the status of our daughter. What about me? After all, I'm only the child's mother.

"She's fine," I replied, trying to hide disappointment in my voice. "In fact, I was just wondering if you could babysit next Saturday? I'm going out for the day."

"Sure," was the response. "Where you off to?"

At last, a modicum of interest in what I was doing. "Una's hen-do. It's an all-day thing."

I actually wanted to tell him: *there'll be drinks, dancing and cocktails. Plenty of talent eye-balling me!* But I didn't want to. That would be going too far. I was, after all, looking for a favour.

"That nutcase Una!" he butted in. "She'll be dancing on the tables by lunchtime."

I gave a gentle laugh. It was a warm moment. A tiny slice of togetherness. Like we used to have. An in-joke. We both knew Una – her bubbly personality. There'd been so many laughs in town with her in the past.

"Yeah, I guess she will. Maybe even before lunch!" I laughed.

"Sure. I'll look after Emma that day," he said. "No problem".

"Cheers. And Liam…" I began.

"Yeah?"

"You'll be careful with her, won't you? Just the flicks and *McDonalds* or something. No beer gardens or…"

"Zoe," he seemed to be spelling it out. "I'm clean. I haven't touched a drink or any bad stuff in weeks. Been doing the meetings. I'm a responsible adult, you know!"

His words were somehow laced with menace. Maybe he was offended. Like I was talking down to him. Treating him like a child.

"That's great, well done on your clean time. Keep it up."

He must have felt like I was patronising him because his reply was sharp and terse: "Yeah, well, I'm just taking it a day at a time."

"Sure," I darted back quickly. "Well thanks, see you Saturday?"

"Yep, will do." The mood reverted to that clipped, matey vibe. "See ya." Click. The phone went dead.

What if you hadn't asked him? Why didn't you realise that he wasn't capable? You knew he was only a few weeks clean. He could relapse at any time. Stupid.

✧   ✧   ✧

"WAS HE SPEEDING?" I ask, out of the blue, as my thoughts whir around constantly. "Liam, was he speeding?"

The female officer turns to face me. "We don't know Ms Waller. Truthfully." Her face is sombre and sympathetic. "We think it might have been a hit and run but we're going to check it out."

"Hit and run?" I repeat, my voice sounding hollow. "Hit and run? Well, did you make the arrest?"

"Hit and run is a spontaneous event, Ms Waller. We're checking out the identity of the driver," Kerry replies.

"But he lives near the Duck and Goose," I blurt out.

"Sorry? So, do you think you know who might have done this?" Kerry asks, her interest piques all of a sudden.

"Oh no, I didn't mean anything, just ignore me," I realise I've over-stepped the mark. Maybe said something I shouldn't have.

"Are you absolutely sure there's nothing you want to tell us?" Kerry persists.

"Yes, I'm not thinking straight." I reply, flustered.

"A passer-by noticed another car drive off so we'll be investigating that," she adds.

Guilt immediately drowns me. There was I, blaming Liam for speeding; for his inability to look after Emma, when really, was it even his fault? Someone just smashed into him and drove on? What bastard would do that? What asshole could bash into my defenceless child and just carry on with his day as though nothing happened?

I could feel the anger boil up inside me like a simmering cauldron.

"And who was this fuckwit?" I say, thinking aloud more than anything else, for I know they won't have had time to find out yet.

"We've already told you Ms Waller. We don't know but we will certainly be looking into it as soon as possible."

"And when he's caught?" I ask.

She looks over at me. "When the driver is caught, well, that will be up to the judge to decide what punishment to impose."

Christ! Not unless I see him first and kill him with my own bare hands.

CHAPTER FOUR

Zoe

THAT FAMILIAR STERILE odour greets us the minute we walk through the hospital doors. The detectives lead me up towards the Intensive Care Unit. I look a sorry sight; pyjamas, shoes, overcoat, no make-up and hair a mess. And if that's not bad enough, I'm flanked by two cops but that's the least of my worries. It's a horrible, surreal feeling. Am I really walking along hospital corridors to see my own little girl in ICU? I'm here but how can I be? How can this be happening?

At the ward there's a sign on the door. Something about restricted entry. Detective Lawlor asks me to sit on one of those rigid plastic chairs while she organises access. She has a muffled conversation with one of the nurses. "Yes... aware of visiting rules..." I hear snippets of the dialogue. "But there was an accident... just tonight... wondered if she could see them..."

And we're in. Through the swing doors where an eerie stillness greets us. A silence except for the beep-beep-beep of machines. Rows and rows of beds, a nurse sitting at the end of each bed.

And then I see them lying there. Liam and Emma. Next to each other. I hear an animalistic sound. A crying, wailing, guttural howl. And then

I realise it's me. A nurse is putting an arm around me. I'm being comforted. Actually, I don't know whether she's trying to reassure me or quieten me down so I don't upset the patients. Probably both.

I stare at Liam and Emma lying there. They're engulfed in a tangle of tubes and wires. They're stiff, still and worryingly lifeless.

"It looks like they're asleep," I observe.

"Yes, they are," the nurse soothes. "They're both in medically induced comas. They're only sleeping."

They're not dead, I tell myself. *They're not dead.* I'm clinging on to the last bit of hope I have left. I hold Emma's hand, careful not to touch any of the attached tubes.

"Oh baby," I say, tears well up in the corners of my eyes and spill down my face. "I love you. I love you so much." I'm hoping she can hear me, but she looks rigid. Perhaps her soul can hear me crying out to her. "Hang on Emma, hang on."

The nurse and the detectives are watching me with pity. I feel drained. I turn to Liam and gently pick up his hand. There was me, thinking it was his fault and all along it could have been a hit and run. A deliberate act by somebody else. "Come on babe," I whisper. "Don't give up on me. You can fight this." I kiss him gently on the forehead.

The nurse comes over. "You should go home and get some rest Ms Waller. They're both seriously ill with concussion and loss of blood. We can't give you a prognosis for either at the moment. We'll know more tomorrow. We're doing tests. We'll call you first thing in the morning."

Her eyes are sympathetic and soothing. I shake my head. "No, no, I don't want to go home. I want to stay here with them. I have to be sure they're okay." What I really want to do is crawl into bed beside Emma, curl around her and snuggle up for the night.

The nurse shakes her head slowly. "I'm sorry Ms Waller but we can't allow relatives to stay, I'm afraid. I hope you understand that in order to give the best treatment, we have to restrict visiting time."

Kerry starts to gently guide me away from the bedside; her hand grips my elbow softly, ushering me towards the door. "It's best if we take you home," she advises calmly. "You can come back tomorrow. You need to get some sleep."

On the way home, the rain lashes against the window and the sound of windscreen wipers thrum in my ears. Kerry's question comes out of blue.

"Zoe, I know this doesn't seem the right time but how was Liam's mental state during the last few weeks?"

I look at her quizzically. "Mental state? What do you mean?"

"This sounds crazy, Zoe, but it's a box we have to tick. There's a possibility, probably unlikely mind you, that he deliberately drove into the wall. Was he depressed? Have there been any episodes in the past where suicide might have been considered?"

My mouth drops open in shock. "No, no, not

with Emma in the car! That can't be the way it was! Just can't be! That other bastard must be involved." I quip back and suddenly wish I hadn't.

There's a pause in the conversation. The whine of the wipers see-sawing is the only sound in the car as we sit in contemplative silence. After a beat, Kerry turns to me again. She won't let the matter drop.

"You seem to have an idea that somebody might have arranged this accident deliberately. I get the impression you have a particular person in mind."

I hesitate at first, then say. "Look, it's just that sometimes Liam gets involved with the wrong crowd. Customers in the pub. It's a hazard of the job. You get bad types hanging around."

As if I haven't enough to worry about, she keeps interrogating me. She won't let it go. And I don't want to get anybody into trouble.

"So, can't you give me a name? Your mind obviously zoned in on someone when we first mentioned it." She's turned around to eyeball me from the front seat.

"No, sorry, I don't know." I close my eyes, hoping that she'll get the message.

"Sorry," Kerry relents. "Let's get you home and into bed. You need your sleep."

Sleep. Sleep does not come.

I kick off my shoes and drop my bag on the floor. Slumping down onto the sofa, I pull a blanket over me. I lie there, staring into thin air. I can't stop thinking. I think about that bastard in the other car, about how he just swerved away

and drove off. I can picture him. And then I can
see the car smashed into the wall; Liam slumped
over the wheel. Oh god, and Emma! I can see it
and I don't want to see it. I can't face the thought
of them suffering. The pain they must be in. It's
just too much for me.

Shock. I'd heard about how it affects people.
It's like a mental buffer. It blocks things out.
Shock convinces me that they're just sleeping.
Everything will be okay. They'll wake up and
come home. Life will go back to the way it was.

And I'll never let Emma out of my sight again.

THE DOORBELL RINGS early in the morning. I must
have given in to sleep at some stage, even though I
feel like I'd been tossing and turning all night.

I stir groggily and push the blanket back slowly. Memories of the night before come flooding in
and jolt me awake. Liam and Emma. In ICU. The
accident.

The doorbell rings again. Persistent. Perhaps
it's the police. Here to tell me that Liam and
Emma have woken up. That everything is okay.
Wishful thinking but I have to cling on to hope.
It's all I have. I pull the door open to see a fresh
faced, smiling young woman standing on the
doorstep.

"Hello Ms Waller. I'm Orla Parker a reporter
from the Post. I'm so sorry to hear about the
terrible accident. We think it's an awful tragedy
but we'd like to do a piece on the events last

night…"

I am about to shut the door in her face. I have a strong urge to tell her to piss off and respect my privacy but just at that moment, she comes out with the magic words.

"We want to help you find out who was driving that other car. Who had the cheek to hit and run? Somebody must know. We can run a campaign. People can phone in if they've noticed anything."

She stands there, smiling, knowing that she has handed me the golden ticket. She already realises I won't refuse this offer of help.

Orla adds. "All sorts of things come out of the woodwork after an incident like this. Someone is bound to notice a damaged car that fits the bill."

"You'd best come in then," I push the door wide and allow her to step through.

"Thank you very much," she smiles courteously. She follows me into the living-room.

I slump back down onto the sofa. She notices the crumpled blanket and the general mess. She appraises the scene and gives me a sympathetic look.

"Oh Zoe, you're obviously wrecked you poor thing. Why don't you let me make you a cup of coffee? You sit there – you've been through enough."

I sink into the sofa and allow her to take over. In fact, in a way, it's quite comforting. Someone to take charge. Take control of this situation. I'm so exhausted I don't even care that a complete stranger is rifling through my cupboards. I let her get on with it.

In the middle of all this, I suddenly remember I need to phone my mum. I have to let her know what's happening. And Liam's mother too. I wanted to phone them last night but I knew they'd have been in bed long before. I didn't want to wake them at that time of night. They'd be annoyed if they weren't the first to hear the news. I make a mental note to get on the phone the minute the reporter leaves.

"I found some biscuits as well," Orla says when she returns. "You'll be needing to get your strength up. I bet you haven't eaten anything yet."

She's right. I haven't.

There is something oddly comforting about this young reporter, barging her way into my home and making coffee and biscuits. I'm numb, almost paralysed. Whereas she swans in enthusiastically and organises me, at least for a short while.

"We're going to find that driver," she promises. "By hook or by crook, we'll hunt him down. We'll make him pay."

That bastard will finally get what's coming to him.

CHAPTER FIVE

Zoe

THE SLOW BEEP-BEEP-BEEP of the machines is the
only sound in the ward. It would feel strangely soothing if I didn't feel so sick. I sit on the
plastic chair next to Emma, my hand gently
touching hers.

Please wake up, I urge her. "Please wake up,"
I whisper the words hoping somehow, she can
hear me. I pray my words are seeping into her
subconscious mind. My mother looks over, her
smile sympathetic. She's sitting on the other side
of the bed, apprehensive and despairing.

The numbness is still with me; a refusal to
believe that this is actually happening. I'm in
denial of the fact that we are sitting here in an
intensive care unit, clinging on for dear life. We
are only allowed two visitors per bed. My mother
and I at Emma's side; Liam's mother sitting at his
bedside.

Even though there are twenty beds in the ward
with two visitors each and a nurse at every
station, there's still an eerie silence. The continu-
ous beeps of the surrounding machinery are the
only sounds amidst the respectfully hushed
atmosphere.

I can't stop thinking about how that other

driver just drove on. Left Liam to swerve into a wall, his head smashing against the steering wheel. My mind keeps going back to that bastard Big Al. I wonder, was it him? He could have been driving that other car. Liam mentioned him on several occasions. There was the night he attacked Liam outside the pub with a couple of other scumbags.

It's one thing trying to get back at Liam, it's another to hurt an innocent young child. Of course, a piece of shit like Al wouldn't think twice about anybody else's life being in danger.

I see Emma lying in the hospital immersed in tubes. If it was Big Al that did it, shouldn't it be his life at risk?

I can't stop thinking about what the detective Kerry said – about Liam deliberately driving into the wall. She doesn't know about Liam's history. And I didn't say anything. I just can't accept that he would do that to me and Emma? How could he purposely do something as crazy as that with our daughter on board?

I wish I could turn back time. To when things were good. When Liam and I first met, he would do anything for me. He chased me with abandon.

I distinctly remember the first time we met. It was our fresher's night at University.

I was glad to get away from home. To escape the crushing claustrophobia of my childhood. Having to tip-toe around my father and his moods. Always walking on eggshells. My mother was so timid and subservient around him, constantly obeying his orders. She used alcohol to cope, hiding a bottle of vodka under the mattress in my room. Sneaking into the bedroom with her half glass of cola and topping it up with the hidden booze.

That first night at Uni, I sat in the student union with my new flatmates, cross-legged on the floor, sipping cold beer from a bottle. A happy fizzy feeling tickled my throat and lit up my insides. I felt like I had arrived. This was where I was meant to be. Free, independent and surrounded by cool, like-minded people.

I quickly acquired a circle of friends. Chloe and Yvette were the confident ones. I had the lucky fortune of ending up in a house-share with these two girls. People gravitated towards them for their charismatic and trendy vibe. Yvette always wore short skirts and huge hats. Chloe sauntered around campus, a long red coat billowing behind her. We all studied drama, but I wasn't a stereotypical drama student. I wasn't loud, confident or gregarious. I was introverted but able to click into character when I needed to. Happy to be the listener in the group; the quiet one.

People flocked around Chloe and Yvette. There was Yvette's boyfriend, Danny and a bunch of his flatmates. And then there was Liam, a friend of Danny's. He was also on my acting course. Everyone thought we were all a big clique. I suppose that's how it seemed. But they were mainly attracted to Chloe and Yvette. They became my friends by proxy.

Liam bumped into me one day as I was coming out of the lift after class. We literally collided.

Almost ran me down. He tried to charge into the lift too quickly and I was dashing out, rushing to my next tutorial.

"Oops! Sorry!" he smiled, with a warm and cheeky grin.

"No worries," I said, ready to dash on.

"Hey!" he said, not bothering to take the lift after all. Instead, he took time out to talk to me. "Aren't you … don't you live with Danny's girlfriend?" he asked, his face wrinkling with recognition.

"Er, yeah…" I said, distracted. I was running late but trying to be polite.

"Cool" he nodded. "They're a good bunch, Danny and co."

"Yeah," I agreed, not sure what else to say. I was so shy back then. The years of strict parenting and being the quiet one at school, meant I wasn't prepared for Uni life. At least not until I had a few drinks. When I hung out with Chloe and Yvette, I could bounce off their confident banter. On a night out with them, I felt great. But in the cold light of day, I was self-conscious and overly aware.

"We should go out for a drink some time." Liam said. "Get to know each other."

I looked at him; his cheeky smile, his confident air. He wasn't my usual type. Dark red hair and beard, and quite tall with a reasonably slim build. I couldn't be sure if he meant 'drink' as in 'a date' or 'drink' as in hanging out with all the gang. I saw myself as the girl next door type. I thought he would have fallen for the likes of Chloe or Yvette.

"Erm, sure," I stammered. "I think we're all going down to the Union on Saturday night. I'm sure we'll see you lot there." I was instinctively vague and stand-offish. I knew that, but I was shy. Guys didn't normally ask me out. I didn't have any cool responses or clever chat-up lines.

He gave a gentle laugh. "I meant a drink, just you and me," he said.

I had to admire his audacity. He was confident, I gave him that. Not one bit phased by my shyness. "C'mon," he teased. "What about tonight? Eight o'clock? I'll come round and pick you up." And with that he jumped into the lift, not even taking no for an answer.

"See you then", he chirped, with a twinkle in his eye. The lift doors closed behind him.

I stood there open mouthed, gawping like a goldfish. Had I just agreed to a date with Liam? Yes, I definitely had. I thought of nothing else as I walked along to my next class. An uncontrollable smile spread across my face. I couldn't wait to tell Chloe and Yvette! They'd find it hilarious!

And they did. They roared with laughter when I told them. "Oh my god!" Chloe exclaimed. "I can't believe you're going on a date with Liam!"

"Wait till I tell Danny!" Yvette squealed in excitement. She already had her fingers on the keypad, dialling his number.

"Oh no..." I cringed. "Don't be telling Danny..."

It was too late. Word had already reached the boys' house around the corner. The guys already knew because Liam had been on to Danny double-checking my address.

"We'll all be sitting a few tables away in the pub, to watch how you two get on," Yvette and Chloe teased. It all seemed so funny then. Of course, looking back, we were only eighteen. We thought we were so mature and worldly-wise. Yet there we were, getting all giggly and ridiculous over a simple date.

Part of me found it entertaining too. I enjoyed being the centre of attention for once. I got off on knowing that the guys found this so fascinating. And I enjoyed the fact that I had been chosen. Liam hadn't picked Chloe or any of the other girls on campus. He had pounced on me. Why?

He turned up at eight as promised. I could smell his aftershave the minute I opened the door. Nice. He'd made an effort. We walked to the pub while he chatted effortlessly, leading the conversation. In the pub, the patter continued. I remember thinking he was actually very interesting and I enjoyed his stories. It dawned on me that we were a good match. He did the talking and I listened.

The other guys sat a few tables away. They kept an eye on us. I found it funny, that they would even bother to come along. Later, after a few pints, we all ended up together. The whole bunch invaded our table and we headed on to the Students Union. A night of drinking and dancing. All of us together.

It was the first time I felt I really belonged. I was actually part of something. I had found my tribe.

On the one hand I was flattered that Liam had

selected me over the others, but another part of me was taken aback. I wasn't like the other girls. Worldly-wise and fancy-free. I was still a virgin at eighteen. Most girls had taken the plunge at fifteen or sixteen. I kept the big V of my virginity a secret. It was uncool, untrendy. I couldn't hang around with the 'in' crowd and be a virgin at the same time.

So, I had sex with Liam. He was the one. Although he had no idea it was my first time.

There was blood on the sheets afterwards. He didn't mention it. He quietly scrunched up the linen and took it to the launderette, not mentioning to any of the boys. I'll give him that. He was discreet.

The sex had been painful and uncomfortable. I wondered what all the fuss was about.

"It will get better, I promise," he whispered afterwards.

Eventually, it did get better, until one night I felt a billowing wave pouring through me. A feeling I had never experienced before. Like my whole body was closing in on itself, releasing every single bit of tension. A sense that I had arrived. He had given me my first big Oh; a crashing orgasm. He looked at me, his face full of joy and pride. I had come.

And after that, I was hooked.
Addicted.

CHAPTER SIX

Kerry

"**W**OW, SERIOUSLY NEED coffee," I say as we get into Simon's car and put on our seat belts.

"Me too," Simon agrees. "I'm exhausted."

Last night was a late one. By the time we drove Zoe home and landed at McDonalds, it was past two in the morning. And now we're on a day shift again, heading back to the scene of the crime. Simon wants to visit the neighbours to see if anyone saw the other car and, even better, if one of the houses has CCTV.

"My turn," I announce. I notice Simon casting a quizzical glance at me so I elaborate. "I'll get the coffee. You bought it last night."

"Oh yeah, nice one. I'll have a grande then," he jokes.

"You must be knackered."

"I am," he says, putting on his sunglasses to shade the unusual early morning sunlight. "Something odd happened last night when I got in."

"Oh yeah?" my interest piques. It's not like Simon to spill out his personal life but when he does, I'm all ears.

"Yeah," he says, flicking the indicator switch

and turning left towards the embankment. "Laura was fast asleep when I got in – nothing strange there. Kids out for the count too. Which was good. But I noticed she had fallen asleep with her phone in her hand and her glasses on."

"Hmm…" I murmur, giving him an indication that I was listening intently.

"So, I go over to remove her glasses gently and set them on the bedside table, trying not to wake her. And I take her phone out of her hand and go to put it on the table too. But then I notice…" He pauses, flicking the indicator again and turning the car into Ravenhill Road.

"Hmm…" I encourage eagerly, dying to hear what's coming next.

"Well, I noticed on the screen there was an envelope icon and I saw the beginning of a message but I couldn't unlock her phone to see the rest…"

"Yeah? And what does it say?"

"Goodnight sweet…."

"Goodnight sweetheart?" I finish, my jaw dropping in disbelief.

"I presume so," he confirms, his face looking hard and annoyed.

"Oh my god," I say, a shocked silence fills the car for a few seconds.

"I know," he eventually mumbles.

"Well, did you confront her about it this morning?"

"Of course not. She'd only deny it if anything was happening."

"So, what are you going to do? Track her

phone?"

"Dunno," Simon grimaces. "I did consider that, I'll be honest."

I let out a low whistle. "Wow, she's mad to mess with a top detective."

"Humph!" Simon exclaims. "Maybe that's all part of the thrill."

We arrive at our destination and park up along the roadside. There are rows of houses all around.

"Okay," he says, changing the subject with his unfailing professionalism, as always. "Let's see if we can get any info out of these neighbours."

"Let's hope so," I unclick my seatbelt and get out of the car. I can't help but admire Simon's ability to switch effortlessly between personal and work life. If that was me, and I suspected my partner of infidelity, I'd probably be a heap of distraction and unable to do my job. Then again, I consider, I've been single for so bloody long, I have no idea what I'd be like in a relationship.

We approach the first doorway and tap loudly on a green door. After what seems like an eternity, we hear footsteps coming down the hallway and a voice shouts "Coming!"

An elderly lady answers the door, smiling but curious. "Yes?" she asks. "May I help you?"

"Good morning ma'am," Simon begins. He holds up his ID badge as he introduces himself. "I'm Detective Chief Inspector Simon Peters".

"And I'm Detective Kerry Lawlor", I say, waving my own badge.

"Goodness me! What's wrong?" the old lady

remarks.

"Nothing to worry about," Simon interjects quickly. "We're just doing some routine checks on the car accident last night. We're wondering if you saw anything?"

"Oh, do come in," she says, holding open the door and waving us through. "Come in, come in, I'll put on the kettle."

Reluctantly we go through. If we had our way, we'd spend five minutes on each door step, ascertain a quick yes or no, and move on. But sometimes, that's just bad etiquette. The elderly lady, who we learn is called Mrs Wright, ushers us to sit at the dining table in the kitchen while she fusses about with a kettle and three cups.

"Terrible tragedy last night," she says. "Truly terrible. I did look out and see the commotion. I didn't go out because I was in my dressing gown, but I was on the phone to Mr Taylor this morning. He filled me in on everything. He lives across the street. He saw the car drive off."

My ears prick up as the old lady finally pours the milk into the cups.

"Is that right?" I ask. "And what number does he live at?"

"Oh, he's just across the way dear," she mumbles the number.

"Right," I say, "We'll visit him next then," I indicate to Simon. He nods.

"Oh, but you'll have your tea first dear," the elderly lady insists, and we feel obliged to sit and listen to her stories. We hear all about her beloved husband who passed away two years ago. About her two daughters who take it in turns to visit every day. And Mr Taylor, the neighbour across the street. What a great help he is and the jobs he does around the house. The poor lady is obviously bored out of her mind. When the doorbell rings announcing the arrival of one of her daughters, we hastily beat a retreat.

"Thanks, so much Mrs Wright, have a nice day," Simon calls back as we head off.

"You too dear, keep me posted on what's happening."

We march straight across the road. I notice the blinds are already twitching and there's a man peering out at us. We approach the door, ring the bell and make the same introductions as before.

"Yes, yes, come in, come in," the man booms as he holds open the door and beckons us through. "Mary!" he calls, presumably to his wife. "It's the Police. About the accident."

An elderly lady hurries out into the hallway where she spots us and nods. "Oh certainly, I'll put the kettle on."

She scurries off while Taylor leads us into his living-room. It is immaculate; everything in its place. His wife is obviously a busy woman who spends a lot of time cleaning and house-keeping.

"Have a seat, have a seat," the elderly man urges with a confident air. "You'll be wanting to know if we saw anything last night?"

"Well yes," I note his determination to lead the conversation.

"Indeed, I did!" he proffers confidently. "I looked out the window and saw the car drive off.

And then I heard a loud bang." He sits forward in his armchair, obviously full of adrenalin and excitement.

"And what time was that, sir?" Simon asks.

"Well, it was around eleven last night, of course," Mr Taylor replies.

I interject: "Did you notice what type of car it was, Mr Taylor?"

"It was red – a sports car. Fancy looking. Sleek. And it just buzzed off so quickly. I had no time to see the registration number."

"No, that's understandable," I assure him. "It was dark after all. But you think it was a red sports car?"

"That's right," he confirms.

"Mr Taylor," Simon begins. "If we were to show you photographs of every model of this type, do you think you would be able to pick one out?"

"Oh yes, of course! I don't know the various makes off by heart but I'd recognise the one if I saw it."

"Well, that's very helpful Mr Taylor," I intervene. "We do appreciate it."

"Oh no problem," he is now gleeful. "I'm happy to do anything I can. I'm always trying to help, aren't I dear?" he looks over to his wife who is dutifully trotting back into the living room. She's carrying a tray of cups and saucers.

"You are, yes," the wife says but I can't help notice a hint of irritation in her voice, as though she's humouring him.

"May I help you?" I ask as she struggles with

the tray.

"No, no it's grand, I'll just set this here."

Just as Mr Taylor launches into a story about cars – types of cars he's owned in the past and types of cars he'd love to own – Simon's phone rings.

"Oh sorry," he says, jumping up. "I need to take this." I know he's not sorry at all. I know he's delighted that he's saved by the bell and I'm left behind having to listen to unnecessary tales.

I can hear him take the call in the hallway. I keep one ear on Mr Taylor and one ear on Simon.

"Hey Orla," I hear him say. "…A piece in the Post? Really? You know we'll have every Tom, Dick and Harry phone up, don't you? … Hmm, s'pose so. Well, if you must. Okay, well keep me in the loop."

Simon returns to the living room.

"All okay?" I probe.

"I'm really sorry, Mrs Taylor. We're going to have to dash. I've just had an urgent call we have to attend to. Sorry about the tea. I'm sure you understand."

"That's no problem." Mr Taylor butts in with a commanding air. "Surely we'll be able to find out who owns the red sportscar then. You'll let me know what's happening, won't you?"

"What was the phone call about?" I ask Simon as we jump back into the car. "Was it actually urgent or just a ploy to get away?" The look on his face tells me that the caller might have annoyed him.

"It's Orla, that reporter from the Post. They're

putting an article out today. An appeal for witnesses to phone in if they know anything."

"You're joking!" I reply.

"Yep. You know what happens when they give out a helpline number. Anyone can phone up."

"And we get inundated with time-wasters!"

"We'll see," Simon says, but he's not looking positive. He's aware that Time-Wasters Anonymous are going to be out in force throwing out every red herring under the sun.

Just when I'm losing the will to live, the phone rings again. This time, it's my own mobile. "I'll just take this," seeing Zoe Waller's name come up on the screen.

"Zoe," I say, keeping my voice low and sympathetic. "How are things with you?"

I wonder for a second if she's called me by accident. I can't hear any words. Perhaps she's muted. But then I hear a sound, a strangled gasp, as though she's crying.

"Zoe? What is it?" I try my best to be soft and caring.

"It's Emma!" she chokes out suddenly. "Emma's dead!"

I raise my hand to my mouth in shock. "Oh no! Oh Zoe, I'm so sorry!"

Zoe is crying continuously on the phone now, unable to say anything else.

"I'm so, so sorry," I hear myself saying again, repetitively, as my body goes cold and her grief washes over me.

"The doctor phoned me," she snivels. "It was

too late. There was nothing they could do. She just slipped away."

I close my eyes and my heart sinks. I can imagine the terrible pain Zoe is suffering.

All the while, I'm thinking that this case has suddenly escalated. Until now, it was a possible hit and run. *Now, it's manslaughter.*

CHAPTER SEVEN
Zoe

"**W**HAT DO YOU mean? She's 'passed'?" I can hardly believe the words coming out of my mouth.

"She's passed away, Ms Waller. She died at five past eight this morning." Doctor Farnham's voice is sympathetic but professional.

"No!" A guttural cry escapes my lips. I stagger back against the wall. "No!" I clench my mobile as I slide downwards.

"I'm so very sorry Ms Waller," I can hear his hushed tone at the other end of the line.

"But... she seemed stable... the machines were keeping her going?" Of course, I have no idea about these things but I'm just plunging around for words, trying to understand. I'll never get my head around this.

"It happens at times I'm afraid, Ms Waller. Her injuries were too severe. Her organs couldn't cope with the impact."

I close my eyes. "No."

I hear footsteps charge down the stairs. It's my mother.

"What's happened?" she asks, even though she can guess the tragic news from my position on the floor. I look up, holding the phone towards her. I can't speak to the doctor anymore. I crawl into the living room and clamber on to the sofa while I hear my mum go over the same news I've just been told.

"I need to see her," I plead, as my mum comes off the phone and I've somehow straightened myself out on the sofa. "I have to comfort my baby."

My mother doesn't argue. She helps me get my shoes and coat and I'm ushered to the door. We bundle into the car and she drives me to the hospital. I can't think straight. All I know is that I need to be beside Emma. Now. To hug her, keep her company and say goodbye.

In the hospital, she looks like she's just sleeping. So peaceful. But the life force has left her. She's definitely gone.

"Oh baby!" I wail. I throw my arms around her. "I love you so much. I love you so much!"

I can hear my mum try to stifle a tear behind me. I know she's finding this heart-breaking to see. This isn't the way things should be. A mother watching a daughter in agony. And a grand-daughter who has passed away.

I presumed I had a lifetime with Emma. She was only six! I thought she'd live until eighty. I hoped she'd be looking after me in my old age.

"Oh god!" I bawl. How can this nightmare be happening? I pull a blanket up close under her neck, as though to keep her warm and comfort her. I carefully curl my arm around her to keep her company.

"Oh Emma!" I cry out in vain. My brain is

scrambled. I can't think straight at all. I wasn't there to look out for her. In her final hour, I slipped up. I should never have allowed Liam to look after her that day. Why did I bother going to that crummy event? I should have stayed with my baby girl. We could've cuddled up on the sofa watching silly movies and eating popcorn. If we'd done that, we wouldn't be sitting here now, with Emma gone.

I wasn't there to protect her when the car hit the wall. The physical pain would've ripped through her. It was my job to shield her and I've failed miserably.

Tears are now streaming down my face and I'm totally hysterical. My mother puts her arm around me but I'm inconsolable.

"Oh darling," she strokes my hair in an effort to soothe me.

We sit for an age. I hold Emma and stroke her soft red hair. I talk to her as I caress her small, beautiful face. I see other visitors looking at us, their expressions concerned yet curious. I'm past caring what other people think. A doctor and a nurse arrive at the bedside. They apologize about the need to take Emma away and are at pains to ask if we've had enough time to say goodbye.

I know what this means. Her body will be stretchered away to the mortuary. Her remains will go into one of those drawers, like a filing cabinet. Then they'll slide the little corpse into a coffin before lowering it into the cold earth.

This is not the way things were supposed to be. She was meant to open her eyes, rise from her bed and walk. For us both to step out of here, hand in hand, maybe go to the canteen for an ice-cream. She had her whole life ahead of her, school to finish and university to attend. And of course, there would've been a wedding to organise, a reception and a honeymoon. Maybe even children of her own.

Instead, she will be carried out on a stretcher to the mortuary.

As they wheel her away, I fling myself on Liam. He's still hanging on. Alive but in some sort of a coma. How am I ever going to survive this? Why am I still alive? How can I continue to live and breathe from one moment to the next when my world is crashing down around me?

"Liam, please, you have to hang on," I beg, hoping that somehow the words are penetrating his skull. "Please, you're all I've got. Don't leave me on my own!"

After some time, my mother manages to settle me. She puts her arm around me, encouraging me to walk towards the door.

"We have to get you home," she is pleading. "You need rest." She's propping me up as we edge towards the exit. "Come on, let's get you home."

I notice the concerned looks on the faces of the staff and visitors. I don't care how I look. I'm just allowing myself to be directed robotically away from the scene. It is when the doors open and we step into the hall that I see a familiar face. Orla. The reporter from *The Post*.

"Zoe" she waves over, jumping up from the waiting room chair as I emerge. "Zoe, how are you love?"

I can feel my mum bristling next to me. "Now is not a good time." She asserts in a menacing tone.

The reporter throws me a sympathetic glance. She knows how to be persistent: "With all due respect Mrs Waller, it is *exactly* the right time! You see, the Police have just informed us that a witness thinks a red sports car departed from the scene that night. It is totally in your interests to try to locate the driver. Especially now, given the very serious circumstances. The tragic loss of Emma."

Orla stands her ground. She's now looking directly at me and imploring me to comply. Despite her plea, the words come across as gobbledygook. My brain is scrambled. I feel like I'm going to explode.

"We need to find out who did this to Emma," she pleads. "We have to catch that bastard. The best chance is to act now before the trail goes cold. I can do that for you." She's starting to talk my language. This is something I can understand.

"We need to lock him up," Orla continues. "For Emma's sake. And for the sake of any other children on the road."

She's getting through to me now. It's beginning to make sense. Despite my grief, she's scaled a barrier. I'm going to go along with this.

"It's okay, mum," I pat her hand. "It's okay, I want to speak to her about this."

Orla tries to contain a triumphant smile from spreading across her face: "Great, shall I get you both a coffee?"

In the canteen, she launches into a discussion about the article she plans to write. "I want to get the public on your side Zoe," she pops two sweeteners into her cappuccino and stirs. "They've got to see your point of view. People will line up behind you. The more they think about your situation, the more they'll want to help. The word will get out. Everyone will hear about it. In time, the story will do the rounds. There aren't too many red sports cars about. Someone will know who it is. There's a very good chance we'll find that driver Zoe. Help the police get the bastard."

"Are you sure this will work?" I clench the coffee cup in my hands as I take everything in.

"You've nothing to lose, Zoe. God knows what the sentence will be, now that we know what's happened to Emma. I hope he gets a long sentence. That's what he deserves. They're tightening up on this type of driving offence." She takes a sip of her cappuccino.

She's on my side. She wants to help me.

"Oh, and by the way Zoe, there's a large payment for this article. We suggest that you set up a fund to help find the killer. The money can go towards this. We can organise it at *The Post*. Every little helps."

I look at her. It's a good idea to start a fund. I'm on overdrive now. I nod automatically. At least someone's in charge. At least somebody can think straight.

✧　✧　✧

THE ARTICLE LOOKS terrible when it comes out. It's tabloid heaven. Orla talked me into doing a photo shoot, *to appeal to the readers; to get their attention.* I look awful in the photos. No make-up, hair a mess, wearing an old jumper. My eyes red raw from crying. I guess that was the look Orla was going for: the tragic, heart-broken mother. I'll never forget the headline: *Who could do this to a mother and child?*

She even managed to sneak a photo of Liam on his back in intensive care with tubes hanging out of him. How they managed that is beyond me, but these newspaper people are capable of anything. I read the comments online. Most of the posts were fine. People sympathising and saying things like: *That poor woman; how will she ever cope? She'll never get over it.*

But there was the other side of the coin. Nasty trolls by the sort of people who have nothing better to do. Vitriol like: *I wonder how much she got paid for the photos? Imagine making money out of your daughter's death!*

I had to steel myself to avoid lashing back at them. I wanted to fight my corner: *I didn't do it for the money, you scumbag! I'm trying to find a killer! Who else is going to get this maniac off the streets? I'm protecting all our children!*

But Orla tells me not to reply to any of these keyboard warriors. "Just ignore it, Zoe," she warns. "Don't say anything. It'll only look bad on you. We're trying to get people's sympathy. Ninety nine percent of the public are behind you. The trolls will always find something negative to say. Ignore them. They have sad, pathetic lives."

I know she's right, but I can't help it. I pour over the criticisms. It's like picking a wound and constantly making it worse. There are radio phone-ins. Talk shows where people discuss the *Emma hit & run case*. One hard-hitting presenter quizzes listeners on the police attitude to hit and run drivers. The theme always revolves around what happens to the guilty driver when found. What should the punishment be? The presenter confidently urges listeners to phone in demanding longer sentences.

"Hang him!" An old lady retorts. "Bring back the death penalty! That's what I say! A life for a life! That poor little girl was only six years old! She had her whole life ahead of her!"

"Yes," an elderly gentleman agrees. "That driver probably had drink in his system. How long before he offends again?"

The words come over the airwaves and fold around me like a comfort blanket.

But there are other callers. Their views hit me like a slap across the face. "Yeah, but what about the mum? Where was she that night? Why wasn't she at home looking after the child? Why leave a six-year-old in the hands of a drunk driver?"

They were hitting me where it hurt the most.

Somewhere deep down, it was starting to ring true. They were right.

CHAPTER EIGHT

Kerry

"A NOTHER DAY, ANOTHER coffee," I reflect, as we cruise up to the drive-through.

"I know, we should have shares in this place," Simon agrees; the car rolls past the large yellow arches.

"Fancy one of those double egg McMuffins?" I suggest, reminding myself that I really should hit the gym on my day off. All this fast food is not helping my figure.

Simon grabs the meal deal from the girl at the window and instinctively hands it to me. I nurse it on my lap until we find a spot in the car park to sit and eat.

"Hello muffin, goodbye waistline," I announce cheerily as I munch into my food.

Simon laughs. "Hey, you've nothing to worry about, don't be silly."

"You have to say that, otherwise I'll be in bad form with you all day."

"That'd be all I need; a pissed-off woman at work and a pissed-off woman at home."

"Oh dear," I grimace. "Laura still acting strange?"

"Mmm," Simon agrees, his mouth full. He takes a sip of his coffee and then confides, "She's just so quiet and withdrawn, I don't know what's wrong with her."

"You've tried asking her, I presume?" I put the question to him tentatively.

"Yeah, but she just brushes it off. I'm convinced something's going on. It looks sorta' suspicious. Like there's somebody else in the picture."

I shake my head. "Maybe you guys just aren't seeing enough of each other. Maybe you should take her out for dinner one night or something."

Simon swallows more coffee whilst watching the people going in and out of the burger bar.

"Oh I dunno. Can you imagine if we got all dressed up to go out and then just sit there across the table from each other with nothing to say? It'd be so awkward."

I scrunch up my wrapper and take his from him too, about to jump out of the car to dump it in the bin. "A few drinks, you'll be relaxed; you'll end up talking about the kids or something."

I step into the fresh air, throw away the rubbish and hop back into the car again.

Simon starts the engine and immediately changes the subject. "So, Mr Taylor, here we come. With luck you can tell us what car our man drove off in."

"Let's hope so," I reach for my laptop on the back seat. We have a bunch of images online. All types of sports cars. Fingers crossed; the witness can pick out the car he spotted on the night.

When we arrive at his house, I notice the blinds twitching already. No doubt Mr Taylor will have called to his wife and told her to put the kettle on. I have a feeling our visit is the highlight of his day.

"Good morning officers!" he booms, pulling open the door as he welcomes us in.

"Good morning Mr Taylor," we reply in unison. I can't help but notice that he seems slightly too cheery for what is now a manslaughter enquiry. But it takes all types to make the world go round. If my time with the police force has taught me anything, it's like they say: *there's nought as queer as folk*.

"Mary's putting the kettle on," Mr Taylor says, somewhat excitedly. "Come through, come through!"

The living room is pristine as before. Mary struggles in with a tray, teacups rattling as she bustles about setting it out on the coffee table. I haven't the heart to tell her that I've just finished an Americano Grande and a breakfast muffin. She proffers a plate of biscuits in my direction and I take one, resolving to spend even more time in the gym on my day off.

"So, Mr Taylor," Simon begins. "We have a collection of images here for you." He opens the laptop and swings it into view.

Taylor sets down his cup of tea and squints steadily at the screen. "Mary, pass me my glasses, will you?"

I notice Mary's frown as she gets up from her seat, crosses the living-room and takes the spectacles from the table beside her husband. She hands them over but he doesn't pick up on her body language. The way she abruptly snaps up the glasses from the table top.

The poor woman must be run off her feet. He seems to have her at his beck and call. Why couldn't he just get off the chair and pick the things up himself?

Taylor makes a big show of putting on the spectacles and perusing the images closely. "Now let's see," he mumbles. His eyes roam from one image to the other, oblivious to the fact that his wife is sitting on the other sofa, rolling her eyes in exasperation.

"Didn't you have a look at that sort of stuff online yesterday?" she interrupts, a hint of annoyance in her voice.

He looks up at her, peering over the top of his half-moons. "Yes, that's right," he agrees. "I went onto the Google and had a look at sports cars to pick out the one I saw."

Simon raises his eyebrows. "That's very good of you, sir, to take the time to do that."

"Have you decided which car it was?" I try to move matters along.

"Yes", he nods definitively.

I feel my heart lift a little. Finally, we are on the right track.

"It was a red Audi A5 Coupe," he proclaims with a confident flurry.

"Okay." Simon says. "Now, you're sure? Some of these marques look alike. All red. For example, there's a convertible A5 with a hood. From the distance, the roof is black. So, you definitely saw a red Audi A5 sportscar?"

"Definitely."

"That narrows the search considerably," Simon turns and catches my eye.

"Yeah, there can't be too many of those running around the city." I agree.

"We should let Orla know, so she can amend her article before it goes out." Simon notes as an afterthought.

"Thank you so much for your time, Mr Taylor," I stand up, signalling to leave.

"Oh, you'll stay for another cuppa, surely?" Taylor asks. "I could show you the photos of that car exhibition I went to last year?"

"I'm so sorry, Mr Taylor, we really must crack on. We have a ton of calls to make today."

"Of course," he tries to hide his disappointment. "Well, do feel free to call around any time and keep us posted on what's happening with the case."

"We will indeed," I reply. Then, turning to his wife, "Thank you so much for your hospitality. May I use the bathroom before I go?"

"Of course," she says, leading me down the hall. "Just in there to the left."

I go in, locking the door behind me. As I wash my hands, I notice the headline on the newspaper lying on the floor. It reads *Carnage on the Ravenhill Road.*

✦   ✦   ✦

"ORLA, BIT OF an update on the Ravenhill crash." Simon throws himself straight into the conversation with the reporter on the speakerphone. I can't help but smile. No niceties with Simon. No *Good morning Orla, how are things with you?* Concise and to the point.

"Well, good morning to you too," Orla's voice booms out sarcastically.

"Sorry, good morning," Simon retreats, suitably admonished.

"So, what's the update?" she asks. I hear the click of a lighter and a sharp intake of breath as she drags on a cigarette. I can almost feel my resolve weaken. I imagine the comforting feeling. The nicotine hit. It's been six months since I smoked, and the urge never goes away. It's also the reason for an unwanted gain of ten pounds. But at least I don't smell like an ashtray. In fact, I treated myself to my favourite *Coco Chanel*. I spray it all over when I feel the urge coming on.

"We think the car was a red Audi A5 Coupe." Simon announces.

I hear Orla blow out another plume of smoke. "Bloody hell Simon. I can't imagine there's too many of those zooming around Belfast."

"Yeah," he agrees. "It cuts down the field quite a bit."

"Quite," she agrees. "Okay, I'll amend the article and we'll get it out to press today. Do you think this Taylor guy would be up for an interview?"

"Oh, he can talk the talk alright," Simon tells her.

"Marvellous", Orla says, her voice thick with appreciation. Another article in the bag for her and another payment. "Keep me posted if you hear anything else," she quips cheerily.

"Likewise," Simon confirms and hits the End button.

"No cheerio, have a nice day Orla?" I tease.

"Shit! I forgot," comes the sarcastic reply as he gives me a cheeky grin.

I roll my eyes playfully. "Right, let's get the official list of A5 owners in town. Then we can pick out who to call on."

"Hopefully it'll only be a few."

WE PULL INTO a sweeping driveway in Holywood. The house is what you expect for that area; an architect's dream, surrounded by shrubs. The views over the nearby coastline are spectacular.

"Wow, nice place," I observe.

"Isn't it just," Simon murmurs, as the car tyres roll along the pebbled path where we scrunch to a halt.

"And there's our car," I spot the Audi parked up ahead.

"Completely unmarked by the looks of things," Simon notes, as he steps out of his own car and shuts the door behind him. We approach the ornate front door and press the doorbell. As we wait patiently, I sneak a glance through the fancy glass panelling on either side of the door. This visit will be an interesting *through the keyhole* experience, if nothing else.

The door opens and a man appears smiling in

the entrance. He's dressed smart-casual in linen trousers and a cotton shirt. His hair is peppered with flecks of grey and his beard is trimmed to perfection.

"Afternoon sir," Simon starts off. "I'm DCI Simon Peters".

"And I'm DS Lawlor". We hold up our ID badges. I notice the guy's smile fade into a quizzical expression.

"May I help you?" he asks, his voice laced with curiosity.

"Who is it dear?" A well-dressed woman appears in the background.

We repeat our names.

"We're here in connection with a car accident that occurred on Friday evening on the Ravenhill Road."

"Accident? What accident?" the woman queries.

"There was a serious car accident in Belfast in which one man was seriously injured and a child was killed. You haven't heard it on the news?"

The woman's jaw drops, her face genuinely surprised. "No, I don't know anything about it."

"Er… sorry, what has this got to do with us?" her husband intervenes, his tone oozing curiosity but remaining polite.

"Sir," Simon begins, obviously aware that we're not going to be invited in. "The accident was a hit and run and we have evidence that the car which fled the scene was a red Audi A5."

The man's car is parked stubbornly behind him, its existence now mocking him.

"What? But…" he stutters. "It can't be… I know nothing about this…"

"May we come in sir?" Simon gestures calmly.

"Yes, of course," he replies, his face now clouded over with worry.

We are led to the back of the house where a plush kitchen merges with a spacious dining area. The walls are floor to ceiling glass looking out over a breath-taking sea view.

"Please, have a seat," the owner gestures. "I'm Richard Foster by the way and this is my wife Holly."

"Mr Foster," Simon begins assertively. "To get straight to the point. We need you to confirm your whereabouts on the evening of Friday the twenty-fourth of July. Between the hours of ten pm and midnight to be precise."

The suspect's forehead furrows as he tries to cast his mind back to that evening.

"Hmm…." He sets his head in his hand as his eyes stare into the distance. "Friday night, now, where was I?"

"Honey," his wife pipes up. "Wasn't that the night you went down to the club with the boys?"

He looks up, starting to gain some recognition. "Of course, that's quiz night at the club."

Something tells me he doesn't sound convinced about that.

"Which club is that, sir?" Simon persists. "And who was with you? Sorry to have to ask you this."

"You have to do your job I suppose. All the lads, we go out most weeks. Mike, Andy, Tom…"

Simon enquires further: "And these friends? Will they be able to verify your attendance that night?"

"Of course!" Foster asserts.

I'm not buying it. Something about his perplexed stare and the body language screams that he's lying through his teeth.

CHAPTER NINE

Zoe

THE ROOM IS stuffy and warm. I want to open the windows but I guess they are closed for a reason. It's deathly quiet. Maybe they don't want the noise of traffic to spoil the silence. Leafy shrubs adorn the reception. Vases of fresh flowers are strategically positioned. Plants, greenery. *Living things.*

With care and compassion, a leaflet on the table advises. I am at the undertakers to prepare my daughter's funeral. It's a horrible, surreal feeling. Living in a moment where everything is real but surely can't be. I shouldn't be sitting in this waiting room, organising my six-year-old daughter's burial.

A box of tissues sits on the coffee table. I take one out, just in case. But in fact, I feel numb. I'm going through the motions. As if I'm outside of things, looking down at myself. From somewhere above, I watch my mother and myself sitting there calmly, on the waiting room chairs; detached and observant. Mum is leafing through a magazine. I'm staring into thin air. The receptionist is making herself look busy. She avoids small talk. She taps gently on her keyboard, head down, concentrating, trying to look distracted.

A door opens and a woman appears. She is dressed in a snug fitting grey suit. Her skirt skims below her knees and her jacket is well buttoned.

"Ms Waller?" she asks, gently.

I stand up.

"Come through."

We enter a smaller room. There is a circular table with chairs arranged on either side. I notice a folder on the table. It's a brochure. A selection of coffins. This can't be happening. I shouldn't be browsing a catalogue to pick my daughter's casket.

I should be at home, bustling around in the kitchen while Emma is on her tablet, picking out the toys she wants for Christmas. *Just let me know what you want*, I would be cheerily calling out. *We'll write a list to Santa later.*

Will Santa bring me everything? Emma ought to be saying, giggling with excitement.

Well, we'll have to ask him nicely, won't we? If you're a good girl, he will be kind to you.

"That one," I say, pointing to a small white coffin. It's actually the first one I see. I want this over and done with as fast as possible.

"A very good choice," the woman replies with assurance. "And about the flowers...?"

"White lilies," I butt in with no hesitation. The quicker we deal with this, the sooner we get home.

She asks more questions. Which day will we have the funeral? The time? Who will carry the coffin? I look at mum, willing her to answer all of this. She immediately takes over. I can't think straight. She decides the details and deals with the other queries.

Meanwhile, I'm staring at the catalogue with all the pictures of coffins. I think back to the beginning. When I saw those two blue lines on the white stick. *Pregnant.*

My hands quivered. I couldn't believe it. And yet in a way I sensed it. My breasts were swollen and heavy. I just felt it in my being. Some women say that, and you think it seems ridiculous, but it's actually true. You just know when you're expecting. I felt it and knew it. From the very next day.

Liam and I forgot to use a condom. We were drunk. It just happened. It was so much better without one. The moment I sat on him and felt his skin on mine, we groaned and I plunged down further. We just kept going. It was too good to stop.

The next morning, in a hungover blur, the memory came flooding back. How we had forgotten to use protection. I half wondered if I should rush down to the chemist and request the morning after pill, but I didn't. I was lazy and broke. I begrudged spending twenty-five pounds on one lousy tablet. After all, what student has twenty-five quid to throw away? Twenty-five pounds would get you a week's worth of food, not a single tablet that you probably don't need.

Besides, Liam was all curled up next to me. We had that lazy Sunday morning glow. The knowledge that there were no lectures or seminars that day. We could have breakfast in bed, then morning sex. Later a pint and pub grub with the crowd down the road. Life couldn't get any better. Studies could wait.

Of course, reality always kicks in. Studies couldn't wait. As a student, you felt you could never relax. You should never stop cramming. There was always another text-book to read or essay to write, but Liam was adamant about Sundays. "We need at least one day off," he'd say and I agreed wholeheartedly. One day of the week lazing with Liam was fine by me.

It was our third year. Finals were fast approaching. The dying days of student life. The end of an era. There was a strange atmosphere. On the one hand, we all felt stressed; studying to pass exams and achieve the necessary grades; hoping to hold the degree certificate in our hands with glee, clamouring to get it over with and announce that we were finally free. Ready to take on the world.

On the other hand, no-one wanted it to end. Deep down, we all had a feeling that this was probably the best time of our lives. Three years of university. Three years of freedom and fun. Partying and mixing with like-minded people. Unburdened by responsibilities such as jobs, children, and mortgages. We were in that lovely limbo phase. Devoid of parental discipline and not yet shackled by pressures of adulthood. The paradise between teenage years and adult strife.

The weeks rolled on. Exams came. So did my expanding belly. It was hard and taut, pushing defiantly against my waistband. My breasts became firmer. I was slowly inflating like a balloon.

Student weight, I grimaced at the girls, trying to bide my time. *That's what I get for drinking too much and eating all that crap.* They nodded agreement; they were all suffering from the student weight gain syndrome.

The second I held that white stick in my hand and set the timer for three minutes, I guessed the result long before I saw it. I could feel it. The two blue lines showed up defiantly quick. Bold and blue. Clear and obvious. They screamed *pregnant.*

I sat there, on the toilet seat, my knickers around my ankles, staring at those two blue lines. *You had arrived.* Loud and clear. Rapidly pulling my pants up, I gathered myself together, not even wanting to think. There were so many worries scrambling around my brain. Where would I start?

Would Liam stick by me? Help me look after the baby? And what about my studies? I still had exams and the graduation ceremony. How would I get a job? And how on earth could I look after a baby with no experience? Where would the money come from? What would my parents say? Too many thoughts, all swirling around, vying for attention.

It seems terrible but I just wanted to get drunk; to feel comfortably numb. Block everything out and pretend it wasn't happening. I'm ashamed to say that's exactly what I did. It was a Monday. Our usual student night at *Zoots.* Happy hour at fifty pence a pint. They were watered down to nothing but that wasn't the point. They were still only fifty pence. We boozed, danced and sang. We repeated the mantra we had been saying for weeks. *Only a few weeks of freedom left.*

We all had a fatalistic, melodramatic attitude. We knew that this was the end and that life would never be carefree again. *How right we were.*

When I was drunk enough, much later on that night, I broke the news to Liam. "I have something to show you," I said, when we were sitting on my bedroom floor, cross-legged, listening to music.

"Oh yeah?" he teased. He thought it was some sort of come-on. That I was going to be sexual and suggestive. *How wrong he was.*

"Yeah," I said. I reached up to the bedside table and opened the drawer. I pulled out the white stick. "This," I said, handing it to him.

I watched his face as it quickly flitted through a myriad of emotions. First, he was jovial and smiling, thinking the object I lifted out of the drawer would be some sort of sex toy. Then confusion as he took the little white stick from me. Finally, the realisation when he saw those two blue lines along the end of the stick. After that, shock and denial.

"No really?" he asked, shaking his head. I nodded back simply and confirmed his worst fears. I was pregnant with his child. Just as we were about to graduate. A ball and chain around his neck at the start of our professional lives.

"No, really?" he repeated. He'd had just enough alcohol that night to prevent him from being diplomatic or sensitive.

"Yes", I confirmed again, allowing the news to

sink in.

"But how? When?" he stammered.

"There was one night we forgot to use a condom," I shrugged.

"Was there? But when? How?"

I sighed, "There was."

He ran his hand through his hair. "Shit. Bollocks."

I rolled my eyes. I don't know why I was annoyed. After all, I expected this reaction. This had been my gut response as well, but I longed for him to put his arms around me. Tell me that everything would be okay. He would take care of us.

"Can we see about an abortion?" His words cut straight through me. Like a slap across the face.

"An abortion? No!" I said, defiantly.

His face fell, realising that we weren't on the same page.

"What? You want to keep it?" he baulked, looking incredulous.

I said nothing but my silence spoke volumes.

"Zoe! We're just about to graduate! We have no money!" He jumped up and began pacing the floor, as though to burn off all his pent-up energy. "No, strike that, not only do we have no money, but we're in tons of debt! Three years of student loans to pay off before we do anything! We can't afford a kid!"

He was terrified. I could see it in his eyes. It was fear that was making him behave this way.

"I'm keeping it, Liam," I announced. End of. No discussion. I could be stubborn when I wanted to. "It's your choice. You can either be in my life and the child's life or not, it's entirely up to you."

"Ha! So, this is some sort of ultimatum is it?" he glared furiously at me.

"If that's what you want it to be!" I retorted.

Where did my strength came from that day? How did I sit there with such inner resolve? I just knew, deep down inside, that I had to fight for you, Emma. Actually, maybe it was you doing the fighting. Perhaps you gave me the inner strength to stand firm.

"I'm going home," Liam said, stomping towards the door. "I can't deal with this." On that note, he flung it open and stormed through, slamming it behind him.

That's right, I whispered through bared teeth. *Run away, like you always do. Run away from your responsibilities. Run away from life.*

I sat down on the bed, feeling heavy and exhausted. I held my hands around my tummy. *I held you.*

"Don't worry," I told you. "I have a plan. I'll always take care of you, little one."

How wrong I was.

CHAPTER TEN

Kerry

"**M**R FOSTER," I pull out my notepad. "Please let us have the names and telephone numbers of the friends you mentioned. Just so we check out your alibi and move on."

His face crumples in annoyance. "But this is ridiculous!" he exclaims with irritation. "They don't want to be bothered with a call from the police!"

"Sir," Simon begins calmly. "There was a serious hit and run accident. A man is lying in intensive care in a coma. His six-year-old daughter is dead. I'm sure your friends will have no problem confirming your whereabouts that night, especially, if, as you say, you have nothing to hide."

"Just a routine chat and we'll be on our way," I assure him. "It's simply to rule you out of enquiries. We'll make sure they know that."

Foster folds his arms defensively but his shoulders sink inwards. He knows he can't argue.

"Here, I have their numbers," Mrs Foster intervenes. She picks her mobile phone up from the worktop and comes to the dining room table, scrolling through the device as she walks. She lifts her glasses from the top of her head and sets them on her nose. "Let's see…" she begins, oblivious to her husband's increasing irritation. "Ah yes, Mike first, here we go. Got a pen?" she asks, cheerily.

I scribble down the numbers as she reads them out. Foster squirms in his seat.

"Oh, and Andy lives at number fifty-one," she adds. "It's just a few doors down. You could call and see if he's in."

"Thanks very much, Mrs Foster," I say. "We really appreciate your help."

When I've taken a note of all the details, we get up to go.

"Oh, one more thing," Simon interrupts. "The barmaid on duty that night? Or the barman? Who was it?"

I can see the suspect is racking his brains for something to say.

"It was Lottie," he blurts out. "Lottie was on duty that night."

Simon nods, his eyes tell me that he thinks we've caught him out. He had no idea who was working that night because he wasn't there. I can tell Simon's thoughts without him even having to voice them.

"We'll be in touch soon," Simon states. "Just to keep you posted on proceedings."

Foster gets up and follows us to the door. "Can I have your card? In case I need to phone you for anything."

"Sure." Simon says, taking a card out of the inside of his suit pocket and handing it to him.

The guy's hand lingers on the card, as though he wants to say something else, but then the moment passes and we're at the front door.

We make our way towards the car. It's only a few moments later when Foster follows us. He looks back furtively, checking that his wife is still inside and out of earshot.

"There's something I need to mention..." he mumbles.

I raise an eyebrow. I knew there was something he wanted to get off his chest.

"What's that?" I ask, trying to keep my expression as open and approachable as possible. I'd heard of this; the 'door knob moment', when an important piece of information would be released at the last possible minute.

"I wasn't with the lads that night," he confesses in hushed tones.

My eyes widen. "Is that so?" I ask. I can't help but notice that his wife is lingering in the livingroom. She's standing just behind the blinds, watching us. She is obviously wondering what her husband needs to discuss with us at the last moment.

"Yeah," he mutters, casting his eyes downwards as though in shame. He runs his hand through his hair. "But I wasn't anywhere near that accident," he says firmly. "I wasn't. Look, I was with a friend. A female friend." His eyes are mainly focussed on the ground. "My wife isn't to know, I urge you. All hell will break loose if she finds out."

I can hear Simon sigh heavily beside me. His suspicions about his own wife's adultery are probably looming in his own mind.

"Well, obviously we're not obliged to tell your wife, Mr Foster," I interject. I try to hide a little disappointment. "But we'll need the contact number of your friend. She'll have to confirm your whereabouts that evening."

"Sure..." he says, taking his phone out of his pocket and scrolling through to retrieve her number. "Her name is Jessica Cook and her number is..."

He rattles it off while I scribble it down on my pad. Simon keeps a stony silence next to me.

"Everything okay?" A voice tinkles out from behind. It's Mrs Foster. She has come out of the front door, her footsteps gently crunching over the driveway.

"Of course." Foster twitches at first, then smiles automatically. "We were just chatting about the Audi, where I got it and stuff." He shrugs nonchalantly. "Boring car talk, you know."

Simon's face remains deadpan and I smile awkwardly.

"Well, thanks for your help," I offer again, as I get into our car. "We'll be in touch."

Simon slumps down into the driver's seat and we reverse slowly down the driveway. Mrs Foster is waving amicably and I wave back.

"Oh dear, she has no idea, has she?"

"Nope", Simon was somewhere else. Perhaps he's thinking of his own situation; how Laura could be playing away. Maybe he worries that it's obvious to their friends. They could be looking down on him. Pitying him.

✧ ✧ ✧

"KERRY, GOT A Mrs Taylor on the line for you," the receptionist at the police station pipes up in her cheery voice.

"Mrs Taylor?" I'm trying to remember who that is.

"She says she lives on the Ravenhill Road. She said something about her husband seeing a red car."

"Oh God, yes, of course. Great, put her through." I'm intrigued as to why this woman is calling.

"Hello, DS Lawlor speaking."

"Oh hello, it's Mrs Taylor, you were at my house the other day?"

"Yes, Mrs Taylor, good to hear from you. How are things?"

"Well, it's my husband you see," she says, in that feeble voice. "I'm phoning while he's popped out to the shops. He'd be annoyed if he knew I was calling you."

My ears prick up with curiosity. "Go on."

"Well, look, I was just thinking... he can sometimes be a little, you know, scatty. It's our age you see, dear..."

A sympathetic smile spreads across my face.

"You can never be entirely sure that he got the red car thing right. He might have thought he saw a car that night, but he would have been trying to help. I'd be a little wary. Just in case he might not be one hundred percent correct."

"I see." I take a deep breath, realising that the

Foster visit might be in vain. "Well, I do appreci-ate you phoning, it can't have been easy."

"You won't tell him I called, will you?" she asks.

"Of course not," I assure her. I close my eyes realising that we are probably no closer to finding the driver than we were at the beginning.

Just as I'm about to say goodbye and hang up, she says, "Oh, there is one more thing…"

"What's that?"

"The neighbours from across the street have returned from holiday. They were in Spain for a few weeks. I think they have CCTV cameras. They might be worth talking to."

Cameras. At the house just across from the accident. At least we have another lead.

"Thank you, Mrs Taylor. That's great to know. I'll get in touch with them."

"I have their number here, dear. I keep it just in case. Hold on." I hear the clunk of the phone as she sets the handset on the table, then goes off to retrieve her address book. After what feels like a century later, she returns to the phone. "Are you still there dear?"

"I am yes," I say patiently.

"Oh, that's good, sorry dear. At my age it takes me a long time to get around the house."

"That's no problem Mrs Taylor, you've been very helpful." I have my pen poised, ready to take down the number.

She reels it off before saying, "Oh, there's his nibs back. I better go, I don't want him to know I've been on with you."

"Of course not, thanks so much." There was a click and silence.

✧   ✧   ✧

"SIMON, I HAVE an update. I heard from one of the neighbours."

"Oh yeah?" he asks, looking up from his computer.

"Remember the place opposite with CCTV? I got the number from Mrs Taylor. It's a guy called Green. It's that place at eight twenty Ravenhill Road. You know the one that we knocked on a few times but no-one was ever in?"

"Oh yeah," Simon says, folding his arms in interest, listening intently.

"Turns out they've been on holiday in Spain. Only just home and heard the news. They had cameras running the whole time they were away. I'm told we can come round to have a look now. Seems the footage might have a good view of the accident. It's directly across from the scene."

"Great!" Simon is already getting up and putting on his jacket. "Let's go!"

I grab my bag and follow him out.

"Shame the Foster thing fell through," he says conversationally. We had visited the girlfriend's house earlier that day. She confirmed that he was with her that night and she had evidence to prove it. Her CCTV showed him turning up at around eight o'clock and leaving after midnight.

"It's always a downer when a lead like that runs dry," he adds.

"Well, let's see what this new equipment can show us," I feel the adrenalin rise as we get into Simon's car and take off.

"WELL, THAT'S NOT an Audi for a start," Simon points out as he squints at the footage. He bends down more closely to the screen. "It's a BMW 4 Series Coupe. Similar to an Audi mind you, and it's definitely red."

"So old Taylor was wrong after all."

"Look, we've wasted our time door-stepping Audi drivers. But at least we've got a BMW to follow up on. That's better than no lead at all."

"An easy mistake for old Taylor to make though. Both cars look the same from that distance late at night."

"But look at this footage. This isn't what I expected at all," Simon gestures.

We look at the screen, peering closely at the pixelated images. The BMW is sitting at a T-junction and has just pulled out onto the Raven-hill Road, turning left. Suddenly, we see Liam's silver Mondeo approaching. It's coming into view from the right. He's belting along at a hell of a speed. The two cars look certain to collide. At first glance, it seems that Liam takes action to avoid hitting the BMW broadsides on. He swerves hastily to his right and crashes headlong into the wall on the other side of the road.

"Wow," I go straight for the replay. "I wanna see this again."

On second viewing, we look more closely at the footage. I turn to Simon: "Liam is speeding but is he completely to blame? Did the BMW pull out too close in front of him?"

Simon considers this for a moment before replying. "He was motoring along way above the limit. We can certainly prove that from the timing of the footage. But was the other car at fault? I'm not completely sure."

I stare at the screen, "So what's the situation if the BMW driver isn't to blame for Liam's actions?"

"Let's get ourselves up to date on the facts first. We'll have to get the road traffic boys to measure up the whole thing. Make a judgement on whether Liam needed to take such drastic action."

"It does look a bit like Liam Fitzpatrick over-reacted some distance away from the other car. Either deliberately or as the result of drink or drugs?"

We looked at each other. If that's the case, there's no other way to say it. *Liam killed his own daughter.*

CHAPTER ELEVEN

Zoe

EVEN THOUGH LIAM hadn't wanted the baby, he came round to my way of thinking eventually. I knew he would. All he needed was time to tire of sitting in denial and to pretend it wasn't going to happen. He felt angry and resentful; hard done by. He wanted his freedom, youth and independence. He was just about to graduate. He lived in London and hoped to start an acting career. London was the place to be. The ability to drop everything and head off to an audition at a moment's notice was important. A baby didn't figure in that scene.

I had studied acting as well and we were on the same course. I didn't feel as hopeful as he did. He had confidence and charisma. Liam could saunter into any audition and charm the socks off the female producers.

I guessed deep down that I didn't have the right look for a raunchy leading lady. You have to be drop dead gorgeous and super thin. I thought I was pretty enough and quite slim but I was shy in a world of extroverts. I could pretend to be confident; put on an act, but I lacked the deep-down self-esteem of other players. I watched competing women on my drama course. They had stunning beauty and naturally slim figures but it was their charisma which landed them the good parts. They usually had parents in the background who encouraged acting careers which built up their confidence.

My father was the opposite; a religious fanatic and very strict. I wasn't allowed to go to cinemas or discos, and make-up or earrings were forbidden. The arts were wicked and debauched – the devil's work. He was the type of father who told you to sit down and shut up. Children should be seen and not heard.

Mum was more open-minded but she never stood up to my father. She agreed with him to his face but behind his back, she'd let me get away with blue murder. She pretended she didn't see me sneaking out of an evening and then covered up for me. She crept downstairs in the middle of the night to unlock the back door, making sure I'd be able to slip back in. She turned a blind eye when I put on a mini-skirt and bright blue eyeshadow. Once, dad caught me wearing a short skirt and said, *That's not a skirt, it's a belt! Put some clothes on!* I pulled on a long old-fashioned skirt that went down to my feet and covered every inch of flesh.

The minute I got to the top of the lane I pulled the skirt off to reveal the mini underneath. I hid it under a bush and retrieved it on my way home.

I knew my father would be appalled when he heard about the pregnancy. He would spout venom, telling me I was Satan's child and a disappointment to the Lord. I didn't have the courage to tell him so I phoned my mum and burdened her instead. I waited until I knew my dad would be out of the house and got in touch with her on the landline.

"Oh dear", her voice was heavy with disappointment. "What's your father going to say about this?"

"He's not going to like it," I stated the obvious. "But what can I do? I'm not getting an abortion."

"No," she agreed.

"I'll send him an email instead. I can't come out with it on the phone. He'll be beside himself." I warned her.

Of course, it was the coward's way out. It was a certainty that when he read the email, fury would be unleashed. I was worried he'd take it out on mum.

"Okay," her words came with an air of resignation. Obviously, she feared the same thing.

His response was as venomous as I thought.

"I am sorely disappointed and disgusted. That a daughter of mine would sin against the Lord and turn towards the devil! Your mother and I will have nothing to do with this baby." He ranted on for what seemed an age but I was already making plans in the back of my mind.

And that was that.

He no longer wanted anything to do with me and I was disowned. I was left with no emotional or financial assistance, and at the time, no support from Liam either. Completely alone, it was just me and my unborn child.

Cradling my stomach, I imagined the baby inside me; her tiny fingers and toes. She had to be protected from the venom spouted by my own father, and from Liam's fear and denial. I had to be the strong one and keep her safe at all costs.

I stood firm and enquired about government welfare and the available support, sorting everything myself. Financially, it's almost impossible to raise a baby living in London, so I moved back home to Belfast and looked for somewhere to live.

Inevitably, my mum would visit after some time. Even if she had to turn up on the sly, she would help. She might slip me a bit of money now and then and she'd certainly provide child-rearing advice, even if it had to be kept secret from dad.

On the flight home, there was no Liam by my side – just the baby in my belly. Staring out of the window as the plane gathered pace on the runway, my thoughts drifted to Liam and the friends left behind. They were probably nursing hangovers and dreading the thought of trying to find work. Whereas, I was flying home and about to move into my newly decorated flat. There were arrangements for child benefit and housing relief – to get the best start in my new life. I was going to make ends meet and would do this all by myself.

A few months later Liam landed on my doorstep. This was always going to happen. He couldn't live without me – his backbone. He liked to think of himself as confident, assured and in control but in fact he depended on me. I was his rock; an anchor who gave him security and comfort.

After a few months of failed auditions, no acting work and dwindling finances, his life of freedom in the capital looked less appealing. His main occupation was waiting on tables to earn a living. He was on his feet all night scraping people's leftovers into a bin. He expected a glamourous life as a celebrated actor with people cow-towing to him. He aspired to dine out in the best restaurants, wearing Paul & Shark shirts and Gucci shoes. What a bitter disappointment to be on the other side of the coin. Other people were wining and dining and wearing the expensive designer gear. Liam was the waiter carrying away the scraps.

"I've missed you," he said, when I opened the door to him that night.

"I know." I retorted gently with a coy smile.

"Can I come in?" he asked, somewhat shyly.

"Well, I suppose so, now that you're here." My voice had a mildly sarcastic tone. He knew I was playing a game.

We sat there on my sofa with my pregnant bulge protruding. I was about thirty weeks with Emma at that time. Those brown eyes seemed to look into me with sincerity. I'd longed for that look. I'd missed his strong arms, soft beard and dark red hair.

"I'm sorry," he whispered.

"Are you?" I teased playfully, holding off. I was dying to pounce on him and smother him with kisses but I knew to keep cool. He would have to work for this; he would have to earn it.

"I left you in your hour of need. All these months, you've been pregnant and having to cope with the responsibility of this all on your own. You're expecting my baby and I deserted you."

I looked at him, my expression soft and almost mothering. "You needed time to get your head around it," I assured him tenderly.

He gave a soft groan. "You're so forgiving Zoe." He placed a hand softly on mine. I could almost feel an electrical connection; a current running through his fingertips and onto my skin but it was important to keep playing it cool. I knew not to scream or shout. I was determined not to retaliate or scold him for his disappearance. In this situation a girl has to be coy and the guy will come running.

I always had the feeling that he couldn't survive without me. London life was too difficult for him. Managing his finances, paying the rent, cooking TV dinners. He'd be lost on his own.

It was an odd aspect to our relationship. We had the romantic side; the sex of course, but there was definitely another side. I was the sensible one; taking care of the finances and putting food on the table. He was the playful one. He liked to take risks and live on the edge. Yet more often than not he returned to the nest; to the safety and security I provided. I was his comfort zone; in a way, almost his mother. With me, he could feel grounded.

"I've missed you Zoe," he murmured again. This time he edged closer, moving his hand along my arm, touching my face. He cupped his other hand under my chin. He was testing the water. He wanted to kiss but was checking if I'd allow it. Would I let him ease in for a kiss? Would I push him away?

I let him ease in. His lips softly landed on mine. He kissed me with all the warmth and apology he could muster. The move told me he couldn't live without me. A kiss that said *I've come home.*

My lips parted slightly and his tongue plunged further in. It swirled around my mouth, sending all sorts of sensations exploding inside me. Our breathing deepened and our mouths blended further, inhaling each other greedily.

"Zoe, I've missed you," he gasped, in the breathing space between kisses. "God, I've missed you."

"I've missed you too." I was breathless. My hands reached down to the bottom of his tee-shirt and pulled it over his head. My eyes travelled over his slim torso, the muscles rippling as his arms moved upwards, the smattering of hair across his chest.

His hands moved between my legs. I melted.

"What about the baby?" he whispered. "I don't want to hurt it."

I slid submissively underneath him. "You won't," I exhaled in pleasure. "Trust me, you won't."

How wrong I was. *How disastrously wrong I was.*

✧   ✧   ✧

"MISS WALLER?"

I immediately recognise the voice. "Yes, is that Doctor Singh?"

"Yes, I'm afraid I have some bad news for you. Are you sitting down?"

I feel the blood drain from my body and my knees immediately weaken. I sit on the kitchen chair.

"What is it?" I ask. "Is it Liam? Has he passed?"

"No ma'am, he's hanging on. However, we've discovered something. Miss Waller, unfortunately Liam had drugs and alcohol in his system at the time of the accident."

"What?" I gasped. "He'd been trying to stay clean. He was attending the meetings and doing so well."

"It wasn't a large amount Ms Waller, but he was over the limit. We will have to add it to the record. The police will want to know our findings, so we are obliged to report it. You understand we must keep within the law."

But I'm already lost in thought.

"Miss Waller? Are you there?" the doctor probes, puzzled by my silence.

"Yes," I say slowly. "I'm just taking it all in."

Drink and drugs in his system. While our baby was in the car.

I'm starting to build a case all of my own.

CHAPTER TWELVE
Zoe

"Zoe, it's Detective Simon Peters." His voice is confident, to the point.

I grip my mobile in anticipation. "Mr Peters." I notice my heart beat a little faster. "Any news?"

"Yes, we do have news, Zoe, but I'm afraid you're not going to like it."

For the second time that day, I feel the blood drain from my face and my knees weaken. I slump down onto the sofa. "Is it about Liam and the drugs?" I ask.

"Yes," Simon says, "but there's more I'm afraid. We've uncovered CCTV footage of the accident and it's very clear that Liam was speeding at the time of the accident. It wasn't a hit and run Zoe. Liam was speeding and swerved into the wall of his own accord."

I close my eyes. It's hard to take in. And yet the minute I close them, I can see the accident clearly in my head. Liam gripping the steering wheel. His pupils dilated by drugs. Emma sitting in the passenger seat, nervous and frightened. I envisage Liam blaring some awful techno music. A hideous racket blasting through the car speakers. I imagine him putting his foot to the floor and the car taking off. Liam acting the big shot, thinking he looks cool. Then the screech of brakes, the squeal of the tyres and a deafening crunch of metal as the car smashed into the wall.

"Zoe?" the detective breaks my train of thought.

"Sorry. I'm just in shock." My world feels blurry and unreal.

"Yes, that's understandable." His voice sounds so normal – so real. This phone-call seems so calm, serene, and yet it can't be happening. Sitting here on my sofa, listening to a cop tell me my partner is responsible for killing our daughter. The magnitude of that knowledge hits me like a tsunami.

Liam killed Emma!

My fists clench in anger. How could he have been so irresponsible? And why am I involved with such a self-centred asshole? I get up and start pacing the floor. There is so much pent-up energy I need to burn off. I'm going to march up to intensive care and tell the half-dead bastard that if he doesn't die all by himself, I'll finish the job for him.

How dare he take drugs when he was looking after our child! The one night I ask him to mind her and he gets off his head! What a selfish fucking prick!

✧   ✧   ✧

IN THE ICU, I whisper into his ear: "Let me tell you…" The staff are getting on with their business all around us. "… you better hope that you don't come out of that coma. Because if you don't die, I'm going to kill you myself."

A nurse walks past, giving me a sympathetic smile. She assumes I'm whispering gentle encouragement; urging him to make a speedy recovery. She has no idea what's really on my mind.

"In fact, I should have a word with the doctor. Maybe see if it's time to switch the machine off? You hear about this sort of stuff in the news. The sick victim fights for life. Haven't you fought enough Liam?" My voice takes on a venomous tone. I didn't know I had it in me. "Haven't you done enough damage?" I squeeze his hand, but not in a comforting way. It's a vice-like grip and I hope it hurts. I get up, the chair scraping back behind me and thunder out in disgust.

My partner and the father of our child, who also happens to be a bloody murderer, is lying still on the bed, unmoving. It's as if he's avoiding responsibility just by lying stock still. That way, the bastard doesn't have to explain himself.

THE PHONE BLEEPS again. I snatch it up from the coffee table.

"Miss Waller?" I recognise the doctor's voice straight away.

"Dr Singh" I hope I'm guessing right. Liam must have passed. Perhaps somewhere down in his subconscious, he heard my threatening words. He'd know he had nothing to live for and might as well slip away.

"Miss Waller, it's good news. Not entirely unprecedented. Liam's starting to recover. There are definitely encouraging signs. His eyes opened last night for the first time and the nurse has been attending to him. He's conscious and aware, and has actually muttered a few words. It's normally a progressive situation. Chances are he will continue to get better although we can't guarantee anything. It's looking quite good at the moment."

"Really?" I ask, my voice deadpan. Dr Singh must assume that I'm in shock because he simply carries on.

"Yes, it happens with a small number of patients who have suffered this level of trauma. He's very lucky."

I can see Dr Singh's face on the other side of the phone. The triumphant smile, the smug grin. This would be a major success for him, a high point in his career.

"I see." I mutter with disappointment. The man does not deserve to be alive; he's a negligent, irresponsible killer. It's only fair that he should die too.

The only comfort I have is that I can go talk to him. Tell it like it really is. Make his life a living hell.

When I click off the phone, I call my mum to tell her the news. Naturally, she wants to come to the hospital with me. I think she looks forward to speaking with Liam, to hug and molly-coddle him.

"It's fine, mum, I'd rather go on my own."

"No dear, I'll come with you."

"What about dad?"

"He's playing golf with the boys; he doesn't need to know where I am."

"Okay," I sigh. She obviously wants an excuse to get out of the house, listen to my frustrations on the way to the hospital and get involved.

"Zoe, it was an accident," she assures me with conviction. "You can't blame Liam."

"That's rich, coming from you!" I snap back. "You and dad can't stand him!"

She gives me a sad look. "That's not fair. It's your father that doesn't like him. I've never said a bad word about him."

"He took drugs and got behind the wheel of the car with our daughter!" The veins are almost popping out of my head with anger.

"Yes," Mum soothes calmly. "But that doesn't mean we should want him dead. He's just come out of a coma, Zoe. He needs love and care."

I decide to keep my mouth shut until we get to the hospital. By that time, I hope I'll have calmed down. Otherwise, I'll say something I regret, something about arranging to have him taken out.

"You're just angry at the moment Zoe," my mum says softly. "It's just so raw. It will ease eventually."

Not in this lifetime, I think, but I remain quiet. I put my sunglasses on and stare out of the window, watching the houses pass by, trying to calm my racing head.

When we arrive at ICU, a man is sitting next to Liam's bed. He's dressed in a suit. He looks smart. A minister? Has Liam gone religious and asked someone to come in and prepare him to meet his maker?

We approach the bed. Liam is propped up. A sad look is etched on his face as he sees us coming towards him. He starts to talk about Emma first.

"I'm so sorry. How could this have happened? To Emma! It's so awful. I can explain."

"I'm sure you can." I can't hide my anger.

"Liam dear," mum interrupts, going over and giving him a kiss on the cheek.

We stand there awkwardly. The suit at the end of the bed is looking at us, waiting for an introduction. Liam is staring at me expectantly, awaiting a hug; a gesture of solidarity.

There's a brief but pregnant silence.

"Just give me a chance to explain," he begs. He's got that nervous look; he probably knows his story isn't going to hold up. I stand glaring at him, feeling everyone's eyes on me.

Then I respond, "Is there an apology for killing our daughter?" My expression is cold and hard.

I see him blink, shocked at my abruptness. I'm not normally like this with Liam. In any other circumstances, I'm the doormat and he's the one that walks over me.

"Zoe." I hear my mother say gently but I detect a warning note in her voice.

"What the hell is going on?" Liam blurts out at the same time.

"Miss Waller," the well-dressed man suddenly pipes up. Now we're all talking at once. How does Liam manage it? They're both rallying to his side.

"Miss Waller, I'm Victor Brown. I'm a solicitor. I'm here to talk to you about what happened that night."

So that's the mystery man. Liam doesn't beat around the bush, does he? I stare at Liam. "Some things never change."

"What's that supposed to mean?" Liam replies defensively.

"Well, you didn't waste time getting a lawyer on board. Covering your back as usual!" I snort.

"Now hold on a minute Zoe," he raises a hand in objection. "When I came round, the nurse filled me in. She said the police were here so I called a solicitor. He said we needed to get started on the case quickly."

I look at him, my face resigned. He's at it again. Never mind Emma. It's all about him. His lawyer's already on the ball. Trying to wiggle him out of every situation he gets into. Get the story right from the start. Whatever will sound good in court.

"So, what about the drugs then? The stuff they found in your system? You drank and snorted up that shit. Then you got behind the wheel with our baby next to you?" I'm stiff, standing upright and barely able to look him in the face.

Liam glances at the legal advisor. His face says it all. He's too tired to talk. At least that's what he wants me to think. Let the smart attorney do the lying for him.

"Miss Waller," Victor Brown stands up to address me. He's probably using a well-practised psychology with punters. Don't stay seated and have them tower over you. This guy's now face to face with me and ready to defend my husband.

"Liam is convinced his drink was spiked that night…"

Before he has time to finish his sentence, I roll my eyes in disbelief. Typical of my beloved arsehole to have some pathetic excuse up his sleeve.

"It's true Zoe," Liam butts in.

Brown continues. "Liam was driving past the bar where he works so he popped in to check his rota. He stopped for one drink. An orange juice for Emma and a half pint of shandy for himself. He thinks that while his back was turned, the glass was laced with something."

I've heard it all now. A lame duck tale. Just what I expected.

"Oh? And who was the evil villain who happened to be standing there? Ready to pop their stash into your drink?" I don't even want an answer. I'm so disgusted.

"Liam believes that the crime was executed by a well-known local drug dealer who was present. His name is Alistair Jones. Apparently, most locals call him Big Al." It sounds strange when a solicitor utters a name like Big Al. The nickname flows awkwardly from a voice which is both formal and educated.

"And why would Big Al want to do that?" My voice mimics the stupid name of the guy. I always knew he was getting far too involved with that scumbag.

Liam shrugs his shoulders. "Revenge, I guess." His voice is weak. Obviously, he is trying to garner sympathy.

My arms are folded. I'm relentlessly unsympathetic. "You're implying that you did something wrong to make him seek revenge!"

"There is one thing, Miss Waller," the solicitor says.

"What's that?" My eyebrows are raised.

"The car at the scene of the accident? The red BMW? We believe that it was driven by Mr Jones. Sorry, I mean Big Al. It's possible he planned to influence Liam's driving in some way. That's why he spiked him with drugs. He actually intended to cause an accident."

My jaw drops. Something in the back of my mind tells me that Big Al turning up at the scene of the accident might not actually be a coincidence. But I still can't feel my heart softening for that stupid bastard. There was no way I'd reach over and hug Liam. Nor celebrate him coming out of a coma. I'm certainly not going to bloody well kiss him or welcome him back to the land of the living. With that, I turn on my heels and walk out of the ward. I'm going to get a hot shot lawyer of my own.

Liam's going to get what's coming to him.

CHAPTER THIRTEEN

Simon

"THERE'S SOMETHING FUNNY about this Liam Fitzpatrick case," I'm looking over at Kerry as I speak. She's holding her notebook and has a laptop perched precariously on her knee.

"Yeah, I know what you mean. There are a few things on my mind too. Tell me what's bothering you and let's see if we're thinking the same thing," she replies.

"Why don't we look at what we've got to date? A guy with his daughter in the passenger seat drives straight into a wall. He's accelerating at the moment of impact. Did he swerve to avoid another car?" I drum my pen subconsciously on the pad of paper in front of me.

"You mean the infamous BMW?" Kerry raises her eyebrows at me.

"That's the one." I nod. "But then the Soco guys pour water on that theory by looking at the tread-lines. They can't be sure."

I start to shuffle through some papers on my desk. "Now something new has come up. Dr Singh phoned from the hospital. He tells me Fitzpatrick had ..." I flick through the papers to find the facts: "...yeah, it's here. He had 80mg of alcohol and what looks like a residue of benzodiazepines. That could come from popping two or three twenty mil tablets earlier in the evening."

Kerry butts in: "Definitely over the limit for driving on both counts." She folds her arms and sits back as though contemplating. "But it's hardly enough to make him go crazy and drive straight into solid objects with his daughter in the car."

I stand up and walk towards our Nespresso machine, popping a capsule into the slot and setting a cup underneath the nozzle. "That's why I'm telling you nothing is cut and dried. We know it's not right but an average guy of Liam Fitzpatrick's weight and build would probably get away with driving home quite normally. Of course, he might have taken a bigger dose of drugs earlier in the day. That would still leave the same trace." The coffee machine makes a gentle whirring sound as a pleasant aroma fills the office. "Want one?"

"Yeah, go on then," she smiles appreciatively.

"You were checking into the cell-phone found on the driver's seat." I pipe up as I fiddle about with another coffee pod for her. "What's the situation there?"

She sifts through some other papers looking for notes. She looks up at me: "The news is good and bad. Firstly, the mobile at the other end was a burner phone." She sounds pessimistic.

"Oh right, a pre-paid phone. We can't trace the other end of the line, then," I muse.

"I'm afraid so. Turns out the device was being used at the time the car swerved and we can't identify the person he was talking to. It's not even certain he was on a call in the first place. It might have been a pocket dial. Just an open line. We could have trouble doing him for use of a phone while driving, or establishing that this caused the accident." She takes the proffered cup of coffee from me gratefully and sips tentatively, careful not to burn herself.

I walk over to the window, my coffee in hand. I can't help thinking of the little girl. I'm pretty sure her death will be punishment enough for that poor bastard lying up in hospital. And as if I haven't enough variations on a theme to deal with already, there's further news to break to Kerry. "I phoned the forensic boys this morning with the news from Dr Singh. They came back a little while later to tell me Fitzpatrick's name is ringing bells all over their system when the drug information was typed in."

"I don't need three guesses." Kerry quips. She doesn't miss a beat, that girl.

"You've got it. He has a history. Not serious as far as drugs are concerned. User only. But we do think he may be going up in the world. He's a known associate of Big Al Jones. Big Al's an A-Lister with the drugs squad and a dangerous guy. I can tell you something else. I asked somebody in the office to give him the go-over. Turns out he owns a red BMW Coupe."

"What a coincidence! But from the quality of the CCTV we have, we can't establish that the vehicle in the picture was his, can we?" Kerry quizzes.

"That's right and it's still a stretch to imagine Alistair Jones zipping around with criminal intent towards Liam Fitzpatrick. Could he have some-how forced Fitzpatrick into that wall?"

"I dunno. You're a bloke. Aren't you guys supposed to know everything about cars?" She gives me a grin. Am I imagining it or is she being slightly flirtatious?

"Hey, aren't you supposed to be a top detective? Didn't you pass your advanced driver's test like the rest of us guys?" I banter back.

She laughs it off and continues, "Touche, but seriously, could he drive in such a way to run Liam off the road? Did he swerve out deliberately just to put a frightener on him? Or did he plan to kill him?" She crosses her legs and I can't help but note her skirt rises a little high. I dart my eyes away, sit back on my chair and focus on my paperwork.

"Let's put it this way. I doubt Big Al would be a considerate road user. With his drug dealing background and criminal past, he's hardly a Sunday school teacher. If he did cause the accident intentionally, Emma's death isn't manslaughter anymore. It's murder."

Kerry takes a sharp intake of breath. "Proving it would be a nightmare without crystal clear CCTV footage." She sets her laptop on the floor and gets up to walk towards the window, stretching her legs.

"There's something else," I interject.

"Go on, Simon. Surprise me," she quips, folding her arms and leaning against the wall.

"I got a call from a Doctor McKay. He's the shrink attached to this station. He has information about Fitzpatrick. It'll not break the case but he wants a word in person."

"I'll speak to him," she offers quickly. "It'll be interesting to hear what he has to say."

✧ ✧ ✧

Kerry

I LOOK AT my watch as I wait for the lift. Two twenty-five. Doctor McKay doctor has arranged to see me at two thirty. I'm curious to hear what this psychoanalyst guy will have to say about Liam Fitzpatrick. His office is on the third floor. I approach the door which bears his name emblazoned proudly on a plaque above a half-glazed upper panel.

Tapping the glass, I see his profile in the background. He comes over towards the door and opens it. I cast my eyes on a middle-aged man wearing a pin-striped suit and sporting perfectly groomed silver hair.

He smiles in greeting. "You must be Sergeant Lawlor. Come in."

"Thanks so much for your time," I reply gratefully.

He signals me to sit down in the chair opposite his desk. He slinks around to the other side of the desktop and seats himself opposite.

"Liam Fitzpatrick," he announces confidently, wasting no time in beginning our meeting. "I understand you're uncertain as to the cause of this dreadful accident?"

"There's various possibilities." I muse. "Are you aware that the child has died?"

"Yes, it's terrible for both the mother and Fitzpatrick himself." His face is sympathetic. "The thing is, he has a bit of a psychiatric history. Depression." He rests his fingers together in thought. "I know there was some talk of the impact being the result of a deliberate act, I thought I'd let you know this is a possibility. Not definite mind you, but it's something you can't rule out." He seems very circumspect.

Possibly a suicide, I reflect. How terribly tragic. *Especially with his little girl gone with him.*

"We sort of did set it to one side. The reason being that his daughter was in the car," I add. "Surely he'd wait until Emma was out of the picture before doing something desperate like that." Even as I voice this, I know it's pointless looking for logic in a complex situation involving mental illness.

"That's probably right. But Liam Fitzpatrick had clinical depression. Sometimes things get so bad that you just don't take your own life, you can take close relatives with you too." His fingers grip together in a relaxed clench. "I've seen this sort of thing before I'm afraid."

"So, you think it could have been a suicide attempt?" I'm repeating myself but with his own child on board, I'm struggling to let it sink in.

The doctor shifts in his seat. "I'm not saying it was suicide. I'm just saying it's possible. It's a mental condition which can happen to anyone. You see stuff like this on the news all the time. A farmer shoots his family and then shoots himself." The doctor shuffles some papers on his desk into a neat pile. He picks up a couple of files and slots them into the cabinet behind him. The subject of suicide is day-to-day business for him.

"When you say mental condition, do you mean Fitzpatrick had PTSD?" I ask.

"Not quite. Depression and post-traumatic stress disorder have similar symptoms but there are subtle differences. Depression builds up. It's usually brought on by a combination of worries all happening as once. Being jilted, money problems, career reverses. Things seem to get on top of people."

"So, what's PTSD precisely?" I have a fair idea but I'd rather hear the explanation from the horse's mouth.

"PTSD is usually triggered by a single massive blow. Loss of a loved one. It can be put into motion by any of the things which cause depression. Usually, the trigger is a one off, a death, a betrayal, something like that."

I flick a glance at my watch, conscious not to take up too much of his time. "Sorry to ask more questions but how can you tell the difference?"

He waves a hand dismissively. "It's fine, no problem about the time," he assures me, although I can't help but notice that his phone is lighting up with an incoming call. "Sometimes you can't, unless you know the history."

I'm getting the impression that he can't really tell me anymore. I'm going to have to make do with the information I have. I stand up, grabbing my files and sling my bag over my shoulder.

"Thank you so much for your time, sir," I offer my hand.

"You're welcome, detective." He shakes my hand. "I think that's all you need to know but if you need any further assistance, please don't hesitate to contact me again. I'm always glad to be of help."

✧   ✧   ✧

Simon

I PICK UP the canteen tray and carefully trace my steps back to the table where Kerry is sitting. "Well, anything interesting from Dr McKay?"

She's stirring her cappuccino intently as she thinks it over. "Yeah, he said Fitzpatrick has a history of depression. He's not ruling out the possibility that the accident could have been a suicide attempt. Even with his daughter in the car." She takes a sip of the coffee, her long nails clinking against the cup.

"That's interesting but we have to concentrate on stuff we can prove. What we've got now is maybe Big Al was involved, or maybe not. The shrink says it might be a suicide attempt but we can't prove it. Even if Liam drove into the wall deliberately, there's still the fact that he was over the limit on two counts. Drink and drugs. With the road safety lobby on our tails, we're going to have to charge him with manslaughter."

Kerry grimaces: "When you look at what happened to the child, I can't say I've much sympathy for the poor bugger."

"We have to go by the book and the book says it's manslaughter. We've no choice."

"Just something more for him to worry about if he survives."

CHAPTER FOURTEEN

Zoe

I WORE BLACK that day. There are those who say you should wear colourful clothes to a funeral. That it should be a celebration. *This was no celebration.*

You didn't live long enough to celebrate life, Emma. Six years is not enough. Sixty years maybe. Definitely not six.

You only had time to get to second year in school. To start learning your spellings, build castles in the sandpit and play hop scotch with friends. You only had a few years at home with me before nursery. Mothers and toddlers. We didn't have enough time to bake cookies and watch TV. You sat at the living-room window one day, watching the other kids walking home from school. You pointed at them and asked, "When can I go to the big school, mummy?"

"Soon, my little one. You'll be going soon."

You had a year and a half of school in the end. The teacher loved you and said you were a good girl, perfectly behaved. At Christmas, you played Mary in the school nativity. We put a tea-towel over your head and used your school tie to secure it. Your friend Jonny was the donkey and you sat on him all the way in. You looked so regal as you arrived.

I turn around and see the black shiny hearse outside. You have certainly arrived. Two men carry you up the aisle towards the altar. Your coffin is so small and white. I can't bear the thought of you inside it. The morbid image of you lying still and silent.

I think back to all the times I called out: *Emma! Quiet! Settle down!* Oh, how I wish I could take those words back. How I long for you to be able to talk as loud as you like. Skip up and down in the aisle until you collapse, giggling and exhausted. Make a racket, why don't you? Who would care about the noise you're making? What does it matter if you're a badly behaved child! That's what childhood is about.

Tears sting my eyes and roll down my cheeks. I dab the already sodden tissue onto my face. A guest darts a glance towards me, doing a double-take when she sees my expression. I'm raw and contorted with pain. Not that I care what anybody thinks of my appearance. I don't give a damn how I look.

I recognise that guest. She's the barmaid from Liam's work. A lot of his colleagues are here even though he's lying up in hospital.

I watch your little casket being carried to the front of the church and placed on the table at the altar. The soothing tones of *Ave Maria* echo out from the wall speakers. The music adds to the sadness.

The minister asks us to sit. Now he's saying a few words about you. You were young, innocent and a ray of sunshine. You put a smile on the faces of everyone who knew you. He offers up the usual comforting platitudes. That God wants another angel in heaven. The Lord needs you by his side. *I can't accept that. I won't accept it.*

What sort of God would want to take you away from me? After the things we've come through. The times I fought for you. Protected you with precious little support from anyone else. Now my failure to do that properly overwhelms me. How could I have let somebody like Liam take care of you that day? Why didn't I cancel that stupid party and stay home with you?

Emma, I'm sorry.

"Forgive us our trespasses..." the minister rambles out the Lord's prayer in the background somewhere, "...as we forgive those who trespass against us..."

But I won't forgive Liam. He chose to take drugs. It was his decision to get behind the wheel of a car. He floored the accelerator. He drove you, our baby, into that wall. He's the one at fault here.

The preacher continues to effuse sad words whilst glancing at the coffin, but my mind is thinking *revenge*. I will make Liam pay for this; for stabbing my heart and crushing my soul.

They begin to carry you back down the aisle. The hearse is waiting at the door. We all follow behind. I step outside and the sun glares harshly in my eyes. I put on my sunglasses and stand there, numb.

Now the awful small talk. People come up to

offer condolences. I should thank them but I'm not in the mood for niceties. My face is a tear-stained mess and I want to retreat to a quiet room. An escape to some sort of sanctuary. A place where I don't have to show gratitude for their attendances.

The woman who noticed me crying in the church comes over.

"Hi, I'm Mia," she says. Her demeanour is awkward and apologetic. "So sorry. I just wanted to pass on my condolences."

"Thanks," I say stiffly.

Mia falters a moment. It's as though she dreads the encounter but at the same time there's something she's itching to ask. "How's Liam?" she adds tentatively.

"He's doing okay," I acknowledge politely. "He's come out of the coma."

I want to blurt out: *Why do you ask? The murdering bastard is the reason we're all standing here today.* But my solicitor has told me not to say anything defamatory. It wouldn't do me any favours if there's a civil dispute between us.

"Oh, that's great!" she replies, her face light-ing up. She gushes it out with a cheery disposition.

I glare at her, deadpan. I'm not in the mood. "Excuse me," I walk off abruptly. I move over to a spot on my own at the side of the church, away from the small group congregating outside. I light a cigarette and put my mobile phone to my ear. I pretend to listen to someone so that no-one comes over to disturb me. I don't want people to invade my space or engage in small talk.

I inhale the smoke deeply. I happen to be standing right next to the gleaming black hearse. Your tiny coffin is resting on the polished oak decking inside it. It's almost as though we're having some quiet time together. All those people can stand over there and witter on about nothing. For them, this is just a sad occasion that will pass. But for me, my life is over. You're gone. It's Liam's fault. My world has crumpled around me. Why does the sun shine so brightly today, when it should be grey and miserable?

In the background, I can hear a lady laughing at someone else's wit. How can they be joking when they should be sad and sombre? Then I see my mother walking towards me. I point to my phone, motioning that I'm busy but she keeps coming. She is now hovering next to me, interlacing her arm around mine.

I continue to pretend that I'm having a conversation with a make-believe person on the other end of the line. "Okay, well, thanks for your kind wishes, it's appreciated," I try to sound convincing. "Yeah, bye." I shove the phone in my pocket and give my mum a gentle smile.

"Who was that?" she probes.

"A friend from work." I look away as I tell the lie.

A silence descends upon the two of us. It suddenly dawns on me that we're standing there, gazing directly at your coffin.

I turn to my mother and ask: "Where's dad?" My voice is laced with scorn.

She sighs. "He's not here but you kind of expected that, didn't you?"

"I suppose it's just as well. At least I don't have to look at his disapproving face all day."

She gives me a glance which tells me she doesn't want to argue, but she knows I'm right. I can picture him scolding. Saying things like, *Well, I warned her. I told her to find somebody worthwhile. If she had met a decent hard-working sort instead of a useless good-for-nothing, none of this would have happened.*

Maybe he has a point.

I inhale the final drag of my cigarette and flick it away. It rolls under the wheel of the hearse.

"Isn't it about time you gave those up?" Mother lectures dutifully as always.

I glare at her disapprovingly. "Are you really going to having a go at me about smoking at my own daughter's funeral? Don't you think I need something to cope with the stress?"

"Sorry, I shouldn't have said anything," she answers apologetically, patting my shoulder.

I suddenly feel guilty about snapping her head off. It's just that there's a well of anger boiling in my gut. Ready to explode. God forbid if anyone inadvertently steps into my path. I'm looking for a fight. With somebody, anybody will do, but especially Liam.

The undertaker comes over to discuss details. He says they're ready to start the funeral cortege towards the cemetery. Do we want to walk behind for a bit?

We follow you. Your tiny white coffin ahead of us. It feels like the weight of the world is on my shoulders. My mother on one side of me, an uncle on the other. They almost have to prop me up; steady my frame and help me to walk along.

I notice that passers-by stop and stare; probably pitying us. They can see the tiny white casket and must realise I'm the mother. They're thinking *Oh dear God, poor woman, that must be her child.*

I don't need their pity. I'd rather have their disapproval. Back to the time when you were running riot through the supermarket. Being a nuisance. I would rather they were rolling their eyes with disdain and saying: *She should have that child under control.*

We're now being ushered into another black car behind the hearse and motoring away. Suddenly we're at the graveside. I'm not ready for this. I can't bear to see your little coffin being lowered into the ground by strange men using spades to toss mucky soil on top of you. I can't believe a small wooden box with you inside is disappearing into the depths of the earth. *Oh God, I can't see your coffin at all now!*

My tears flow unstoppably. I'm sobbing inconsolably as you slip out of sight. This can't be happening. You're gone. *Forever.*

I now feel completely drained, like a balloon that's just been burst. We arrive back home and slump into the armchair. Mum is there, along with relatives and friends. She is fussing around making sandwiches but I can't face the thought of eating. All the energy has left my body. You have gone and I am hollowed out.

"I'm going to lie down if you don't mind," I give a dismissive wave to my mother as I brush past her on the way to the bedroom. My eyes are glazed over. I'm living a nightmare.

"Of course, dear, you go and have a rest." Her words trail behind me.

Everyone in the room glances nervously at each other. They understand.

I wish sleep could take over. I pray for unconsciousness to engulf me but I lie awake. My tortured mind replays the burial scene incessantly. The sight of the little white casket. The horror of it being lowered into the ground. The dirt so easily flung on top of you.

And then I think of Liam. Comfortable in hospital. Having caused it all. Anger boils furiously inside me.

Some people have to be made to pay.

CHAPTER FIFTEEN

Zoe

EACH DAY BEGINS to feel like Groundhog Day. I sit endlessly at Liam's hospital bedside, day in, day out.

I'm supposed to be the doting partner, praying for a speedy recovery. I bring coffees and magazines, bottles of Lucozade and sugar-laden traybakes. Between taxis, treats and drinks, my wallet is emptied out continuously and I'm exhausted.

Liam might be the one lying on his back, unable to move; his body trying to recover from the accident, but I'm worn out too. They often say that it's not just the patient who suffers; the family go through just as much. All the trekking to and fro, the emotional drain; it's just as much a burden for the visitors.

When the nurse passes, I nod politely, acknowledging her sympathetic glances and warm smiles. In reality, I'm secretly spouting venom at him through gritted teeth.

"How could you do this to me? Why did you get behind that wheel knowing you had drink and drugs in your system?" I'm holding his hand but I realise my grasp is too tight; my pent-up frustration is channelled into the grip.

Liam sighs, his head sinks further into the pillow. "We've been through this a million times Zoe. It was an accident. I'm as devastated as you are. Don't you think I'm totally traumatised about what's happened to Emma?" He closes his eyes.

I can tell he's trying to fight back tears but I can't stop myself continuing to dish it out. "Maybe if you hadn't taken drugs in the first place or pushed your foot against the accelerator so hard, perhaps you wouldn't be traumatised," I hiss.

He spells his next words out slowly and resolutely. "My drink was spiked. I've told you that already."

"Why were you in the bar in the first place? Why didn't you take Emma to a *McDonalds* or something?" I'm being persistent and pushy; an absolute nag but I can't help myself.

"Because I was going to check on my rota, for god's sake. I told you before!" he glares at me, exasperated.

"I never should have let you look after her that day. What was I thinking?" I shake my head and close my eyes. My body is deflated.

"No, you shouldn't have," Liam spat back. "Cos you're so perfect and such a great mother."

I look up at him abruptly. "What's that supposed to mean?" My eyes drill into his.

Liam sighs and looks away. "You know exactly what I mean."

I fold my arms, defiance screaming out of every pore. "No I don't as a matter of fact. Why don't you enlighten me?"

"Well, let's see…" Liam begins "…Let's talk about the night the neighbours called the police, shall we? Do you remember that?" His eyes widen and the anger seeps out of him. He despises me; I can tell. In this moment, he absolutely detests me.

Of course I remember. How can I forget? I recall the precise moment there was a loud knock on the door.

✧　✧　✧

"POLICE HERE, CAN you answer?" A deep voice boomed from outside.

The cops wouldn't understand it. It wasn't my fault I had a knife in my hand; it was Liam's. He brought out all the frustration in me. I wasn't actually going to do anything; I was just trying to scare him. I had tried everything to make him stop using drugs – being angry, placating, coaxing, trying to build him up. Anything to discourage him from stealing money and wasting his life away. Wasting our lives away.

If drugs hadn't turned him into a selfish, self-seeking, lethargic prick, he wouldn't be so impossible to live with. If he was clean and sober, I could have peace and contentment. A normal existence.

It turns out that some nosey neighbour over-heard our domestic and called the police. Talk about making a drama out of nothing!

We used to fight like cats and dogs. On and off like a light switch. The night the Police turned up was the night I broke off our engagement. I threw the ring back at him. It was probably a cheap trinket bought off the back of some lorry anyway.

"Over my dead body will you ever get custody of Emma!" I shouted at him.

He bawled a mouthful back; something about me drinking too much and not being a suitable mother.

That was when I slapped him; hard and fast across the face. It stung; I could tell. His face broke into a pained expression and his hand darted up to his cheek.

"You bitch!" he yelled. "What's got into you? You're out of your head!"

"For Christ's sake! You're the one that's always out of your head!" I yelled back. "You and your bloody dope! You don't care about anything other than drugs and partying! Well, you know what? If you want to party with fucking Gaz that much, then go! Piss off to his place then!"

"Yeah, I will!" he retorted furiously, grabbing his coat and making to leave. "I'm not gonna stick around listening to some crazy bitch…"

His mumbling was cut short when I suddenly grabbed the kitchen knife from the holder on the counter and pointed it towards him.

"Get out then!" I screamed. "Get out!"

The blood was pumping through my body, adrenaline pulsating from head to toe. The knife shook in my hand.

"Zoe…" Liam said, in a shaken voice. "Put the knife down…" His eyes were bulging and his shock was obvious.

That was the moment the police knocked the door. *Saved by the bell.*

An officer asked a ton of questions and took statements. Liam decided not to press charges but he did clear off to Gaz's to live.

Initially, I was glad to see the back of him. Good riddance to the drunken rows. The end of having to hide my purse. No more nights when I would hear Emma crying because of our arguments.

That resentment didn't last long. The anger dissolved with the loneliness. Too many long nights lying in a big empty bed took its toll. It's easy to romanticise about the good times when there's a gaping hole left behind.

How is it possible to love someone and hate them at the same time? To be so attracted to someone; his strong jawline, his dark red hair, his confident stance, and yet at the same time, resentment seething from every pore.

A friend once remarked that my attraction for him bordered on obsession.

I romanticized about all the good times; the mornings that he cuddled up to me in bed; the laughs we had together; day trips to the beach. Picnics, drinks and strolling home after a lazy summer day, our skin tinged by the sun and faces glowing. The love-making. The quiet slumber. A long lie-in and breakfast in bed.

It was when Emma came along that things changed. In some ways for the better but in many ways for the worse.

In some respects, it bonded us. We would be

forever entangled because of her. Destined always to have that connection, no matter what. When the arguments started and the break-ups began, we still had to communicate about Emma. Even if it was a simple text to say "are you coming to collect her today?", we connected.

At first, he idolised Emma. Spent every waking moment with her; cuddling and feeding her, even changing the nappies. We went for walks and he carried her close to his chest in one of those body slings. He looked so adorable. Men have no idea how sexy they look when they carry a baby around. They come across as protective and manly.

But after some time, he changed. It wasn't anything Emma did, obviously, it was the responsibility that came with her, the financial struggle. The inability to take off at a moment's notice. I think he felt trapped by Emma and me. He resented us.

He saw his other university friends getting acting roles. Nothing spectacular but one of them, Ben, landed a part in a TV soap. Liam went to visit Ben one weekend and came back in a stinking mood. He saw the way girls flocked around Ben. How he threw his money around; fine dining in the best restaurants, a flashy car, designer clothes. I think he saw Ben as a sort of parallel universe. *The life he would've been living if it wasn't for us.*

Ben was being offered tons of money to pro-mote men's clothes and aftershave, whereas Liam worked in a bar, carrying dregs of drink and stacking pint glasses for a living.

When we were lying in bed one night, I whispered to him in the darkness, "Maybe you shouldn't visit Ben again. It just seems to get you down."

I meant those words to bring comfort. I was only pointing out the obvious but Liam sat bolt upright. His blood was boiling and there was no way he'd get to sleep now.

"Oh, so you're telling me who I can and can't visit now, are you?" he spat, his voice laden with anger.

"No, Liam, of course not..." I said this softly, trying to coax him back to bed, but he stormed out of the bedroom as I was speaking.

"I can't sleep," he seethed, and I heard him go down the stairs and into the living-room.

Five minutes later, I could smell the distinct aroma of marijuana coming up the staircase. I tutted. I told him he shouldn't smoke that stuff in the house. I'd said it a million times before. It wasn't healthy for Emma to be inhaling passive smoke.

I sprinted down the stairs and flung open the living room door. He was sitting there in the armchair, his face like thunder; a can of beer in one hand and a spliff in the other.

"If you're going to smoke, can you go outside?" I snapped angrily, my voice shaking.

"It's my house," he said stubbornly. "If I want to sit in my armchair and smoke a joint, I will."

I gave a derisive laugh. "It's not your house honey," My voice was laden with a patronising tone but I didn't care. "It's a rented house and we don't own it."

He glared at me. I could practically see his blood boiling. That's the thing about being in a relationship with someone for that long. You know exactly what to say to hurt them. You know the right buttons to push. And I'd just hit him where it hurt. I'd bruised his ego and damaged his pride; drew attention to his inability to provide. It was a low blow, but I was angry.

He stood abruptly. For a split second, I honestly thought he was going to hit me. He stormed across the room in my direction and his face came right up close to mine.

"Cheers bitch, thanks for reminding me."

His breath stank of beer and drugs. I blinked back as if he had spat on me.

"And may I remind you," he seethed. "That you're an unemployed single mother."

He charged through the kitchen and out the back door where he stood to smoke the rest of his spliff.

He was right, technically. Even though we lived together, we weren't married, so for all intents and purposes, I was a single mother. It was on nights like this, when we had terrible rows, that the pressure of that responsibility really got to me. I knew that at any moment he could get up and walk out. That I would be left on my own, holding the baby.

Well, at least he took his filthy smoking outside like I told him to. At that point, I retreated upstairs. Somehow, Emma slept through it all. I peeked in at her, lying in the little single bed. She looked so cute and peaceful. I kissed her gently on her forehead.

"If we are left on our own, sweetheart, we'll be okay," I whispered. "We'll manage."

Liam's huffiness continued into the following day. I was delighted when he cleared off to work. I was glad to get him out of the house.

In fact, he stayed out of the house for three days that time. I had no idea where he was but suspected he had probably gone to some house party which went on far too long. Part of me didn't even care. The house was so blissfully quiet without him. No blaring football on the TV, no sound of racing cars tearing around a track over and over again. It was just me and Emma. Peaceful.

Of course, he returned after the three days with his tail between his legs. He walked in the door, his expression apologetic and guilty.

"I'm sorry," he said, the tone genuine.

I looked up at him. I was sitting with Emma cuddled next to me.

"Daddy!" she cried excitedly. She jumped up and ran over to hug him. "You're home!"

"Yes, I am sweetie," he grinned, picking her up and planting a kiss on her cheek. "Did you miss me?"

She nodded enthusiastically.

"Did mummy say where I was?" His question was tentative; testing the water, wondering if I had bad-mouthed him. Of course, he knew better. I would never run him down in front of Emma.

Emma nodded. "Yes, she said you were away

working again."

He looked over and me and mouthed a grateful "thank you."

"That's right, I was," he agreed happily. "And I brought you back a present."

"You did?" she grinned. "What is it? What is it?"

"Well, now, why don't you run into the kitchen and see what I left on the table for you," he said, giving her a playful tap on the bum. She scampered off while he stood there looking at me.

"I'm so sorry," he repeated.

"We'll chat about it later," I whispered, "after she's gone to bed".

And we did, later on, when Emma was fast asleep. We sat on the sofa, me with a glass of wine and Liam with a cuppa. We had a heart-to-heart.

He confessed that he'd gone to a party that turned into a binge. He woke up hungover and on a comedown. He regretted every minute of it. He knew deep down inside that this is where he belonged – with me and Emma. He didn't want to be a drunken scumbag lying in some drug den. He yearned to be a good father and a reliable partner. He promised he'd change. Things would be different this time.

"Why don't we get married?" he blurted out.

My breath caught in my throat. "What?" I giggled.

"Let's do it Zoe, let's get married," he grabbed my hands and clutched them in his. "We are meant to be together. It's always been me and you, hasn't it? We'll always be together."

I was half laughing, half crying. Tears were stinging out of my eye sockets and running down my cheeks, but they were happy tears. Tears that let out a ton of emotion – surprise, relief, happiness. Finally, he'd come back to the nest. Whatever he had to get out of his system, he was rid of it of for once and for all.

He was home.

✧   ✧   ✧

"Do you want a sip of water?" I ask him. His mouth looks dry. He's making a slow recovery. Suddenly, guilt makes me want to nurse him.

"Yes please," he replies softly.

I lean gently towards him, placing the plastic straw in the direction of his mouth. He takes it gratefully, and sucks. Such a simple act and yet one that's laden with emotion. Him so vulnerable; me the carer.

"Thanks," he says, when he leans back on his pillow.

What are we like? I think to myself. Love and hate. Up and down. A pair of magnets that can't help being pulled towards each other.

But sometimes magnets line up poles apart. Sometimes magnets repel.

CHAPTER SIXTEEN

Zoe

"**A**LL STAND." THE Clerk of Court bawls to the assembly. "Judge Johnston presiding!"

The Criminal Court is now in full session. I'm sitting with my solicitor beside me. He insists on being there although I am not involved directly in the proceedings.

I notice that the two detectives, Simon and Kerry, are sitting near the prosecution team. Just a job for them, another day at the office. I hope they've done their homework and Liam gets his dues.

The judge announces to the court:

"Dreadful business this. Everybody that matters seems to be here. Counsel for the Prosecution, please get on with it. It's a tragedy, so don't bog us down with waffle. The world and his uncle know what happened from the press so get started with the basic facts and move on."

A long-drawn-out procedure commences. The judge asks for Liam to be arraigned. I learn that "arraigned" means charges will be read out. Illegal substances, dangerous driving and manslaughter. He pleads not guilty on all counts. Now he is walking back to his seat where the defence team are sitting. The Director of Public Prosecutions attorney gets to his feet and adjusts the hideous silvery wig before speaking.

"Ladies and gentlemen of the jury, this is a straightforward case. The Defendant, Liam Fitzpatrick, that you see in the dock, is charged with manslaughter. On the evening of Friday 24 July 2020 at 11.14pm, he drove into a wall. We all know the tragic consequences. I will be able to establish that he was driving under the influence of drugs and alcohol. This caused the death of his own daughter, Emma Waller, who was only six. Mr Fitzpatrick has already paid a severe price in terms of bereavement. But the law must take its toll."

"Will the defendant please take the witness box?"

I watch Liam get slowly to his feet. He's more or less fully recovered by now but he's not one hundred per cent. He doesn't look nervous but I know he is putting on the usual show of bravado whilst quaking inside. He's just been arraigned for manslaughter in a Court of Law but he'll brazen it out. The seriousness of the case seems to have no bearing on his behaviour.

I look at the stony faces of the jury sitting to the left of the dock. One of them is a woman in her fifties, hair greying at the temples. Her face takes on an expression of disgust as the charges are being read. I assume she's dwelling on the thought of a father killing his own daughter. Good. That's one vote against Liam. One down, eleven to go.

The public prosecutor hits Liam with a charge

sheet he can't deny. The evidence is there in black and white. Medical reports confirm he had alcohol and benzodiazepines in his system. The CCTV footage proves that the car was speeding at the time. Sadly, mortuary reports show that Emma Fitzpatrick, aged six years and forty-three days on the date of the incident, became unconscious and died as a result of the collision. She was brain-dead from the moment of impact.

Liam doesn't have a leg to stand on but his stance remains defiant. His face is calm and his manner controlled. At this moment he is called to the witness box.

"Mister Fitzpatrick," the prosecutor continues. "I will now ask you a number of questions. Please remember that your answers should be addressed to his Honour Judge Johnston. Now, tell the court about events prior to the accident that evening. Explain your whereabouts from seven pm onwards."

I fold my arms, staring at Liam. What lies will he come up with? How will he worm his way out this time? The evidence is piled high against him. He has nowhere to go but he tries his best. He claims that at eight thirty that evening, he called into the pub to check on his rota.

"That's the *Duck and Goose*?" counsel interrupts. "Can you confirm to the Court that this is your place of employment? Am I correct?"

"Yeah, that's correct," Liam confirms. "I planned to call in for a short time, maybe half an hour or so and then head on."

"Please continue," the lawyer prompts. "Tell

us exactly what happened there."

"Emma was thirsty so I thought we'd have a quick drink each while we were there. I asked the guy behind the bar for a *Coca Cola* for me and an orange juice for her."

"A quick drink Mister Fitzpatrick?" The learned counsel repeated. "And what happened after that?"

"We were there for quite a bit longer than I intended. I remember taking Emma back to the car later and getting in. We headed off. We drove for a bit in the general direction of Emma's home. I started to feel woozy. I was about to pull over. The next thing, I woke up in the hospital. I'd obviously been plied with something."

"Plied? With what? Mister Fitzpatrick. What exactly?"

"Objection, your honour!" the defence barrister now jumps to his feet. "My client is truthfully trying to recollect details of a very harrowing event. He is not qualified to identify substances which my learned colleague will no doubt attempt to infer that he may or may not have ingested. There's medical evidence on the table. Various reports will follow. Prosecuting counsel is well aware of these documents."

"Sustained," the judge mumbles matter-of-factly.

The defence counsel purses his lips and clasps his thumbs under the lapels of his robe in an almost theatrical manner. He then sits down as quickly as he has risen.

"Very well, your honour," the prosecutor

returns to the fray. "Let's resume where we left off. You say you felt woozy? Have you suffered symptoms like this before?"

Liam seems to gather confidence. "What I'm saying is I didn't take anything. I mean, I didn't take drugs of any kind. I believe my drink was spiked. It had to be. There is no other explanation."

A distinct murmur ripples across the courtroom. People are expressing surprise or disbelief.

"Quiet please!" his honour pipes up. "Please remember that this is a court of law."

Silence immediately descends as the prosecution resumes its line of questioning.

"Mister Fitzpatrick, people would find this hard to believe. Why would anyone do this? Do you have any idea who might have spiked your drink? By the way, just to make it clear to the jury, when you use the word 'spiked', you mean somebody introduced an illegal substance to the glass from which you were imbibing?"

Liam nods and his eyes divert to the back of the room. "Yes, and I believe I know who it was. I believe it was Alistair Jones."

I look around and my eyes follow the path indicated by Liam. There at the back of the room sits the infamous "Big Al", arms crossed, a smug look plastered across his face.

"And why do you believe that this particular person spiked your drink, Mr Fitzpatrick?" the prosecutor presses on.

For the first time Liam looks uncomfortable. "We er... put it like this, we've had a few disagreements in the past."

"Your honour!" the advocate wheels away from Liam. He glances at the judge and looks around the court with some confidence. "May I present to the jury the CCTV security footage of the *Duck and Goose* pub on that particular evening. It does in fact show this Mister Jones…" The learned brief gesticulates behind him like he's shaking a salt cellar over his shoulder. "… is actually seen to hover near to the defendant's glass whilst his back is facing the camera. It confirms that Jones was present. But there is no evidence whatsoever that he interfered with anyone's drink." At this point, the prosecutor rounds back on Liam: "It's plain to see on screen, is it not?"

For once, Liam has nothing to say. Counsel goes on.

"So, I put it to you, Mr Fitzpatrick, that the idea of some character conducting a vendetta conveniently on the night you were driving negligently is nothing more than a fantasy designed to get you off the hook? After all, you've had enough time since your arrest to dream this up."

There is a brief pause. The type where you could hear the proverbial pin drop.

"Now, Mr Fitzpatrick," this time the prosecutor adopts a bored tone. I guess he wants to emphasize the incredulity of Liam's account of events. "The question of spiking the drink is not the only matter of doubt, is it? You say you ordered a *Coca-Cola*. However, there is absolutely no doubt that there was alcohol in your system. If eyesight serves, it was actually a glass of beer on the counter beside you. Did this mysterious interloper also remove the *Coca-Cola* and substitute the lager?"

A humorous murmur of the crowd ripples across the hall.

Liam squirms: "Well, I did have half a pint whilst I was there."

"I see," the prosecution announces with a smattering of glee. "But I observe from the CCTV that the bar tender actually handed over a pint of beer to you. Do you deny that the glass on the countertop was a pint glass?"

"I didn't drink it all," Liam protests. "I ordered a Coke at first but the bar guy knows me and was just being friendly. He offered me one on the house. That's all. I told him I was driving and I'd only drink half."

"So, whilst your six-year-old daughter was sitting by your side on an uncomfortable pub stool surrounded by men drinking alcohol, you drank beer and chatted to your mates. Would you say that this is a responsible way to be minding your daughter, Mr Fitzpatrick?"

I feel my insides burst with joy. *Take that!*

Liam shakes his head defiantly. "It was a quick chat and then we headed on. She was quite happy playing games on her kids' tablet."

"There's no hard evidence that this fellow Jones, or indeed anyone at all, dropped any sort of substance into your drink. Isn't it the case that this particular establishment is well known for a trade in substances of the sort you are quite obviously alluding to? In fact, it's not out of hand to suggest that you acquired the drug all by yourself at some point and popped it into your own drink. And that you drank more than you're admitting. Isn't that a far more likely scenario Mr Fitzpatrick?"

Liam shakes his head again. "No, definitely not."

"Well, we will have to ask Mr Jones. And I guess it will be your word against his." Peering over his half-moon spectacles, the barrister darts a condescending glance at Jones. The latter appears to have no qualms about being involved in the dialogue. He even appears to be puffing his chest out, enjoying the notoriety.

Liam shrugs his shoulders defiantly. It almost looks like a stand-off might emerge between him and Jones. Liam doesn't usually back down.

"Please tell us why Mr Jones would have wanted to spike your drink? Who would want to let you have the gift of a free drug hit?"

Another tinkling of laughter breezes across the room.

"We've had a few disagreements in the past," Liam shifts uncomfortably.

"Disagreements about what?" the lawyer persists.

Liam shrugs his shoulders once more. "Just silly stuff, I suppose." It is clear he trying to make the explanation as obscure as possible.

"Silly stuff, you suppose?" the prosecutor replies with a sceptical grin. "Well, let's find out if your supposition is correct." At this, he glances to the back of the room and back to Liam: "You may step down for the time being Mr Fitzpatrick. I think we will now call Mr Alistair Jones to the stand. Perhaps he can enlighten us as to why he would place free drugs in your drink."

The Clerk booms: "Alistair Jones to the witness box please!"

There then follows a rigmarole of making the affirmation of truth as the Clerk holds up the card. All this palaver although neither of these first two witnesses have probably ever told the truth in their lives.

Big Al comes to the witness stand. He's decked out in an expensive suit which fails to conceal the dark billowing tattoos which creep all over his neck and down to his wrists.

"Mr Jones, could you confirm if there was any issue of dispute between yourself and Mr Fitzpatrick? Please go into as much detail as possible, sir."

"He got off with my missus one night," Jones announces in a thick Belfast accent.

"Now, let me get this clear Mr Jones," the prosecutor nods. "I want the jury to fully understand what's going on, although I'm sure they a perfectly worldly-wise group of citizens. So, when you say "getting off", you mean he had a sexual relationship of some sort with your wife on, do we say, one occasion? Or perhaps more than one occasion?"

"As far as I'm concerned, the bugger better not have done it more than once!"

The judge intervenes. "Do I have to remind you Mr Jones, that this is court of law and your answer has to be respectful as well as accurate. Threats are out of the question. I have to add that you must change your attitude or you will be charged with contempt of court. I promise you will regret that if it occurs." He reverts to the prosecutor, "Now please proceed."

The advocate resumes: "I will take it then that you believe that a sexual encounter took place just once to your knowledge."

"Yes, that's right sir."

I close my eyes. I wonder when exactly this happened. Probably when I was sat at home minding the baby.

"Now Mr Jones, having said all this, does that mean you would want to spike the defendant's drink with some sort of illegal substance?"

"No sir, in my experience, I'm pretty sure Liam is quite capable of taking a helluva' lot of drugs all by himself."

This time there is more than a ripple from the gathering. There is a distinct flare-up of laughter. The judge doesn't appear to be concerned.

The prosecutor appears satisfied that the point has been made. "No more questions, your honour." He sits down and nods to the defence counsel, "Your witness, sir."

The defence counsel stands. "I have no questions for this witness." He turns to the judge, "With respect, unless you have any questions your honour, the witness may return to the floor."

There then follows a parade of other witnesses, endless reports and technical stuff. It appears that Liam was quite definitely not in a fit state to drive when he killed our daughter.

✧ ✧ ✧

"Has the jury decided on a verdict?" The judge asks the foreman of the jury to rise: "Have you reached a verdict on all three charges?"

"Yes, your honour." The female juror responds with an air of gravity.

"Please tell us your verdict and answer the clerk in sequence. We start with the charge of manslaughter. Please read out your conclusion as shown on the card handed to you by the clerk of court."

I look over at Liam. He keeps his gaze firmly ahead but I can tell that his nerves are finally starting to kick in. My palms are covered in sweat and I brush them slowly down my trouser legs.

"Your honour, on the first count of manslaughter, we find the defendant..."

I hold my breath. I watch the juror's lips move as though the whole thing is in slow motion. I look over at Liam and see his Adam's apple bobble up and down as he gulps with fear.

"Guilty."

Liam closes his eyes. My hand shoots up to my mouth in shock. My solicitor looks over at me and displays a triumphant smile.

I should be happy. I ought to feel a wave of relief. Instead, I feel nothing. I find no triumph in this result. There is no victory in the fact that the man I fell in love with is going to prison for killing our daughter. What's to celebrate about that? The only good outcome would be if none of this happened at all.

In a perfect world, there wouldn't have been a custody issue. Liam wouldn't be an addict and I'd never have gone to Una's party. Emma would be alive and well today.

He is pronounced guilty on the other two counts; over the limit and speeding. A police officer snaps handcuffs around Liam's wrists and escorts him out of the courtroom. Liam glances over at me but quickly looks away. I feel as though my insides have been ripped out; like a pumpkin carved up for Halloween.

"Liam..." I open my mouth to speak but he's gone, led through a door at the back of the courtroom. I imagine him being taken down to a cell; being told to strip and shower. A set of prison clothes being left out for him to wear. I blink back the tears.

"Good result?" My solicitor says with a comforting smile.

My expression is glazed over. All I can think about is Emma's white coffin.

"Yeah, a good result." I mumble in a resigned tone, trying to disguise my sarcasm.

The solicitor doesn't heed my tone. He is packing up his things and getting ready to leave. "I'll be in touch," he says with another cheery smile. He walks away.

My mum appears at the court door. She laces her arm in mine and we walk quietly out of the building. I stand on the steps outside. The grand stone staircase sweeps down to the bustling street.

Life goes on. People hurry about, getting on with their busy lives.

I suddenly spot that woman from the funeral. The one that worked with Liam. She is standing with a friend. They are both drawing on cigarettes and deep in conversation. She glances over at me. I return a stiff smile but she looks away quickly, as though pretending she hasn't seen me.

"Come on love," mum directs me towards the taxi rank. "Let's get you home. You need a cuppa."

I'm going to need more than a cup of tea. I can think of something better.

Like a stiff drink, a handful of Valium and a dose of revenge.

CHAPTER SEVENTEEN

Kerry

"HEY, GOT YOU a coffee," I smile at Simon as I approach him. He's waiting for me outside the courthouse. It's a clear, crisp autumnal morning. Overhanging trees show off their beautiful orange and burnt red leaves. Nature is bursting with colour. The beauty of the fall is like a creator splattering his canvas with brush-loads of paint.

"Thanks," Simon takes the proffered coffee cheerfully but seems distracted. We fall into step together, walking towards the main entrance.

"Wonder how this will pan out today?" I muse in an effort to make small talk.

"Hopefully they'll send him down," his tone seems clipped and professional.

The thing about working with someone for some time is that you pick up their mood quickly. You can usually tell when a colleague is in form for banter. You know when a joke will be taken well, and levity gets the right response. Similarly, it's obvious when your colleague prefers to keep things subdued; when he's sullen or has something on his mind. Perhaps mulling over a problem at home, brain-dead and unable to focus.

Simon is having one of those days. He is quiet

and withdrawn. His thoughts are elsewhere and I don't need three guesses to figure out what it is. It's probably about Laura. We stroll along in silence save for the click clack of my stiletto heels underfoot.

I'm wearing a new suit, bought especially for the day in court; a figure-hugging pencil skirt in deep blue, with a matching jacket and cream blouse. I love wearing new clothes and always feel better in a suit. It empowers me as a woman and I need to feel empowered today.

My mind turns to another female facing to-day's drama, Zoe Waller. I dread to think of what she must be going through. She would want to cry out in court about her child dying, but how can she, when her partner is the killer?

We are attending Liam Fitzpatrick's trial. As expected, we will be called as witnesses and I, for one, would like to see closure for Zoe.

In the main, the court case is tedious. Endless waiting around. Yawning through monotonous legal jargon. Coffee of the bad vending machine variety. Simon stays quiet and introspective. I resort to scrolling emails on the cell phone and trying to get up to date on my outstanding caseload.

It's a relief when the jury return to the court-room at the end of the day. First, the manslaughter charge. That's the real deal in the bag. Liam is guilty as charged. Then the other two counts. Over the limit on drink and drugs. A hat-trick and it means a win for us. But there are two losers in this game, Zoe and Emma. A little girl's life lost and a mother grieving forever. We can't do anything about that.

I pick up my bag, slip on my coat and check my watch. Four o'clock. There's no point heading back to the station now. The day shift has just ended.

"Fancy a quick drink?" Simon ventures, out of the blue, as if he's just read my mind.

I raise my eyebrows. "Sure." I'm somewhat surprised by the offer. After all, he's been pretty quiet and reflective all day. At no time did he strike me as being sociable. Maybe he fancies a drink just to let off steam.

We walk over to the nearby *Malmaison Hotel*. I eyeball the lovely bar on the ground floor. It's dripping with plush velvet upholstery and classy chandeliers. The place oozes a dark, moody atmosphere.

I settle on one of the comfy corner sofas whilst Simon goes up to the bar to order drinks. He re-appears holding a cocktail and a pint of lager.

"Oooh, nice!" I take the beautiful frosted glass from his hand.

We toast the court victory and lapse into small talk. We go over the case and descend into idle gossip about colleagues. The cocktail is going down far too quickly and when my glass empties, Simon dutifully asks, "Another?"

I shake my head. "Oh no, it's my round, I'll get it." I stand up, fumbling with my bag and making a to-do of putting it over my shoulder. "Same again?"

"Aw go on! You've twisted my arm," he

quips.

Already I see that he is starting to relax. I'm surprised he wants to hang about for another but I guess the alcohol is doing the job; melting his mood. Two drinks turn into three and cocktails are switched for wine. A mixture of crisps and dips appear in front of us at the same time since neither party has had the chance to eat dinner.

Three drinks on an empty stomach means only one thing. I'm getting tipsy; the lovely mellow, relaxed state of mind where you feel you could chill out on that sofa all night. There is nowhere else I'd rather be. This cosy, classy, atmospheric bar is a secret little corner of heaven and I don't want to leave. Simon and I lapse into that unselfconscious world where defences go down and conversation opens up.

"So," he poses, raising an amused eyebrow. "What's the latest on the dating scene?"

I roll my eyes. "Oh my god, the dating scene! You're really asking me that? As though I have any clue?"

"Come on, fill me in on the recent dates, who are the lucky guys? Give me a laugh at least."

I hit him playfully on the arm. "Well thanks very much. My dating disasters are not simply there for your entertainment you know!"

"Aren't they?" he grins mischievously. "Go on, tell me."

I sigh. "Oh, alright then!" I take a deep breath, ready to launch into my latest escapade. "Well, apart from all the utterly banal first messages. You know. *How are you. Where are you from? What part of town do you live in?* The same repetitive questions over and over again."

His lips crack into an amused smile as I continue.

"So, I went on a date with this guy. Just a coffee mind you, so I can escape quickly if it's a disaster. He turns up and looks nothing like his photo. It happens all the time."

"Well, what did he look like?" Simon queries.

"The photo must've been taken ten years ago. Forget dating, he could've been married and divorced twice in between!"

"Not at all picky," Simon interjects jokingly.

"I've no problem with age, I just think it's silly to show a photo from a previous life! Why lie?"

"Maybe the truth doesn't work like a lie does." Simon shrugs with a funny look in his eye.

"So, this guy and me; it's like pulling teeth. I'm having to ask all the questions and he's dishing out one-word answers. Horrendous!"

Simon grins. "He was probably intimidated by your looks."

I give him a demure look which shows maybe he's taking the piss out of me.

"It was just too painful," I continue. "I made an excuse to leave, went across the road, walked into *Ann Summers* and bought myself a vibrator instead."

Simon laughs out loud. "Did you really?"

"Of course, I did!" I stare back cheekily. "What else is a girl supposed to do?"

"Wow," Simon gasps. "The dating scene. Glad I'm out of it."

"Yeah, alright Mr McSmug," I tease.

He nudges me. "Would I be right in observing that I'm the guy who probably hangs out with you in pubs more than any other fella?"

I ponder the question. "God, you're right!" I say in an attempt to sound horrified. "What an awful thought!"

"Watch it you," he flirts. "I'm not that bad and I'm heading to the bar to get another round." He springs up and saunters over to the bar. I can't remember how many drinks we've had by now.

"Nice one," I say to his retreating buttocks. "Some more snacks while you're at it please."

"Yes ma'am," he proffers a deferential salute, like I'm in command.

"So, what *is* your type exactly?" Simon resumes. He's returned from the bar and we're sipping the two fresh drinks.

I glance at him, "The usual stereotype, I guess. Tall, dark and handsome." *A bit like Simon*, I think, but give nothing away.

He raises an eyebrow. "I see..." The acknowledgement comes with a knowing smile on his lips.

"There's a couple of other points on the checklist. Men that aren't married for one, and men that I don't work with." I wink flirtatiously.

"Shame," he smiles, softly. He starts to fidget with his drink.

There's a swirl of excitement in the pit of my stomach. He's got to be flirting with me? "I could be flexible on the second point. In the right circumstances of course." To cover my embarrassment, I quickly move the conversation along.

"By the way, you haven't told me about your love life lately."

He groans. "It's terrible." He runs a hand through his hair. "I'm one hundred per cent certain Laura's having an affair."

"Really? Why?"

He takes a deep breath. "Because I read one of her texts one night." His voice a mixture of shame and defiance.

"You did? Surely everyone locks their phone these days?"

A look of embarrassment clouds his face. "She's got a thumb-print lock on her mobile. I pressed her thumb on it when she was sleeping. She'd had a few drinks and was out for the count. Couldn't believe I got away with it."

My hand darts up to cup my mouth in surprise. "You didn't!"

He nods his head regretfully. "Yep. Sorry to have to tell you. I've turned into one of those arseholes."

"Wow," I shake my head in disbelief.

He shrugs his shoulders and continues: "It was all going through my head. There was something about the fact that she was checking her phone constantly. I knew something was up."

"Why didn't you ask her about it?" I probe.

"I could have but she would have denied it," he shrugs. "Anyway, if she admits it, then what? That's it? We split up? We get a divorce? I see the children even less than I do now? Become one of those dads who only gets to take the kids to *McDonalds* on a Saturday afternoon?" He is now shuddering. "I'm not ready for that yet."

I look at him in amazement. "So, you're going to let her carry on seeing another man, just for the sake of the children?"

There's a pause while he considers this. "Pretty much, yeah."

"Wow," I say softly, sinking back into my chair, taking in the ramifications of what he's just said.

I bite my lip. "Actually, there's something I need to tell you, Simon" I say.

He looks at me. "Uh oh, why do I not like the sound of this."

I take a deep breath. "Yeah, it's about Laura. I saw her. When I was on one of my coffee dates, she was there in the café…"

He's looking at me intently, a mixture of dread and curiosity.

"She was with a bloke," I blurt out. "They didn't seem to be just good friends. It looked like they were flirting." My eyes dart uncomfortably. I don't like to dish the dirt on another woman or be the bearer of bad news but I feel I should give it to him straight.

"Look Simon, it was more than flirtatious," I go on. "She didn't see me but I saw her. When they got up to leave, he gave her a kiss. Not quite a full-on snog but it was a kiss on the lips. Definitely not the sort of thing you'd do with a friend, if you know what I mean."

"Shit," Simon sighs, under his breath, his jaw sets into a firm line.

"I'm sorry," I lean a sympathetic hand on his.

"I'm sorry I have to be the one to tell you."

He shakes his head and places his other hand on mine. "No, I'm glad you told me. I'd rather it came from you than anyone else."

The moment seemed to stand still. For a few seconds my hand is sandwiched between his. A current of electricity sizzles between us.

"So, what now?" I ask, my breath catching with anticipation.

"I don't know," he replies. He moves his hands away slowly and takes another sip of beer. "She'll probably blame me."

"Blame you?" I counter. My expression is confused. "Why in heaven's name would you be to blame?"

He shrugs his shoulders. "For not spending enough time with her. For working too hard. For being married to the job. You know, the usual bloody things."

"Do you really believe all that?"

He somehow manages a small laugh. "You know what I should have done? I should have married someone in the police force. At least then, they'd understand my shift patterns."

Someone like me, you mean? I want to ask this, but I don't dare.

He looks at me. "Yes. Someone like you."

A gentle laugh escapes from my throat. "Okay, you're definitely drunk," I grin.

"I might be. But it's the truth, and you know it." His voice is a heady mixture of seriousness and sexiness. The way that he looks at me. The way his face hovers close to mine. Our lips are millimetres apart.

"Simon, you're just…" I begin, but he quietens me suddenly. His lips press on mine and we kiss. Soft, passionate, gentle. Then harder and more searching. It is exquisite. As delicious and pleasurable as I thought it would be. Just the right combination of lips and tongue. Tantalisingly slow at first. Then gaining a hurried momentum.

"Wow," he says, afterwards.

"Yes, wow indeed," I smile lazily.

"Why didn't we do that sooner?" he asks.

"Yeah, we should've been quicker off the mark," I joke.

He kisses me again. My insides fizzle with pleasure. All I want to do is lie back and open my legs. Let him climb on top of me and have his way. Here we are, in a fancy joint, trying not to get carried away.

"I'll have to make sure you get home safely, tonight." He whispers softly.

"Yes, I think I'll need a strong man to take me all the way." I attempt to look bashful.

"Sure. First thing you'll need a taxi. Then I'll have to help you get into it. I might even need to carry you to bed."

The taxi journey is a delightful mix of frustration and tension.

We sit next to each other in the back seat. Nothing is said. His hand is on my knee, exploring the soft flesh under my skirt. I badly want to press my mouth against his. But the cab driver is eyeing us up in the rear-view mirror. My insides are throbbing while Simon's hand moves slowly up my thigh.

I can't believe this is finally happening. After all the pent-up desire. The chemistry bubbling between us. We're finally on the way.

As soon as I open the front door, he kicks it closed behind us and pins me gently against the wall. Our lips frantically meld together. Suddenly he is carrying me to the bedroom. He lifts up my blouse and tosses it away. His fingertips track down to my bra and pushes it out of the way, finding my nipples. I groan. My head falls back in almost unbearable pleasure.

Finally. He is plunging inside me. We're coming. And together.

I don't even care if we regret it in the morning. Or if tomorrow never comes. I'm not thinking this shouldn't be happening. In fact, I'm not thinking straight at all. I'm just feeling. The skin-on-skin contact. The frisson of pleasure. I'm living only for the moment.

And now we lie here. Panting, satiated, spent.

CHAPTER EIGHTEEN

Zoe

"LET'S GET THE kettle on," my mother says in a soothing tone as we arrive home.

"Forget it mum, I want a proper drink," I follow her into the kitchen and straight to the fridge.

"Zoe, love..." she watches me open the door. I grab a bottle of white wine and pour myself a large glass.

I glug back the first mouthful and top up the glass right away just for good measure.

"Zoe, darling, you can't drink this way you know..." she pleads.

"Can't I?" I bark back stubbornly, walking away from her into the living room. "Watch me."

Following my stomping frame, she comes and sits down next to me on the sofa. "It'll only make you feel worse tomorrow."

I glance at her, my expression weary. "Mum, I really appreciate you coming along today but I'd rather be on my own now. So, if you don't mind..."

She looks at me realising what I'm suggesting. "Are you asking me to go?"

"Yeah, sorry. I just need to be on my own right now. You know how it's been today."

"Okay, if that's what you want." She stands up in a fluster. It's not hard to tell she's hurting, even if she's trying not to show it. Putting on her coat and placing her bag over her shoulder, she picks up her mobile and phones for a cab.

My heart has started to crumble into a million pieces. I know I'm pushing her away and she's only trying to help, but all I want to do is to sink into a swamp of self-pity and never surface again.

I hear the taxi pulling up outside. "Bye then," she says, hesitantly.

"Yeah, bye," I murmur, gazing at her walking out the door. Guilt overwhelms me as I see her disappear, yet I'm powerless to call her back. Engulfed in pain, I hear the car drive off and slug back another gulp of chardonnay.

IT'S THE FOLLOWING evening, when twilight is melding into darkness. I'm in the kitchen, about to pour myself a glass of wine. A strange feeling comes over me. I've got a hunch someone is watching me. As I peer out the window. I swear there's somebody standing out there in the shadows. Turning off the kitchen light, I squint out into the darkness, hoping that the absence of glare will help me see in the black night. Nothing. I see nothing at all.

Why am I so spooked? Would Liam arrange something? I know he's annoyed to be locked up in prison, whilst I'm walking free. He's the type who will think that if I hadn't asked him to babysit Emma that day, he wouldn't be in jail. The sooner the thought pops into my head, I dismiss it. Liam is safely banged up; there's no way he can get at me, even if he wants to.

But wait a minute. If it's some sort of revenge he's after, there are other ways he can manage that. He doesn't have to turn up in person. He could arrange for somebody else to come and do the dirty work. God knows the sort of people he's been mixing with these days.

I shake my head and push that thought away. That's ridiculous. Liam is a nutcase but despite everything, he wouldn't get up to intentional murder. The killing of Emma was unintentional – an act of negligence.

Pouring myself a generous top-up, I close the blinds and retreat to the sanctity of the lounge. I endure endless crap on TV: a reality show, then a drama, followed by a soap opera. It's not helping my brain to switch off. Questions pop into my head again and again. I can block out the television screen with a zapper, but the problems inside my mind keep resurfacing.

What am I going to do now? How on earth do I go forward from here? What am I going to live on? Whatever cash Liam sent from time to time will dry up now that he's in the can. No more child support with my lovely daughter gone. Not another penny coming in and I haven't worked in years. Who'd want to employ me anyway?

I knock back the next glass of wine at twice the speed.

Waking up in the middle of the night, crying, I

realise I must have been dreaming about Emma and Liam. My own sobs waken me. Tears flow until I cry myself back to sleep.

The next morning, I phone the doctor and plead, "Could I have more tablets and can it be stronger medication?" I didn't think it would be that easy. One phone-call, a simple request and my prescription is upped. That's what happens when you mention dead child and partner in prison.

"You can't keep doing this," my mum announces when she comes around the next day.

"Do what?" I ask. I'm lying on the sofa, a duvet over me. It's where I spend most of my time; on a couch, booze in hand, a stash of tablets on the coffee table. The TV remote helps me to flick from one mindless programme to another.

"Getting the doctor to increase your prescription all the time. You can't live on pills forever." She darts me a disapproving look and her eyes divert to my drink. "And you certainly shouldn't be drinking when you're taking tablets."

I close my eyes to block out her disapproval. I only wish she would stop visiting me; all she ever does is scold me.

Nausea rises in my stomach. "Er... hold on..." I say, as I push back the duvet and make a run for the bathroom.

"What is it?" she calls after me, concern lacing her words.

I lunge towards the toilet bowl and heave as I watch a torrent of vomit slews down the white porcelain.

"Ugh," I groan. I grab some toilet roll and clean around my mouth.

"Zoe, you see?" she lectures softly. Her voice is laden with criticism. "You shouldn't be drinking on medication. Your body can't cope."

"I know," I moan as I flush the toilet and slowly go about washing my hands.

I know and don't care. Why get uptight about health when there's nothing to live for? My insides are falling apart so who cares about alcohol intake or life expectancy? Just take me out of this world and let me join Emma in hers.

Everything feels sore: head, heart and mind. Every part of me aches; even my boobs are sore. If mum wasn't here, I'd pop some more painkillers. I'll wait until she goes into the kitchen, then I'll quickly swallow a handful of pills and wait for the whole thing to end.

"You'll have to eat something Zoe," she persists.

"I'm not hungry mum," I whine.

"A wee toastie. Something to settle your stomach."

"Oh, alright then," I agree, realising it could be an opportunity to swallow a bunch of tablets.

She returns with a tray of food. I eat the toast slowly and we watch a documentary about people being trapped in a house together. At some point, I must have fallen asleep because when I wake up, mum has left a note on the coffee table.

Couldn't wake you. Hope you sleep well. See you soon. Love you xx

My heart breaks with love and guilt. She gives me unconditional love, no matter how ungrateful and miserable I am.

I look around at the mess on the coffee table. An empty wine glass, a packet of tablets and a plate with my half-eaten toastie. My stomach lurches, I'm going to be sick again. Making a dash for the lavatory, I hurl the contents of my stomach into the cistern. How did I turn into such a lightweight? At what point did it become impossible to have a few drinks without throwing up like some inexperienced teenager?

The cogs in my foggy morning brain start to churn slowly as a thought suddenly dawns on me. Could it really be? Is it possible that I'm pregnant? I have that feeling.

There was one time recently that we were together; a one-night stand. An evening not long after our split when we drank too much. It just happened. Is it possible that Emma's brother or sister is a little dot of life inside me?

My hands shake as I retrieve a pregnancy tester from the first aid box in the corner of the bathroom. I sit on the WC watching for the thin blue line on the white stick. I set a timer on the iPhone and wait. My heart pounds. Am I really doing this? Checking to see if I have another bun in the oven? Maybe about to have a child with a man who has just been locked up in prison? A jailbird?

Yes, I'm doing this. The two thin blue lines are starting to form with a bold definition.

The tell-tale streaks are unquestionably blue. And God, yes! There's two distinct lines running across the card.

I'm pregnant with Liam's baby.

CHAPTER NINETEEN
Zoe

"**H**YDEBANK PRISON, PLEASE," I pull the cab door closed behind me and click on the seatbelt. I notice the taxi driver casting a curious glance back at me through the rear-view mirror.

Oh, here we go. Get ready for the small talk. Questions as to why I'm visiting prison.

"They're not locking you up, are they?" His face breaks out into a grin.

I smile back half-heartedly. "Not yet," I snap. I hope the short, sharp answer will deter him from further questioning. No such luck.

"Going to visit a relative?" he probes.

Oh, wouldn't you like to know, I think. You'd just love to hear the gossip; that I'm going to visit the father of my unborn baby. He also happens to be the murderer of my first child. Maybe that'll interest you!

"Yeah," I reply casually. I fish the mobile out of my bag and flick through it, hoping my body language and a one-word answer will scream at him: *just drive the fucking car and mind your own business*!

He finally gets the hint and switches on the radio. An easy listening rift fills the car. I close my eyes in gratitude. It's not his fault, he's only trying to be friendly. The problem is my irritability and restlessness. *How long will this pain go on?*

I remember one of the times Liam and I jumped into a taxi together. We had been to the Christmas market, knocking back mulled wine and scoffing kangaroo burgers. A time full of joviality and Christmas spirit. The cabbie asked if we'd had a good night. We were full of chat. We talked about the market and asked about his Christmas plans. We gave a bloody good tip because we loved his banter but this journey couldn't be more different.

We drive in silence except for the sound of the music coming from the car stereo. Before long, we swing into the prison grounds and sweep up the winding road which is overhung with trees. I spot a couple of squirrels scampering playfully. It would look idyllic if it didn't lead to a jail. When we arrive at the front entrance, I pay the driver. There is no conversation. I get out of the car and close the door gently behind me.

Approaching the double doors, I see the sign pointing to the *Family Visiting Centre*. My heart starts thumping in my chest.

"I'm here to see Liam Fitzpatrick please."

A uniformed female officer asks me to stand with my legs and arms apart while another guard pats me down. One looks inside my handbag and roots around it. The other then makes me walk through more security barriers and x-ray machines. Finally, I get through to the centre itself and see Liam sitting at one of the tables. As I approach him, my legs feel like jelly.

"Hi." I sit down opposite him at arm's length, as the rules dictate.

"Hi," he replies.

There's a moment of silence. I guess we're both sussing each other out and gauging the atmosphere. Is he furious with me? Am I still mad at him?

"Thanks for visiting," he says finally, his words breaking the silence.

"S'alright," I sigh. "How are you getting on?"

He shrugs his shoulders. "It's boring as hell, but that's to be expected."

I nod, not knowing what else to say.

"What about you?" he asks, tentatively.

"It's tough," I admit. "I miss Emma so much."

He nods. "I know, I do too."

There's a silence then. I awkwardly fidget with my hands under the table. I look around at the other visitors, all chatting animatedly. They don't look as awkward as we do.

"I am sorry, Zoe. I know you don't believe me, but I really think my drink was spiked."

"I know you're sorry." I take a tissue out of my pocket and press my fingers tightly on it. I feel tears welling up, but I will them to stop.

"Did your solicitor tell you how many years you're gonna have to actually serve in the end?" I ask.

"He says the ten years might be reduced to six, if I behave myself."

Six years, I think. Our new baby will be five years old by the time he's released.

"Are you behaving yourself?" I try to smile

but those tears are threatening to smudge the corners of my eyes.

"I'm doing my best," he shrugs. "There's nothing else to do around here. If I'm a model prisoner, do the rehab bit, that sort of thing, I'll make it out in six."

I lift my Kleenex and dab a tear away from the corner of my eye.

Justice has been done but there's nothing to celebrate here. No victory that he's locked up. I didn't win the court case; there are no winners, only losers. He's banged up and I'm in hell.

"I'm trying my best, Zoe. I'm going to use this time to get clean, once and for all. I've been going to meetings. People from the Twelve-Step group come in and visit every week. I'm twenty-five days clean."

I look at him with surprise. "Really?" I ask.

"Yeah," he beams.

"Well, that's great," I respond softly. I'm not going to get my hopes up. I've heard him say the same thing time and time again.

"Liam, I've something to tell you." At last, I summon up the courage to come straight out with it.

"What's wrong?" his face clouds over with worry.

"I'm pregnant." There, I said it. The words are out of my mouth; blunt, cold and abrupt. His mouth falls into an 'o' shape.

Squeezing the tissue in my hands, I knead it into different shapes. I'm trying to get rid of my nervous energy.

"Do I assume it's definitely mine?" he ventures.

I give him a startled look. "Of course," I reply. He should know me better than that. I'm not the type who sleeps around with other guys.

"Sorry," he cuts in quickly.

Now, I don't know what to say. I just sit and watch his face move from shock to puzzlement.

"That one night?" he queries. "The night we got drunk and...?"

"Yep, that's the one."

"Fuck!" he exclaims.

Yes, fuck. Fuck is right. Fuck just about sums up the fact that here we are; he's in prison for six years and our first child is dead by his hand. Now our second baby is on the way. Everything's just hunky dory, isn't it?

"Yes, fuck" I whisper softly.

"And you're going to keep it?" His words creep out tentatively.

"Of course," I reply tersely. God, can his questions get any worse?

Liam nods quickly. "Yes, I thought so."

My crumpled hankie is now pressed into a small, tight ball.

After a moment, Liam utters, "Well, you know I'll do whatever I can to support you, in whatever way I can..."

"I appreciate that." I try to sound genuine but a wary voice in my head is saying: *I won't be letting him drive this baby anywhere, will I?*

His face breaks out into a grin at this point. The news is finally hitting him. "Wow, a baby on the way. Thanks for telling me that Zoe. That has really brightened my day. That's something that will really keep me going in here."

I give him a shy smile, willing tears not to fall. Damn hormones must be kicking in already. I try to remain dignified and in control.

"Well, I guess I better head on, Liam. Good to talk to you." My voice sounds formal and strained, nothing like the Zoe and Liam we used to be.

"Yes, thanks for coming," he says, almost as though he's an interviewer thanking a candidate. "Keep in touch, yeah?"

Keep in touch? Of course, I'll keep in touch! You're the father of my unborn baby.

I get up and walk away, willing myself not to turn around and look back. On the way out, I notice someone. It's that damn woman from the court that day! The one who was at the funeral.

"Hey Zoe," she says, her voice a mixture of a polite smile and odd curiosity. "I'm surprised to see you here."

"You are?" I ask. "Why's that?"

She looks flummoxed but says, "Well, with the court case, and you two being against each other and everything..." She trails off, obviously realising she's stepping out of line.

"And I'm surprised you're here," I retort. "It's very good of Liam's bar work colleagues to take the time to visit him." My words are laden with mistrust and animosity. Why is she always around? Why would a work colleague bother to visit someone in prison?

"Well, we're all very good friends in the *Duck & Goose*," she smiles. "I'm Mia, by the way," she holds out her hand. I can't help notice how glammed up she is for a visit to a prison. Her freshly washed, long blonde hair, dances around her shoulders with an eye-catching gloss. Tight fitting jeans and a sprayed-on leather jacket show off her figure to perfection. I feel mumsy and fat next to her. I'm wearing a baggy jumper and worn-out leggings. I couldn't even summon the energy to wash my hair.

"How's he doing today?" she seems almost conspiratorial. As though we are both the carers and he's the patient.

"He looks okay. Bored more than anything else."

She nods. "I brought him in some chocolates to cheer him up." She lifts a bag and opens it slightly to show a wide array of chocolate bars. I immediately feel guilty that I haven't bothered to bring him anything.

"That's very good of you," I say stiffly, before adding, "Well, I better head on."

"Oh sure," she smiles. "Good to meet you."

"You too", I lie.

I head straight to the visitors' restrooms to get out of sight. My breathing is laboured and anxious. In the bathroom I catch my reflection in the mirror. It's as if I'm truly examining myself for the first time in weeks; my face is puffed up from too much alcohol; hair – dank and dirty. I haven't bothered to put on make-up. I'm a mess; much older looking than my twenty-nine years. I've officially let myself go. I wonder what age Mia is. Twenty-five? Younger? Her make-up is so perfectly applied. It's clear she spends a lot of time on herself, perfecting every inch of her appearance. I'm sick with envy.

What the fuck is she doing visiting him in prison?

I walk away but can't help take a moment to peer through the glass security wall of the visitor's area. I spot them sitting next to each other at the table. Liam is smiling at her. She is gesticulating gregariously. I feel sick.

I rush back to the visitor's toilets and throw up. The damn morning sickness kicks in all the time now. Still, better to get it over and done with before the taxi ride home. I pray for a quiet cabbie. One who will just sit there and keep his mouth shut.

Thankfully, this doesn't bother with small talk. The only noises I hear are in my own head; thoughts burling around and around, nagging me constantly.

Why's she so friendly with the father of my child? How come they get on so well?

What's that bitch doing here?

CHAPTER TWENTY
Mia

"**M**IA MATTHEWS?"

"Yeah, Hydebank prison, please," I clamber straight into the taxi. The driver looks at me in the rear-view mirror.

"Off to do a bit of visiting are we?" his voice is jovial and friendly.

"I am, as a matter of fact." I take the mirror out of my bag and touch up my lipstick. I checked it five minutes ago but nervous energy is making me fidgety. Anyway, in this type of situation a girl can't spend enough time on her looks and I've never visited a prison before.

When Liam sent me the details in a letter, it felt surreal. *Visiting Hours: Monday to Friday 2pm – 4pm.* A list of do's and don'ts. *Prohibition of illegal substances.* In other words, don't smuggle in drugs. The same for sharp objects. *Take this correspondence with you. Bring photographic identification.* And so on. The sort of stuff you would imagine from watching police shows.

When I was getting ready, I kept reminding myself that I was dressing up to see a guy in jail, not dolling up for a date. Old habits die hard. I had a long soak in the bath the night before, then re-applied my fake tan. After getting up early and spending ages curling my hair into pretty waves, I put on my make-up carefully. I curled my eyelashes and delicately applied mascara, to make sure I look my best. Mixing with men in prison tracksuit bottoms doesn't mean I should go in looking like shit. It's always important to dress to kill. I don't even go to the corner shop without doing myself up. It's a lack of confidence thing but at least I'm aware of that. You never knew who you'll bump into. Imagine if you meet the love of your life at the deli counter but happen to look awful; a great opportunity goes to waste.

"What's he in for?" the cabbie has the nerve to ask. He pulls a cheeky grin to suggest that he's just being friendly but I still feel uncomfortable.

"Oh, it's serious," I reply. I wish he would keep his nose out of it. "But it wasn't his fault." I add hastily.

"They all say that don't they love? Remember that film: Shawshank Redemption. You know what they all agreed on? *Everyone in here is innocent!*" He chuckled.

I shift in my seat and try not to fidget. "He really is innocent," I protest. "That happens to be a fact." That stopped the conversation in its tracks. I make a point of taking out my mobile and scrolling frantically through Facebook. I hope that'll stop his prying. It works. The rest of the journey pans out in silence all the way to our destination.

"Just be careful love, yeah?" he can't help adding as I hand over some cash and get out of the car.

"Yeah." My voice is tinged with annoyance. *What business is it of yours, chum?*

I clutch Liam's letter to my chest as I locate the entrance. Going through the double doors I feel my heart quicken as I see prison officers and the security station. A series of checks and barriers. It's actually quite exciting; like in a movie.

"Over here, madam," a female prison officer calls over. She notices my lost-puppy-dog look. "Who are you visiting? Got your ID?" Then the more personal request: "Spread your legs. Sorry but we have to do a search."

She whizzes through the procedures and points me in the direction of the visitors' room.

That's when I spot Zoe. She's coming out of the visiting room and heading towards the toilets. She looks like she's falling apart. Understandable I suppose, given what's happened.

"Hey Zoe," I call.

She spins round and I notice her expression move from confusion to recognition. She obviously remembers me from the funeral.

"I'm surprised to see you here." The words are out of my mouth before I can stop them. Of course, she'd be here. Why wouldn't she be? Now I just sound like a bit of a smart-arse.

"You are?" she asks. "Why's that?"

She looks terrible. I can tell she's done nothing whatsoever to get ready this morning. It's a shame. A woman with her looks should make an effort but she's wearing baggy, over-sized clothes. Her face is bloated and she hasn't even put on her make-up.

I'm not sure what to say so I find myself stammering, "Well, with the court case and you two being against each other and everything." My implication is: he's the killer of your child and surely you must hate the bastard?

She mumbles something about being surprised to see me too. Her tone is abrupt and unfriendly. The conversation is cut short. She dashes off to the *Ladies* as quickly as possible. I stand there watching her go. What on earth Liam saw in her, I'll never know. *Why he'd ever choose her over me is a mystery.*

Pushing the thought aside, I walk towards the visiting room and open the door. I see Liam sitting there. Bored shitless and lonely. He glances over and catches sight of me. His face lights up like a Christmas tree and I give him one of my smiles.

I walk towards him putting on my best cat-walk stride and notice that a few of the other prisoners look over at me.

"Hello you." His eyes linger over my tight jeans and figure-hugging jacket. "Wow, you look hot," he grins hungrily.

"Thanks, you don't look too bad yourself." I casually throw back at him.

"In this get-up, I don't think so!" he laughs. He nods down at his grey tracksuit with an apologetic shrug of the shoulders. I agree the prison clothes aren't exactly Ralph Lauren but he'd look good in anything. It's still Liam; his chiselled features, sculpted beard and kissable lips. And of course, the come-to-bed eyes.

"I saw Zoe," I announce with an attempt at aloofness but my voice sounds more jealous and insecure than I intend.

He squirms and throws back an apologetic smile. "Sorry you had to bump into her."

"Why's she visiting? What does she want?"

Liam looks awkward. If this was a normal conversation, he'd turn up the volume on the football or head into the kitchen to click open another beer. This time, he's trapped on the other side of a table and he can't run away.

"You know Zoe."

I cross my arms. *No, as a matter of fact, I don't. We've only met a couple of times.*

He picks up on my defiant body language: "I dunno Mia, I guess she's lonely, she still wants to keep in touch. She hasn't got over Emma. She won't for some time."

I raise my eyebrows. "So, she wants to keep in touch with you? After watching you go down? I thought she'd never want to see you again."

"She has no-one else." He leans over to take my hands but then remembers the guards are watching.

"Have you told her about us yet?" The words are out of my mouth before I can stop them. I know I sound clingy and insecure but I can't help it.

He breathes out slowly and momentarily looks away.

"Well...?" I persist.

He shakes his head. "I don't feel like it's the right time."

"The right time?" I parrot, rolling my eyes. "When have I heard that before?"

I notice one of the other prisoners looking over at me. My arms are now folded. My body language must scream nagging, insecure bitch, but I don't care.

"Mia," Liam coaxes. "Why are you getting so annoyed? She only wants to be friendly. She's in shock. She's not in a good place at the moment. It's not like she wants us back together or anything." He takes my hand, forcing me to unfold my arms. "C'mere baby, don't be like that. I'm so happy to see you."

I feel myself melting despite my annoyance. "When are you going to tell her about us, Liam?" I whine.

"Soon, I promise," he leans towards me and repeats it again reassuringly, "Soon."

Then he breaks the rules. He reaches over and kisses me.

"The guards will see us!" I protest.

"I don't care," Liam whispers with a glint in his eye. "Let them watch. They'll all be dying of jealousy."

I giggle and lean towards him. "Okay then," I whisper.

He kisses me, long and hard with his tongue. He has all the confidence of a man alone with me, not surrounded by a bunch of prisoners and guards.

I hear a few cheers and somebody shouts "get a room!" My lips crease into a smile but Liam pulls me even closer. My insides flutter with excitement. All I want to do is sit astride him and feel him plunge inside me.

"Oye, cut it out!" I hear the harsh tones of a prison officer. We quickly pull apart. Next, the sound of a bunch of them scraping back their chairs to clear a path.

Two male prison officers step between us abruptly at that moment. A third, uniformed female, pulls me aside and opens my palms. She pats down my skirt. She's probing my mouth with a wooden stick. They shake Liam down even more thoroughly. Finally, they allow us to sit down again. The dope check is over.

"Fuck," Liam grumbles. "How fucking frustrating."

"I know," I agree.

"Jesus, how am I going to manage in here without you?" he pleads. "Some other bloke is going to snap you up in an instant!"

For the first time I really see his vulnerability. He's genuinely afraid he'll lose me. I feel my heart melt as I look at the fear in his eyes.

"No bloke is going to snap me up," I whisper affectionately. "I'm all yours."

He closes his eyes momentarily. "You say that now but six years is a lifetime babe. I'd understand if..."

I shake a finger to interrupt him mid-sentence. "I'm not going anywhere. Get that into your head."

He looks at me with gratitude, as though drinking me in.

"And besides," I add with a coy smile. "I'm

pregnant."

I watch his expression move from shock to surprise and then, I hope, to delight.

"You're what?" he repeats.

I nod and my eyes fill with tears. "Yup. Bun in the oven." I joke. The tears well up and trickle down my face. I take a tissue out of my pocket and dab my cheeks. "So, you're stuck with me now."

"Oh my god!" he exclaims. "You really are pregnant?"

"Yeah, five weeks."

"Jeez," he mumbles.

"You're happy about it?" I ask, my voice tentative.

"Of course, I am," he shrugs, diverting his eyes to my waistline. "You're not even showing yet."

"Oh, I am," I argue. "I have a little pot belly going on underneath these jeans."

"Hardly," he teases.

A bell rings. It's the end of visiting time. I hear chairs scraping back and Liam stands up. It's just an inkling but something gives me the impression he's glad the conversation's over.

Saved by the bell.

"Good visit?" The taxi man grins at me in the rear-view mirror.

"Yeah, great." I reply dismissively. But a few questions begin to churn in my mind. *Is he really happy about the baby? Is he ever going to tell Zoe about me? Well, he'll have to when the baby comes along!*

"Visiting your boyfriend?" the taxi driver asks, tentatively. New cabbie, new questions. Same old, same old.

"Yup," I reply.

"What's he in for?" he asks.

"Manslaughter," I answer. "But it wasn't his fault."

His face is sceptical. "That's what they all say, love." The tone is soft even though the words are harsh.

"No really, he didn't do it. He's not responsible," I answer. My tone is certain and assertive. He didn't intend to hurt his child. Only I know the truth.

I know Liam isn't to blame because I'm the one who is responsible.

It's my fault the little girl is six feet under.

CHAPTER TWENTY-ONE

Liam

I COUNT THE stains on the ceiling; thirty-one blue tack marks. The guy who stayed here before had obviously decorated the ceiling with pictures of nudes; his very own porn channel. The same images to wank over, night in – night out.

I lie on the top bunk, hands behind my head. I can't stop thinking. Along the corridor, a noisy din goes on all day. The sound of men shouting, the clunk of gates slamming. One minute, laughter and banter; the next, screaming and aggression.

How has it come to this? My daughter dead. She's six feet under and I end up in this shit-hole.

I think of my mate Ben, living my parallel universe in London. Ben has the lifestyle that I should be enjoying right now. If Zoe hadn't got pregnant and I hadn't had to leave London, things would have been different.

I'd be holding down an acting job in the West End, working my way up nicely. A producer would have spotted me by now. I could have been a soap star with loads of money. Fans following me everywhere I went and the pick of any woman to shag. Living in a penthouse apartment in Chelsea with a wardrobe full of designer clobber, a walking model for Hugo Boss and Gucci.

Instead, I'm lying on the top bunk of a prison cell counting fucking blue tack marks on a ceiling and having to put up with those noisy bastards on the landing.

I'm doing my fucking head in with negative thoughts. It'd be great if I could flick a switch and turn the whole lot off. There's nothing else to do but think. It's just me and the four walls.

I think about the move back to Belfast. About Zoe's face when she opened the door. It had been three months. I'd hung around in London doing numerous auditions. My only luck was with crappy TV ads or standing on street corners handing out flyers. No sign of any soap opera parts, never mind a role in the West End.

Money started to dry up and I couldn't afford the rent. I'd lie in bed at night stressed about my increasing mountain of debt.

I missed Zoe, actually craved her and longed for that caring, calm support. The way she'd hold her arms around me and say that everything would be okay. Her knack of effortlessly cooking meals and sorting bills. That girl just made shit happen. She made life look so easy and always landed on her feet. I yearned for all that. She was like a lucky talisman; someone I wanted to hang around for a long time in the hope that her luck would rub off on me.

Of course, I thought about the baby, when Emma was just a bun in the oven. I tried not to dwell on it by drinking the worries away. I found it hard to accept the little dot of life that was growing inside Zoe's belly. I tried to banish the idea of the responsibility and the tasks I would need to take on, the money I should be earning and the lifestyle I ought to be providing. Every time a worrying thought surfaced, I'd drown my sorrows, tell myself it wasn't my fault. After all, I didn't plan the pregnancy; she should have been more careful. She was supposed to be taking the pill; it was her fault.

The following morning, in the cold light of day, I'd wake up hungover and stone cold sober and the guilt would drown me like a lead blanket. My baby was growing inside Zoe and I had ghosted her for months.

I tried to sleep it away and by sleep, I mean shag. I shagged any other woman who would have me. I told myself that sleeping with someone else would erase Zoe from my mind but it didn't. Her face appeared to me in my dreams; a reminder that she was still there and wasn't going away anytime soon.

My agent phoned me around that time: "I have a job for you."

"Oh yeah?" I said hopefully, imagining a TV role.

"Yeah, it's not the best job in the world I'm afraid, but the money's not bad and it will tide you over until something better comes along."

My heart sank. It seemed that my agent started every conversation with this line. "What is it?" I asked, failing to hide disappointment in my voice.

"It's for a well-known fast-food company. They need some actors to dress up as clowns and hand out food samples in the town centre on

Saturday…"

"No," I interrupted harshly, before she even had a chance to finish her sentence.

I heard her taking a heavy sigh at the other end of the phone. "Liam…" she began, her tone tinged with annoyance and frustration. "You can't keep saying no to these jobs…"

"Yes, I can," I snapped back moodily. "Would you like to dress up as a clown and stroll around town?"

There was the usual uncomfortable silence from her at the other end of the phone. "Liam, I'm not the actor, you are," she reminded me, with a patronising tinge in her voice.

"An actor, not an arsehole!" I retorted.

She sighed. "Liam, I don't know what to say. You expect to get lead roles straight away, but quite frankly, those parts don't crop up every day. You've got to be realistic. Take smaller roles. Give it time."

I couldn't contain myself: "Maybe if you knew what you were doing, I'd have got something decent by now! Perhaps I should look for an agent whose parts don't need chicken outfits!"

I hung up. Just like that. In one swift, sponta-neous, self-destructive moment, I'd managed to cut my career with a metaphorical knife.

I knew I couldn't call her back. She'd drop me from their books for my attitude. I'd need to phone her up and grovel if I really wanted to be considered for anything from that moment on.

And what if I did? What if I sucked up to her and all she ever gave me was cheap shit street work? Fuck that.

So, I decided to go home; to return to Zoe in Belfast; to be there for my unborn child and act responsibly for once in my life.

I wanted to man up and do the right thing; bring my child up in a world where he or she felt loved and cared for. I didn't want to be like my own dad or repeat his behaviour. I didn't want to be neglectful, abusive and violent, a carbon copy of the father figure he had been to me.

My child wouldn't cower in fear. I'd never be drunk or angry nor would I strip off a belt and lash it over any little one. I wouldn't humiliate a kid for wetting the bed by hanging his dirty sheets out the window. I didn't want this youngster to hear taunts of disgust and disdainful laughter; the name calling and the bullying.

Zoe welcomed me back with open arms. I knew she would. I didn't even get any grief. That's the loving, warm and beautiful soul she was. She was simply glad that I had got it out of my system, whatever 'it' was; probably the fear of being a father.

She said she knew I'd do the right thing eventually; that I'd see sense and step up to the plate. Truth be told, I didn't have much to do. Zoe sorted everything. She'd arranged accommodation and obtained all the available benefits. Bought loads of baby books and read up on what to do. All I had to do was be emotionally supportive.

I did get a job though; as a bar man in the *Duck and Goose*. Just a temporary position. Not what I really wanted. But it would tide me over until something better came along.

It was only meant to be a few casual hours, just a bit of extra cash but it turns out I was good at it. I chatted easily with people, was quick on my feet, and able to do a good night's shift. Before I knew it, I was promoted to supervisor. The other staff said I was a good team leader; friendly and fair without being over-bearing. They said they liked working a shift when I was in charge. Staff knew they'd be appreciated.

Months whizzed by and before I knew it, I was bar manager. I remember working one night and caught a reflection of myself in the window. I was bending down, picking up empty pint glasses. There was this bloke sitting on the sofa; one arm around a woman, the other holding a pint. I couldn't help but think he was looking down on me. I remember noticing his shoes; shiny and pointy. They reeked of money. I imagined this couple had probably just arrived in from the theatre or some expensive restaurant. Now he was looking at me as though I was dirt on the soles of those fancy shoes.

Fury rose up in my gut. A red mist fogged my mind. I wanted to punch him.

"Got a problem, mate?" I asked, with contempt oozing out of me.

The guy shifted in his seat, suddenly uncomfortable. "Er no, it's all good," he said. He looked at the girlfriend, his eyes darting with fear. "We were just heading on actually," he said, lifting his coat and nudging her.

"Bye then," my voice was laced with sarcasm

and aggression.

"What was all that about?" I heard her whispering as they walked off.

What was it all about indeed? It was about me hating myself. The image in the window was me in a place where I didn't want to be. The months flew by like lightning. My dreams of becoming an actor were so far removed, it felt like they were gone forever. I was just a lowly bar man. The other guy wore the expensive shoes. He was the person I should have been. The person I was nothing like.

I felt resentful about the job in the pub. It was a noose around my neck. It stopped me from going to auditions; prevented me from pursuing my dreams. With every shift I clocked up, more time was wasted.

The only way to cope was to drink. When each shift was over and the punters were gone, there was booze. We could sit around, have a few beers, relax and unwind. Staff could talk about the annoying customers and have a bit of banter. The minute the alcohol seeped into my system I felt the warm, woozy liquid reach right down to my toes. I could relax. It didn't matter about the broken dreams or the wasted existence. I could just be.

At first it was easy to sneak a beer here and there. Before I knew it, the job was too convenient to leave. It provided the free alcohol and ready-made social life. Instant friends who would party with me every night and access to women who liked to have fun.

On a merry-go-round to nowhere.

CHAPTER TWENTY-TWO
Liam

NORMAL PEOPLE DON'T understand. They can't comprehend the problem about needing drugs. They think it's something akin to *wanting* the stuff. The right word is *craving which is* something entirely different. It's not a question of choice. An addict doesn't just wake up one morning and decide to stick a needle in his arm. That's not how it works.

In reality, an addict's daily routine goes something like this:

One day your head is pickled and negative thoughts fly around like confetti. The brain is a washing machine on full spin. You decide that a drink or a tablet will fix it. Knocking it back, a woozy, calm feeling drifts over you like a warm mist. Momentarily, the pain slips away and the negative thought cycle settles down. The voices stop. Peace.

You like the feeling so much that another shot seems like a good idea. If the first shot can do this much, why not take another? Things should get better still. And so, you take more. And more.

Until you've woken up the next day not sure how much you've taken. You've overdone it. Then a blackout. Loss of memory and no recollection of the immediate past; what you've said or what you've done the night before is a total blank. You check your mobile for evidence of what might have happened; appointments not kept and calls not returned. The things you should have done but didn't.

The washing machine drum in the head starts spinning again. Fear, guilt and shame burl around in a whirlpool of confusion. Suddenly everything goes into a full cycle spin. Your only solution?

Take another drug.

And the cycle of addiction begins again. That was how things happened on the day that Zoe told me about the first pregnancy with Emma. I woke up hungover and on a comedown. I rushed to the toilet. My insides felt like they were collapsing; my head ached, my stomach lurched like it was going to explode. My mouth opened and a torrent of liquid hit the bowl; a green, foul smelling liquid; remnants of the food I'd eaten mixed with a cocktail of vomit.

Cleaning my mouth and moaning, I flushed the whole foul concoction away, feeling horrendous. Lying down on the bathroom floor with the cold tiles next to my cheek, the world was spinning. Please let me fall off. No-one should ever feel this bad. Please God, I prayed. If you get me out of this, I'll never touch another drop.

The nausea dragged on for most of the day. I divided my time between the bedroom and the bathroom. If I tried to hold down some tap water, it shot straight back up again.

Finally, about seven that night, I managed a

slice of toast. It stayed down. As the hours passed, normality slowly returned.

I'll never drink again, I promise. Never again.

A few days later, the memory of the physical trauma began to pass. My body started to get stronger but my head had some way to go.

A picture of Zoe and the baby clouded my mind. How would she cope? She expected me to leave London. To give up my dreams of becoming an actor. She wanted me to move back home.

The cycle of negativity spun around again. Like the devil on my shoulder, whispering constant put-downs. You think you'd do a better job than your own father? You can't even look after yourself, never mind a baby!

The thoughts went on and on like a bully taunting me all day long. If only I could ignore those voices but they were too real and too overpowering. I wonder where they came from? Perhaps the words of my father were echoing back to me from the days when he relentlessly talked down to me as a kid. *Sit down and shut up! Children should be seen and not heard! You must be stupid!*

And so on and so forth.

Perhaps his voice had distilled into my brain. Like an earworm; an annoying song that becomes lodged in the head. It hangs on in there no matter how many times you try to dislodge it.

It only took a few days but the craving for the bottle returned. My prayers had been ignored. The promise never to drink again abandoned. *A drink would take the pain away.*

Just one cold beer. A golden pint with conden-sation trickling down the side.

The spirits lift with just one drink. *Just one and then I'll stop. After all, one beer doesn't do any harm, does it?*

Then I bumped into a mate who said, "One more?" By the time he'd said it, he was already on his way to buy another round. Before we knew it, we had scored some gear and were snorting a line through rolled up ten-pound notes.

By that stage, the pain had gone. What pain? I'd forgotten. The bad thoughts had disappeared. They vanished like a pebble into a pond.

What started with emotional pain now became physical dependency. Without my fix every day, life was unbearable. Withdrawals would kick in. I was restless, irritable and discontent. I needed the coke just to get by. Without the stuff, I was below par. Far from getting euphoria, the gear merely got me back to normal.

The average person doesn't understand that. Ordinary people have the joy of being okay all the time. Addicts need substances just to bring them back to normal; to get them up to par.

Of course, there's the question of money. It's not a case of stealing money – it's a case of telling yourself you deserve it. You need cash so badly, it's your human right to have it. You'll help yourself at any opportunity. You're entitled to it.

If some drunken plonker pays for his pint and forgets to wait for the change, it's no problem slipping it into your own pocket. It's amazing how much a bloke can scrimp and save when he keeps his eyes open and his hand in the till.

Zoe started to suss the situation. She began to hide her purse, cleverly putting it in different places; first underneath the mattress, then the airing cupboard and even under Emma's crib. But I always found it. It was like our own little game of adult hide and seek.

I tried the meetings. Loads of times. Losers sitting around in a circle talking about how grateful they were to be clean. Drinking cups of lukewarm tea and munching cheap biscuits. Weekends consisted of hanging around coffee shops, smoking and watching the world go by.

They were missing out. On that first line of coke that hits the back of your nostrils and travels down in a chalky glow. The first rush. Feeling like you're ten feet tall. You could take on the world. You can walk into a nightclub and pull any god-damn woman in the joint. And if she doesn't take the bait, that's her loss. Shagging someone against a wall in an alleyway makes you feel like the biggest stud on the planet.

Then there was the horror of coming-to the next morning. Insides about to explode. And worse, there's a damp patch on the sheet – you know you've wet yourself in the middle of the night.

You turn around and see a woman asleep on the other pillow. When she wakes, she'll feel the wetness underneath. She'll know that you've pissed yourself in the night.

The old man's voice resonates again. *You've wet yourself! How many times have I told you to go to the toilet instead!* You hear the unbuckling sound as his belt is freed from his waistband and whips through the air.

The woman is still fast asleep. Who is she? What is her name? You don't remember, but you do have a vague recollection of chatting her up. You recall at the time, she looked like a model; long, dark hair and a stick thin figure.

In the cold light of day, you realise she's not Kate Moss. There's saliva oozing from a corner of her mouth. Her eyes open slowly. She smiles awkwardly. Her expression says she has no idea who you are either. You could be Ted Bundy for all she knows.

There's the awkward interval which follows. She's pretending she doesn't notice the puddle in the bed. Making polite small talk and ignoring the elephant in the room. You want to tell her to forget the patter and leave. *Just end my humiliation and disappear.* But she stays on wittering endless drivel. In denial of the fact that we're total strangers with only one thing in common – a nightmare hangover.

You don't have the nerve to tell her to just leave. The drink's worn off. The only thing that will get you through this is the hair of the dog. The first drink of the day will calm everything down.

Finally, she goes. You pull a beer from the fridge. It's ten o'clock. Never mind the kettle and the coffee, let's go straight to the booze. Gulp back the first sip. Strip the sodden bedsheets. Turn down the volume on the vile words ringing in your ears. The old man's vicious diatribe.

I'm going to hang your bedsheets out the window so the neighbours will see!

The sheets get slung into the washing machine. You slam that glass door and hit the start button. Tears start to pour out. You crumple onto the floor and whimper. A pathetic heap of a man. A supposedly mature adult, crying in front of a domestic appliance and slugging beer for breakfast.

You really need help.

CHAPTER TWENTY-THREE

Kerry

A CAR ALARM rings somewhere in the distance. The sound worms its way into my sleepy head. Consciousness slowly takes over and I realise I'm awake. The scratchy feeling at the back of my throat and a dull ache in my head reminds me that it's the morning after the night before. I turn to the pillow next to mine: empty. Simon has gone, but there's a note on the bedside table. I pick up the little piece of paper and read the handwritten scrawl: *Sorry, didn't want to wake you x*

Christ! It's half nine! As my brain registers the fact, I spring into action. I'm very, very late. I should have been in work half an hour ago. My feet propel me out of bed as I rush into the bathroom. I'm in a cold sweat as adrenaline courses through me. I throw myself together in super quick time.

I've no time to contemplate the previous night – the kiss; the fact that he had come back with me and we had unforgettable sex. I don't have time to laze over a coffee and dreamily reflect on what happened. Nor to ponder how I'll behave in front of him or how this could affect our working relationship; whether we'll be able to work together at all.

Didn't want to wake you. Why *didn't* he wake me? He knows I need to spring up and get to the office just as much as he does. Unless he hoofed it in the middle of the night while I was fast asleep. Probably worried about what he's going to say to his wife.

Pushing that guilty thought aside, I grab a coffee and croissant from the corner takeaway. Hurrying into the station and up to my desk, no one seems to notice or care. Tearing open the paper bag and biting off a piece of croissant, a storm of flaky pastry scatters over my desk. Just as I'm tucking in, Simon walks past.

"Hey Ker," he raises his eyebrows.

"Hey," I mumble, my mouth full.

He serenely cruises past throwing a casual smile in my direction. My brain goes into over-drive. How come he didn't stop to chat? Does he regret last night? Is he embarrassed or just being professional?

At that moment, my phone buzzes to life. I quickly swallow the piece of croissant and pick up. It's a colleague requesting an update on a current case. I launch into an explanation, telling myself to forget about last night for now; to push those thoughts aside and get on with the job.

✧   ✧   ✧

Simon

LAURA AND I are sitting in a waiting room. There's

a box of tissues on the coffee table, next to an assortment of magazines. I can't help but notice the headline on the front of one of the publications: *Suzie's third marriage! How she knows that this is the one!*

It jars to read a headline like that. We're in a therapist's office, going into our first marriage guidance session. Shouldn't the selection of reading material be more appropriate, like Interior World, or something with fancy décor and ideal lifestyles? Not trashy rags full of tacky celebs and their kiss and tell.

Mentally, I kick myself for hypocrisy. Have I not just been unfaithful to Laura? Whilst musing this thought, I remind myself that she's been unfaithful to me and for longer.

The door opens and a woman emerges. She's short and round, with a mass of curly hair and a friendly smile: "Mr and Mrs Peters?"

"Yes," we stand up to greet her.

"Simon and Laura, isn't it?" she confirms. We're led into the office and she beckons us to sit on two pre-positioned chairs. To begin with, there is a polite discussion. The type where everybody is civil to each other, but it's not long before we've settled into the blame game.

"He doesn't spend enough time with us, that's the problem," Laura whines. "I feel like I'm a single mum."

"Hold on, that's not true," I pipe up. "I work very hard for all of us! Who pays the bills?" I run my hand through my hair in exasperation. It's the same argument we have on repeat, every single day.

"Okay, you do." Laura talks down to me like a parent disciplining a child. "But we need more than just money. We need your time!"

"I can't split myself in two!" I lash back. "I'm either at work, earning money, or trying to relax at home!"

The therapist follows the dialogue as the atmosphere rises to a crescendo. "Okay," she interjects calmly. "This is good, we're establishing the problem here. It's good to communicate. Now, let's talk solutions. A compromise?" She looks at us, searching for answers. We remain sullen, like a couple of sulky teenagers.

Then she speaks again: "What about you Laura? How can Simon show willingness to spend time with the family?"

Laura looks bemused: "Dunno. Maybe book Saturdays off? Take the kids places at the weekend?"

The therapist nods. "Take them where specifically, Laura?"

She shrugs her shoulders. "The cinema, or the bowling alley. The kids love stuff like that. And there's always the swimming pool."

Panic rises in my chest. I use weekends to catch up on paperwork. If I don't get up to date, Mondays are always hell.

"Yes, I see," the counsellor acknowledges. "And what about time for you, Laura? What about a date night together? Time for the two of you to connect?"

Laura casts a sideways glance at me: "Yeah, I

suppose that might work."

Wow, don't sound so enthusiastic! I think this but manage to keep the gem of a thought to myself. After all, we're trying to make a go of this. I don't want to end up as one of those Saturday dads. My kids split between two homes, batted back and forth like a ping pong ball. I don't want them to have the upbringing I had; a bedroom at mum's house and another at dads. I had to listen to them bad-mouthing each other day in, day out; arguing about who got custody and on which night. That's just not going to happen to my children.

"Yeah, sure," I decide to go along with it. "Let's have a regular night. We can start by getting a babysitter and heading out on Saturday night."

CHAPTER TWENTY-FOUR

Liam

"**A**RE YOU BEHAVING yourself in here?"

My mother asks the question in a low whisper. Her eyes dart around, self-conscious and awkward. She hates the idea of having a son in prison. That look of fear, as though one of the other inmates might jump on her with a knife. She doesn't get it that security guards watch our every move.

"Of course I am, mum," I grumble back in a monotone whine which says *don't talk down to me as though I'm five*. Her face is anxious and tense and her hands are clenched into fists, knuckles white and taut.

"Relax, I'm okay." I say, managing something akin to a smile. It's ironic that I'm the one trying to reassure her. She won't be returning to a tiny cell that smells of piss.

"I know, I know." Her words belie her body language. "I just worry about you son; you know I do." It takes a moment before she braces herself for the next question. "You're not going to do anything stupid, are you love?"

I raise my eyebrows. "What? Like kill myself or something?"

It wasn't the first time she'd asked me this.

Ever since that one incident, the same subject keeps raising its ugly head. She shifts in her seat. My abruptness makes her uncomfortable.

"Well, you know, after that last time..." she trails off awkwardly.

"Mum," my voice is calm and low. "How many times do I have to keep telling you, that was in the past. A long time ago."

"I know you keep saying that but..."

I roll my eyes and interrupt forcefully. "Anyway, the whole thing was dickhead's fault, not mine."

She visibly winces at the word 'dickhead'. It's a word I always use to describe my father. Her husband. *The dickhead.*

"Liam, you shouldn't call him that..." she protests.

"Why not? That's what he is." I fold my arms. We always revert to this; me slagging off dad; her defending him.

"He was a bit harsh on you over the years but he's still your father at the end of the day."

"So that makes it okay for him to beat the shit out of me as a kid?" I spit the words out. Anger bubbles inside and I can't contain it.

"He still provided for you financially," she counters.

"Yeah, and not without a song and dance about it. The number of times I had to grovel for a bit of pocket money."

She takes a deep breath and steadies herself for the next revelation: "Well, he's planning to visit you in here."

A laugh escapes from my mouth in the form of a cackle. "He's going to come into prison to visit me? You're joking!"

I can't picture it. The Great Almighty being patted down by prison guards; someone so haughty enduring the embarrassment of being herded through barriers like an animal in a farm.

"Apparently so, yes," mum affirms. "He wants a word with you about ..." The pause tells me she is trying to remember the exact words dad used. "...your conduct."

I grunt. "Well, you can tell him to fuck off. I don't want him coming anywhere near me."

She cringes visibly at my language.

"Seriously," I persist. "If he turns up, I'll walk straight out of the room. Make sure he knows that."

"Okay," she relents. "I'll ask him not to visit. I don't know what he'll do."

An awkward silence follows. Silence, but deafening in its own way. That's the moment I pop the question she doesn't want to hear.

"Does he hurt you anymore?" I ask, suddenly.

She looks mortified. "No, no, of course not," she persists.

"Good," I think it better to soften my tone. After all, it's not her fault I'm locked up. I don't know why I'm taking this out on her.

"Sorry mum," I add. "I'm a bit grumpy."

She looks at me, a gentle smile lighting up her face. "It's okay son."

I take a sip of tea from the paper cup. It's rank – too milky and weak.

"It's just that..." she looks more intense now, deep in thought. "... the night of the accident... I was wondering. Were you trying to..." She struggles for words before lowering her voice and adding "...end things?"

I widen my eyes. "For God's sake!" I exhale in a low voice. "Do you really think I was trying to kill myself. And not only that, take Emma with me as well?"

A rash starts to creep up her neck. "I just thought that maybe ... with the custody battle and everything... maybe you hadn't taken your medication. Who knows?" She realises she's said too much. The whole thing about killing Emma is a bridge too far.

"No mum." My words come out colder and more hostile than I intend. "I didn't try to kill myself. It makes me sick that you think I'm capable of hurting Emma. I had a phone call when I was driving that distracted me and I lost control of the car. That was it." The moment the words are out of my mouth, I know I've already said too much. I shouldn't have mentioned the phone call.

Her eyes widen. "Phone call? What phone call? Why were you talking on the phone whilst driving?"

I sigh. "I had the speaker phone on. The conversation turned into a bit of an argument. I got worked up." I cover my face with my hands.

"An argument with who? Zoe?" She's trying to imagine the scene. "I can't believe you were talking on the phone whilst driving! And with Emma next to you in the car! My heavens! How could you?"

"Mum," I roll my eyes. "I thought you were here to visit me, not give out to me."

Her tears are coming, I can sense it. Sure enough, she roots around in her pocket for a tissue.

"It's just that…" she begins. And we're off, her tears flow freely. "…if you had seen Emma's little white coffin at the funeral that day…"

Frustration and anger bubble up inside me. "Don't you realise I think about that all the time? Don't you know that it's all I see in my head when I close my eyes? Her coffin! Don't you know how gutted I was not to be at my own daughter's funeral? Everyone thinks it's my fault she's dead! My nerves are wrecked!" All I want to do now is storm out, but I can't leave until an officer calls time.

We sit there in stony silence for a while. My arms are folded tightly; my mother is clutching a tissue.

"Were you taking your prescription at the time?" her voice is low but persistent.

I look at her, unable to answer. She's right. Somehow, she always knows. When I forget to take the medication, my behaviour becomes erratic. Zoe would never have let me look after Emma, if she thought for one moment that I was off the tablets.

I lower my head slowly: "I might have forgotten for a day or two."

She nods and her look confirms her thoughts: "On your head be it." Her hands are shaking.

She's never spoken like this before; never directly accused me.

"So, it's a blame game now, is it?" My lips curl with disdain. "It's my fault is it, that Emma's dead?" I can't believe how I'm spitting this out.

She raises her eyebrows. *Well, if the shoe fits.*

I lean my elbows on the table and look directly at her: "Let's talk about who's really to blame, shall we?"

She makes a big deal of re-arranging herself in the seat.

I go on: "Let's talk about why I have to medicate, why don't we? Let's have a friendly chat about Dad and how he used to beat me black and blue. About the fact that you didn't have the balls to take us away from him. You didn't protect us. You let us stay in the same house as a violent abuser. Day in, day out. For years!" My face is up close to hers. The tension is unbearable: "So, whose really to blame? You or me?" The words explode from my mouth.

She closes her eyes, sits back and attempts to compose herself. When she looks up again, I hear the words: "I'm going to have to leave now. Take care of yourself." Her chair scrapes back, she stands up and I watch her walk away. She looks so tiny and fragile. Her little frame on thin legs heading towards a security officer; a man with a bald head and a huge stomach.

Don't go, a voice in my head says. *Wait, mum, I didn't mean that.*

But she's gone, the double doors are opening, her head is disappearing through them. My heart feels heavy. One of the other prisoners catches my eye. He's sitting opposite his wife and looks at me with pity. I'm sitting on my own and my visitor has fled before time out.

I push my chest out and clench my jaw. Lifting the Mars Bar from the table top, I peel back the wrapper and bite off a huge chunk. I'll show him I'm not bothered. Nothing wrong here; just another visitor that had to leave early.

The metaphorical shutters are down. The hard casing is back on. I return to my shell.

But somewhere deep down inside me, a little boy's voice screams.

CHAPTER TWENTY-FIVE

Liam (Then)

"LOOK AT ME when I'm talking to you!" my father's voice boomed out menacingly. I felt his breath on my face. The words flew across the table and hit me right between the eyes.

I looked up, my hands trembling. To any six-year-old like me, he seemed like a monster; towering, threatening, over-bearing.

"If your mother says finish your dinner, you finish it. Don't whine about it! Do you hear me?"

"Yes dad."

"Say it louder!"

"Yes dad!" I said, raising my voice.

"Now eat!"

I raised the fork to my mouth and stuffed in a large clump of cold mushy potato. It was so disgusting, I felt like gagging but forced myself to swallow. Then the next forkful and the one after that.

I looked across at mum; I'm sure she felt guilty. Her eyes displayed the pretence that she was on his side, but I knew his harsh words would upset her.

When I had finished stuffing mounds of stodgy mashed potato into my mouth, the old man started on me once again, "Now get to your room. And don't moan to your mother ever again."

I got up from the table and darted away. I was more than happy to retreat to my room; to get as far away from him as possible. I would escape into magazines and books and, that way I could shut out the world around me.

I never complained to my mother again after that day. I always finished my dinner – every single morsel, but it wasn't enough. I still got into trouble for other things, like the first time I wet the bed.

I couldn't help it. I just woke up one morning and the sheets were soaked. I didn't remember the feeling of needing to pee during the night. I didn't do it on purpose. There was no intention to let it all just trickle out.

I did have dreams though, like the one where I was floating on a calm lake. I heard dad scream-ing in the distance but the surface of the water was still and quiet. I would start drifting down the lake, weightless and serene; a feeling of relief would wash over me. Perhaps that was the time I was peeing; the moment I had let go.

"What have you done?" he shouted merciless-ly the following day. He was watching my mother load sheets into the washing machine. "Did you wet yourself?"

I could feel my legs quiver as I faced his fury.

"It was an accident," I squeaked.

"An accident!" he exclaimed. "A bloody acci-dent! What's stopping you just getting out of bed like the rest of us and going to the toilet? Are you so lazy that you have to piss the bed?"

I cowered as he came forward and stood over me. I knew what was coming. He would hit me. And he did. A sharp sting landed on my cheek as his hand met my face. And he did it again. And again.

"Steve!" I heard my mum call. "Don't! Don't! It's okay! I'll wash them!"

There followed relief tinged with fear. Relief that she was defending me; coming to my rescue, but fear that she would be at the brunt of his anger next.

He rounded on her. "Don't tell him it's okay Jenny! He'll just keep repeating the same behaviour if you tell him that! Do you want to wash pissy sheets for the rest of your life?"

She winced at the words. "I don't mind," she whimpered in a voice laden with fear.

He pointed his finger at her and his face was up close to hers: "When I discipline our son, I expect you to be on my side. Don't defy me by making excuses for him."

Her body slumped backwards in resignation. "I'm sorry, Steve."

My relief turned to defeat. My only defender had given up already. I was on my own. The bed wetting went on from age six to twelve. There was even the time he hung my wet sheet out the window. With a permanent red marker, he wrote on the sheet: *My name is Liam and I wet the bed.* That sheet billowed in the wind. The kids in the neighbourhood could read about my secret. The old bastard was literally washing our dirty laundry in public. Some kids laughed and taunted me and the bullies had a field day. Other children were polite and said nothing. One little girl was even sympathetic.

One of the neighbours was disgusted. "Is that any way to treat a child?" she challenged. She was told in no uncertain terms that it was none of her business.

"Well, it is my business when you're bullying and humiliating your own son in full view of the street!" At least she had the guts to bite back.

I tried not to wet the bed. Really, I did. But each morning regular as clockwork, I'd wake up to the clammy wet feeling around my legs. I lifted the sheets with dread and felt butterflies in my stomach every time I saw the wet patch.

I tried cleaning it up by myself. From a young age, I learned how to pull the sheets off the bed, roll them up in a ball, and stuff them into the laundry basket.

But he always found out.

"How many times have I told you?" he shouted, grabbing me by the wrist and dragging me up the hallway. "How many times have I told you to get the hell up and go to the toilet?"

There was the inevitable unbuckling of his belt; the slick sound of the belt whipping from his waist. A slap around the face was not enough this time; he was going for the belt.

"Please, dad, no!" I yelled, pleading for him to stop. "I won't do it again!"

Mum was standing in the background. Her face screwed up and anxious. I knew she felt guilty. She wanted to stop him but didn't know how.

The strap came slashing down on me. Ripping against my back. Stinging me in agony.

"No! No! No!" I cried. Over and over again.

But he'd never stop. Once was not enough. The lashes kept coming. Finally, when it was over, I looked up at him. He was drained and spent, as if he'd gotten something out of his system. The anger or frustration had dissipated. I'll never forget that look on his face. After every beating, relief washed over him. Somewhere deep in my gut, I realised I was a punching bag; the butt of his anger, his way of letting off steam.

It dawned on me at some point that nothing I did would ever be good enough for him. Even when I stopped wetting the bed, or set my alarm every hour on the hour to make sure I went to the bathroom. Even when the mattress was dry, there was something else to scold me about.

There was always a reason to punish me. From the age of six, right through to sixteen, something always angered him. It was one thing or another; the TV was too loud, I stayed out too late, hung out with the wrong crowd. The belt would come off and he would let off steam.

At first, I tip toed around, walking on egg-shells. I tried to second-guess every possible mood. I stayed out of his way, skulking in my room and delving into books. But that still didn't work, he sought me out. He was a man on a mission; looking for ways to release the pressure. And if it wasn't me, it was my mother.

Until the night I hit back.

I had discovered drugs. Someone gave me a line of coke. I hung out with an older crowd. The minute the powder went up my nostrils, the tingling sensation took over. Minutes later, I was walking on air. Striding through the room like I owned it. Fear and self-consciousness instantly melted away. I could take on the world. And I did.

Late one night, I arrived home and was buzzing off my face. I heard the old bastard giving off to mum. Ranting and railing about god knows what. This time, I had no fear. I stormed down the stairs and swung open their bedroom door like a demon possessed. She was sitting there in her nightie, cowering. He had his walking stick in hand and was holding it over her. Ready to strike.

"Stop that right now!" I bellowed.

He burled round and took me in. His face shifted into a mixture of sneering amusement and disdain. A half-laugh, half-snort sprang from his mouth: "Oh yeah? And what the fuck are you gonna do about it?"

"I'll tell you what I'll fucking do." The drug fuelled adrenaline pulsated through me. I found myself reaching down and whipping the shoe off my foot. I hurled it at his head. It bounced off his skull with a satisfying whack. The force of it caused him to fall backwards.

I lunged forward and ripped the walking stick from his hand. I turned it on him. It was like a rush of ecstasy. I smashed the stick down on him time and time again. His body shuddered with pain underneath me. The years of being the brunt of his abuse had turned full circle. I was old enough and big enough to fight back. And I was high on drugs.

"Liam! Stop! That's enough!" Mum intervened. "Please stop! You'll kill him!"

Eventually, I did stop. Astounded, I realised that the old man was unconscious. Somewhere in the background I heard mum say "Ambulance please".

"Fuck." I sat at the edge of the bed and looked at him, slumped on the carpet. There was blood on his face and his body was crumpled into a heap. I was strangely satisfied. Like a computer game with too many levels, I'd finally defeated the dragon.

The utopia didn't last. The sound of sirens wailing and the flash of blue lights alerted us. The ambulance had arrived, and with them – the police.

"Excuse me sir, what's been going on?" I realised a cop was talking to me. As he spoke, he was taking in the scene; my father being carried out in a stretcher and my mother quivering in her nightie. And there I was, sitting on the edge of the bed, walking stick suspiciously lying at my feet.

"I was defending her," I said, simply. "He was going to kill her."

The police officer looked me over. He meticulously took in my dilated pupils, sussing my age, observing a frail mother weeping in her night clothes.

"Sorry sir, but we'll have to trouble you with a statement," he advised.

I wandered into the kitchen to make tea. My mind was still a heady mix of adrenaline and coke. When I lifted a cup, I didn't even realise I was squeezing it tight. It broke in my hand. *Holy fuck, I'm a superman.* I watched as the pieces of china imploded over the floor.

That was the feeling I just kept chasing.
That first hit.

CHAPTER TWENTY-SIX
Mia (Now)

"WE HAVE A habit of bumping into each other." I breeze to Zoe in the supermarket. I had spotted her five minutes earlier but kept my distance, watching her. She hadn't seen me; she's too engrossed in the baby clothes.

For a split second, I feel a pang of sympathy for her; standing there, the bereaved mother. I think back to that small white coffin having been lowered into the ground. Here she is looking at children's clothing in a supermarket. I suppose she's reminiscing, re-living the time she bought clothes for Emma; the pink booties and cute little bibs.

"Oh, hi," Zoe says, distractedly, her face deadpan. There's no smile of recognition but I detect her annoyance. She's probably wondering why Liam's female friend keeps popping up out of nowhere. I look at the shelves and then back at her. My face creases in sympathy. "It must be hard." My voice is laden with pity.

"Huh?" She murmurs, looking confused.

"It must be very hard with Emma gone."

She grips her hands tighter on the trolley. Her face sets into a look of steely determination. "I'm fine." She sounds resolute, then walks away.

I stand, watching her go. A trace of a smile spreads across my face; I've gotten to her. I've probably ruined her day; thrown her off balance. In a sense, it serves her right. After all, the number of times she spoiled my day without even realising. I think of the occasions I was pushed aside just for her benefit.

Quietly humming to myself, I brush my fingertips lightly over the baby gear, trying to decide which garments to buy. The little pink jumper? Or the dinky blue jeans? My little bean will grow out of them very quickly, but they're so cute, I just have to buy them.

At the till, I spy Zoe again. This time she sees me. Her expression is now clearly one of annoyance. She looks away and I smile smugly. It's her problem if she wants to be jealous.

✧   ✧   ✧

"Saw Zoe again," I tell Liam when I call up for a visit.

His eyes widen. "What? Again? Are you stalking her or something?" The awkward laugh is meant to show he's joking.

"Have you told her yet?" I ask the question.

He shifts in his seat. "Told her what?"

He pretends he hasn't a clue what I'm talking about. "You know damn well."

He raises his hand to his face and subconsciously starts chewing his nails. "I can't seem to find the right time."

I roll my eyes. "There's never gonna be a right

time. Just spit it out and tell her."

"She'll go through the roof," he retorts.

"So what Liam? I'm having your baby. I need your support."

He shrugs his shoulders. "What support can I give you in here?"

"Emotional support for a start!" Do I have to spell it out for him? "It would help if you could at least acknowledge that we're going to have a child together."

He runs his hand through his hair. "There's one problem." He is looking at me nervously which makes my heart quicken. His voice has a different tone and I don't like the sound of it. "What's that?"

"Don't crack up when I tell you."

"Just get on with it, Liam, what the fuck is it?" *God, what the hell is coming?*

He takes a deep breath. "It's Zoe. She's pregnant too."

I glare back, flabbergasted. It's as though the world has stopped spinning. I can't breathe.

"She's what?"

"She's pregnant too," he repeats tentatively.

I sit and stare at him, unable to grasp the words. Did he just tell me that Zoe and I are both pregnant by him?

"No, she can't be!" I shake my head, as shock and denial coil around me. I'm suffocating with disbelief. He squirms with embarrassment.

"And is it what I think you mean? Her baby, is it yours?" I stutter profusely. The walls are closing in on me like I'm the one trapped in the prison cell.

His eyes are full of shame. "I'm sorry." His voice is so low I can hardly hear it.

"How and when?" I search his eyes for a credible explanation. "When did you two have…" I can't finish the sentence. I can't bring myself to say *when did you two have sex*? I don't want to think about them fucking each other. I can't stand the image in my head; Liam inside her and that woman panting underneath him. I just can't…

"It was just once." he mumbles. "An accident. We were both drunk. It didn't mean anything."

I close my eyes. "Stop! Stop with all the fucking clichés, please."

I hold my head in my hands, my eyes closed, taking deep breaths. "Bloody hell, this can't be happening."

He reaches over to take my hand but I snatch it away.

"Don't touch me!" I somehow look up at him.

"It just happened."

"How could you do this to me?" I look up at him defiantly.

The bastard is clueless, squirming and blank. He shrugs his shoulders: "I'm sorry, Mia."

"I can't even look at you!" I scrape my chair back, stand bolt upright and stomp away. Anger pulsates through every sinew. I don't even look back once. I just thunder on out of the visiting room, away from the prison and down the path. I don't even think of phoning of a taxi. I just keep walking. I'm boiling with anger and adrenaline is pulsing through me.

Its history repeating itself. Like the night of the accident. That was the last time he made me this mad. I know I need to be responsible for my own behaviour. I have to keep burning off this anger.

Or there's going to be another accident.

✧   ✧   ✧

Mia (Then)

THE TEXT TO Liam said: *You haven't forgotten, have you babe? xx*. I pressed send. My watch said twenty past six. Typical of him not to get in touch. He never checks his phone and even forgets to charge it.

I sat at the dressing table and combed out my wet hair. Taking a bulldog clip, I piled one section on top and I clicked on the hairdryer. I put on some dance music and hummed along with it. Between drying strands of hair, I sipped at my glass of wine, getting myself in the mood.

Tonight, was going to be a big night. It was my friend Sarah's birthday and a crowd of us were hitting Bar Red for drinks. The plan was to go clubbing afterwards but nothing was set in stone and we'd take the night as it comes.

Liam promised he'd come with me. It would be the first time my friends would meet him properly. I'd moaned about it on so many occasions: "When are you gonna meet my mates? How can we all get together? When are we going to make this official?"

He body-swerved it many times. He used witty

jokes designed to evade the awkward questions: "I dunno," he'd say. "Maybe I should pump myself up in the gym first. Gotta look good enough to be your fella!" He'd laugh and wink to show me that he was joking. I'd give him a playful nudge on his arm and he'd get away with it again.

"Come on Liam, you know it's important to me." I'd persist. Usually we'd be curled up in bed, post coital, the glow of sex still glistening on our bodies.

"I know," he'd say softly, taking a lock of my hair and twirling it. He always had a way with him. "I do worry about the work thing though, you know that."

I sighed. "But everyone in the pub knows we're an item. It's long past the time we can keep it a secret."

His dark eyes bored into mine, the face placid and understanding. "I suppose you're right," he hushed. "But there's also the Zoe problem." His eyes averted to one side.

I tutted. *Zoe! Why did he always have to bring her name into the conversation?* Even while his sperm was still tricking down my leg, another woman's name was on his lips.

"So what? She's in the past. You're allowed to move on, Liam," I tried to hide the annoyance in my tone.

I got that look thrown back at me again. The teacher talking down to the pupil. "But she's not in the past Mia. You know that. Not in the true sense of the word. As long as Emma is around, Zoe will always be in my life. She's the mother of my child." The tone was sympathetic but the words cut into me like a knife.

Not in the past. Mother of my child. I'd forever be second best to that fucking woman and her kid!

I sat up in bed abruptly, unable to contain my annoyance. Suddenly I felt naked, exposed and totally vulnerable.

"Where are you going?" he asked, as I pulled up my knickers and reached for a top.

"For a pee." My tone was brittle and terse.

"Mia..." he coaxed. "Please..."

I was already stomping out of the bedroom. I couldn't stand the sight of him anymore.

I hurried down to the kitchen. I perched myself on a stool, Chardonnay in hand and listened to the hum of the traffic outside. A night bus rumbled past. In the distance, I heard laughter from youngsters spilling out of a pub. For other people, the night was cruising along whilst I gazed into my glass, asking myself where I was going in life. What was this 'thing' with Liam? Was it even going anywhere? Would he ever change his Facebook status to "in a relationship"? His profile picture was a photo of his daughter. The one true love of his life.

Maybe the only true love?

I don't know how long I was sitting there. Long enough for the hairs on my arms to stand up and for my nipples to harden under the vest top. At that moment, the kitchen door creaked open.

After a silence, I finally heard him say, "Okay then."

I looked up. His expression was soft and compassionate. "Okay, what?" I croaked back.

"Okay, let's make it official. I'll come meet your mates." He was standing in the doorway, wearing only his boxers. I was completely won over at that moment in time. I walked towards him and we kissed. Gently at first, then hard and passionate. Our tongues played with each other. He reached up and felt my taut, hardened nipples. He carried me back upstairs and we made love all over again. This time it was even more intense, grasping and passionate. Now I was sure he was really mine. He had finally given himself to me.

That's how good things could have been.

Except for that one night. The night of the accident. The night where I was at fault.

You always wonder what might have happened, if you could turn back time, if things had panned out differently. Hindsight's a wonderful thing. The accident should never have happened.

But then again, maybe on a subconscious level, I willed it to happen.

Maybe I wanted Emma to go.

CHAPTER TWENTY-SEVEN

Liam

DRUGS LURE YOU in. They provide ease and comfort and make you feel powerful. You feel like arrived; you've come home. You've finally found a best friend; a soulmate; the thing you can always turn to when lonely or depressed but you also pick it up when you're happy. Good times are enhanced by the presence of this new best friend.

Then, all of a sudden, your best friend turns on you; immediately ghosts you; stops taking your calls and finds other people to hang out with. In a short time, the drugs stop working for you. Your tolerance increases to a level where you need double the dose. Gradually, the double dose stops working too. You demand more and more.

For bigger doses, you need more money. You'll do anything to get cash; beg, borrow or steal. Even crime. You find excuses for breaking the law. Your mate Gaz is a dealer. He talks you into doing one small deal. He gives you a bag of coke. He mentions another bloke called Packo who will come into the bar that night. He'll wear a green hooded jacket and sport a beard. This guy will order a Blue Sapphire. You'll get handed a few bank notes. Surreptitiously you put one tenner in the till and slide the rest into your pocket.

When you hand back a small amount of change, you'll pass the cocaine pack discreetly across his palm. That's it. Job done. Easy.

You tell yourself it's a one off. But you tell yourself that every time. You're just gonna do this one deal; a single transaction to get enough cash for one last hit. After this one, you'll stop.

Packo winks at you and walks off. Your heart hammers with fear and excitement. You did it! A drug deal and no-one noticed a thing! One quick sleight of hand and you've earned yourself a tidy sum. It becomes addictive. You tell yourself you'll do it one more time. Just one more deal will get you enough gear for next week. You won't need to rifle through Zoe's purse.

It's like a game. The stakes get higher. It's like playing Monopoly; first you have the little green houses on low rent Old Kent Road. By the end of the game, you need red hotels on *Park Lane* and *Mayfair*. You're aiming high. The sky's the limit.

Gaz starts to tell you about higher-grade stuff coming in. Stronger dope which hits the spot quickly and does the job faster. You snort it and feel the buzz like never-before. That first rush is back; a feeling of power; the ease and comfort; like you can take on the world.

It's a balancing act. On the one hand you have Zoe and Emma. You're trying to be the perfect dad, bringing home the bacon and helping Zoe around the house. On the other hand, there's Mia; sexy, slutty, passionate. She parties, takes drugs and has mind blowing sex with you. The down-side is that she's texting constantly. She's got expectations and wants a full-on relationship.

And then there's the job. The boss, Roger, takes a shine to you straight away. He knows you're a good manager and the staff respond to you. You work hard and put the hours in, but even Roger is starting to suspect something. He comes out with all sorts of stuff; asking me if everything is okay. He remarks that I don't seem to be myself these days; wants to know if things are going well at home.

You reassure him that all is well. You're just tired because you were up late looking after your sick child. You promise profusely that you'll put the hours in. What you actually do is snort more coke to perform better.

But he's at you again in no time. He mentions that you're opening the bar late occasionally; you seem hungover.

You keep promising you'll work harder but he won't let go of the subject. You get more resentful. He's one ungrateful son of a bitch. He can lounge around in his fancy mansion doing fuck all, whereas you're doing all the grafting. You've no option but to do more deals from behind the counter. The web of deceit expands and with it your guilty conscience. The only way to quash that feeling is to snort more drugs.

And then there's Big Al. The hard-faced drug dealer with tattoos crawling all the way up his neck and stopping at his chin. You made the unfortunate mistake of shagging his girlfriend when you were drunk. When they had an argument, she spilled the beans to piss him off. It pissed him off alright. The bastard came looking for you at closing time one night. Trouble was, he had a metal pole in one hand and two thugs on either side of him. They held you up against the wall and made it clear that if you went anywhere near the girlfriend again, they'd rip your balls off. They dished out a bit of a beating for good measure and cleared off. Their idea of a warning.

Then there's Zoe; piling more money pressures on you. An endless list of necessities for Emma; school uniform, lunches and gymnastics. An ongoing merry-go-round of presents for Christmas and birthdays. It never stops.

On top of that, there were constant arguments with Zoe. It would usually start with snide comments. A reminder that things weren't as romantic as they were years ago. Paranoid remarks which told me she suspected there was another woman.

To top it all off, there's Mia; always vying for attention. She's continuously demanding to know where you were, how you were, what you were up to; a constant flow of texts seeking permanent reassurances. *Yes, you do want to fuck her and yes, you will see her on Saturday night.*

And last, but not least, your mother is worried about you; breathing down your neck all the time. She says you look terrible, and you're losing too much weight. She's moans that she's lying awake at night wondering how on earth you cope.

Maybe the old man was right all along. Perhaps you're a stupid waste of space after all. It would be better if you were no longer around.

Better for everyone – Zoe, Mia, Mum, even the boss. Better for Emma too. What hope did she have in life? Growing up in a home where dad was never around. You only swoop in occasionally, take her to swimming classes and fill her up with fast food afterwards. Would she inherit your addict riddled genes? Would she turn into a full-blown user herself and, God forbid, end up working the streets at night?

By now it's clear your mind is fucked. Everything which passes through your head is negative. The doctor calls it *clinical depression*. All you know is, you want to go to sleep and never wake up.

You consider throwing yourself off a bridge. If you could just take one small step over the edge, the pain would end. Your legs quiver. You don't have the nerve to jump. You can't even do that right. You don't even have the guts to kill yourself.

Then there was the night of the accident.

Zoe asks you to look after Emma. She is going to a hen-do. You're glad to look after Emma, glad to get the chance to spend time with her. In no time at all during the day, you can tell she's bored. She wants her mummy, her own bedroom and her toys. You take her to McDonalds; that kills some time. Then the cinema. You fill her with chocolate and sweets which isn't a good idea as she becomes hyper. You pop into the bar for a swift half. You need to do a quick drug deal. It would be over and done with in no time.

Emma wants a soft drink. You both sit on the

bar stools and wait for Packo. There's no sign of him and time drags on; Emma is getting bored and restless. Big Al turns up – aggressive and arsy. He swears in front of the kid. You eventually leave the premises. You haven't done the deal and Gaz will be raging. You get into the car with Emma and take off. A strange feeling comes over you. Did someone spike my drink? A woozy buzz. The mobile rings. It's Mia. For fuck's sake. Not again. She's phoned fifty times already today. I better answer it for once and for all. She's fuming and drunk; ranting and raving about some irrelevant shit. Telling you she's sick of you and she's had enough.

You don't blame her. You're sick of yourself too and you've also had enough. Wouldn't it be so easy to just slip away? Take Emma with you? Just put us both out of this misery for once and for all?

A car comes out of nowhere. You try to swerve but you're too slow. You can hear Mia shouting in the background. Whatever they've put in that drink has hit you. You give in to it. The woozy feeling and the way the car seems to be driving itself. You stop fighting it. You give in. Relax. Let go.

There's a thud. *Then nothing.*

CHAPTER TWENTY-EIGHT
Liam

"**G**REAT TO SEE you. Can I get you a cup of tea?" the bloke holds out his hand. I take it and shake it limply. "Yeah, sure." I'm feeling slightly disorientated. It's been a while since someone was so pleased to meet me, but this guy's enthusiasm is unnerving.

Various blokes are sitting around a table, on the middle of which is a collection of mugs, milk, sugar and biscuits. Some of the guys are prisoners I've seen on the landings. Others are outsiders; in other words, normal folk; visitors who are leading the meeting.

They've set a pile of leaflets on the table. There's a picture of two hands gripping prison cell bars and the words: *Freedom is Possible*.

The visitors look happy. They're joking and laughing with each other.

I sit there, arms folded. My lips are curled with disdain. Do they get a buzz out of waltzing in here and bragging about freedom? Obviously, they see us as a lost cause trapped in hell. They've the nerve to turn up and expect us to feel grateful for their presence.

"Liam, what brings you here to the meeting today?" The first stranger smiles patronisingly.

"It's great to see you."

I keep my arms folded and glare. "Any excuse to get out of the cell."

They all chuckle; even the guy who asked the question. "Fair enough," he chortles. "Might as well have some biscuits then." A packet of chocolate cookies gets passed my way. They're tasty alright, with a thick layer of chocolate, not the cheap crap you usually get in here. I take one greedily. The outsider is unperturbed by my cold exterior. He moves on to the next guy.

"Jimmy, what about you? How are you getting on?"

Jimmy smiles. "Doing okay mate. Day thirty off the drugs now. Feeling a bit better."

The visitors grin. "That's fantastic mate! You're doing so well! Thirty days clean! That's thirty miracles in a row!"

For some reason, I keep going to these meetings. Every few days, the outsiders bring us chocolate treats and make tea. It passes the time. I start to get friendly with the fellow inmate, Jimmy. My instinct tells me he's a good ally to have on the inside. He's tall, with a huge neck and bulging muscles. Tattoos creep up to his jaw-line and down to his knuckles. He looks like a threat just standing still but he's actually the nicest guy you could meet; protective and helpful. He always looks out for me.

"I'm dying for a joint, mate," I admit to him while we're doing our daily exercise in the yard.

"Yeah, but where's that gonna get you Liam?" he reasons. "You'll only wake up tomorrow feeling like shit and needing more."

We walk around the yard, watching the other blokes play basketball. I shake my head. "So what if I wake up tomorrow feeling that way? There's nothing to live for anyway. Every day's the same. Groundhog Day. Stuck in here, day in, day out."

Jimmy shrugs his shoulders, lights a cigarette and inhales deeply. He offers me one and I accept gratefully.

"That's one way to look at it mate," he reflects. "Here's another. You could use the time to get clean. Sort your life out. Then you wouldn't get yourself in the shit again."

Hanging my head in shame, I can't help sliding into denial. "But it wasn't my fault. I shouldn't be in here. I'm innocent."

Jimmy looks sideways at me. "Why's that mate?" His tone is soft but his words are harsh. "Was it someone else got behind the wheel of the car and drove it for you? Some other guy who blew the powder up your nostril? Maybe some other punter opened your mouth and forced the booze down your neck?"

I look skywards and close my eyes for an instant. I know what he's referring to, of course. Emma. If I hadn't driven the car that night, she'd still be alive. If Emma wasn't dead, I wouldn't be in a place like this. How can you argue with someone like Jimmy? Built like a brick shithouse, he's too overpowering to disagree with.

How can I ever convince him that my drink was spiked? That Mia's phone-call distracted me? That another car came out of nowhere?

Jimmy takes another drag and continues watching the basketball game. He looks peaceful and content. I bet there's nothing eating him up. His mind doesn't churn with anxiety, like mine does. My brain spins with 'what if's'.

What if Mia hadn't phoned at that moment? Would I have lost control of the wheel?

What if the old man hadn't knocked me around? Would I have turned to drugs?

"We have to take responsibility for our own stuff," Jimmy goes on calmly, as if he had been reading my mind. "Lots of people have shit happen to them but they don't end up in here. They pick themselves up and move on. That's what I plan to do."

I know he's right but I don't want to hear what he's saying. Emma is six feet under. Her coffin was lowered into the ground and I wasn't even there to pay respects. Zoe's walking around with my baby in her belly, and as if that isn't enough, so is Mia. How did I get into this mess? How come I've so royally fucked up my life?

Jimmy shoots another sideways glance. Nudging me, he remarks, "Hey, it could be worse."

I look at him, confused. "What could be worse than Emma dying and me being in here?"

He shrugs. "You could be six feet under, mate. You could be history too. You can never bring Emma back but you've a chance to sort things out with Zoe and Mia."

I know he's right but when I tell Zoe about Mia, all hell will break loose.

CHAPTER TWENTY-NINE
Mia (Now)

"**M**Y NAME'S MIA Matthews. I have an appointment with Doctor Sanders at eleven." I keep my voice low, ashamed for even being here.

The receptionist looks down and starts tapping on her keyboard. She gives me a professional smile; the type that is laced with sympathy.

"Okay," she replies in a friendly tone. "Let me just check the records here. What's your name again?" She puts on her glasses and squints at the computer. She's attractive, with sleek black hair. Mid-thirties. I wonder why she wants to work here, of all places – an abortion clinic. Maybe she had an experience of her own in the past. "Oh right, yes," she smiles, locating my name on the screen. "You're nice and early."

Depends what you're talking about, I think. I'm not that early – nine weeks, and if I don't get a move on, it'll be too late.

As if she is reading my mind, the girl at the desk clears her throat. She must realise her *faux pas* because she quickly corrects herself, "It's only ten thirty, you have plenty of time. Would you like tea or coffee while you wait?"

I shake my head. "No thank you, I'm fine."

She nods and points to a door. "The waiting room is just in there. Dr Sanders will be with you soon."

My knees feel like jelly as my legs carry me forward. One small step at a time; each a step closer to the termination.

The waiting room is plush. There's comfortable chairs and low lighting. Pleasant floral paintings adorn the walls and soft music plays in the background. There's another client waiting. She looks up briefly as I walk in. She gives a nervous smile but quickly averts her eyes back to her magazine. Clearly, this is not the time or the place for small talk.

I plant myself on one of the comfy chairs and lean across to pick up a magazine from the coffee table. As I flick through it, I realise it's pointless trying to read. Nothing's going in. My mind reels with thoughts; the baby, Liam, and the termination.

Abortion. Why couldn't I just say the word?

Thoughts bounce back and forth like a ball on a ping pong table. On the one hand, nobody wants to terminate a foetus. It goes against a woman's natural instinct. On the other, I need to end the pregnancy. I have to do this; walk away from Liam for good and accept the fact Zoe will always be in his life, with or without a child.

There's a strange magnetic force between those two. She's like his mother; his carer – he's lost without her. Now she's going to have another baby with him. If I go full term and have mine, we'd end up like a bunch of freaks on a reality talk show. Liam, Zoe, myself and two infants. It would simply be ridiculous; the sort of stuff you read about in tacky magazines.

There was also the night of the accident. I can't get it out of my mind. Sometimes I wake in the middle of the night in a cold sweat, racked with guilt and remorse. What if I hadn't phoned him at that particular time?

Would Emma still be alive?

✧ ✧ ✧

Mia (Then)

"YOU HAVEN'T FORGOTTEN, have you babe? xx" I had tapped out that text to Liam. I looked at my watch: Six twenty.

Tonight was going to be a big night. It was my friend Sarah's birthday and the crowd were about to heading out to Bar Red as planned. Ten minutes rolled by. No reply from Liam. I tried phoning him. No answer. I tutted to myself. Why did he never answer his bloody phone to me? It was so annoying! I texted again. "Babe, please get back to me. You're picking me up at 8pm yeah? xx"

I could feel the frustration prickling my skin. Bad vibes began to take over me. Female intuition, they call it. Intuition, or simply knowledge gleaned from getting to know him? Previous experience of Liam told me he was unreliable. Our history together demonstrated that any time I relied on him to do anything with my mates, he let me down.

It was as if he was ashamed of me; embarrassed to be seen in public with his girlfriend. Did I look that bad? That dreadful? Deep down, I denied the real reason. I knew that Liam lead a double life. One world featured Zoe. And a parallel existence traipsed alongside me.

With Zoe, he could pretend to be *Super-Dad*. She was like the wife. They weren't actually married, and they didn't live together, but she still had a hold over him. I played the role of the new girlfriend – the bit of stuff on the side. Zoe still came first.

I lifted my mascara and applied it to my eyelashes. I don't know why I bothered. Part of me knew, deep down, that tonight wasn't going to happen. It would be too much to ask for. The romantic fantasy of turning up on Liam's arm, and introducing him to my friends, started to fizzle away into a pathetic dream.

Instead, it was a cert I'd be turning up alone and empty handed. I imagined the pity on all their faces when, once again, Liam wasn't able to make it. I could predict the exchange of sideways glances. Those looks that said: Is there really a boyfriend at all? Is he a figment *of her imagination*?

I gazed at the dress hung delicately over the edge of the bedroom door. For weeks I had planned the outfit; trudging around all the boutiques, taking in the latest designs. Finally, I decided on one; black, with a daring slit up one side; figure-hugging and sexy. I dieted for weeks to be able to fit into it. I starved myself on lettuce and apples in an attempt to look at skinny as possible. I also scrimped and saved; at one hundred and fifty pounds a pop, dresses like that don't come cheap. Then there was tanning sessions and the nail bar. Tons of pre-planning and a pile of money had gone into this one evening; the night that Liam and I would make it official. We're a couple.

I checked the time on my phone. Six forty and no sign of him. I phoned the silly bastard again. He didn't pick up. I fired off another text. Nothing.

I slugged more wine. Was there any point in squeezing into that tight-fitting dress? The phone finally bleeped and my heart soared with anticipation. But as soon as my hopes were raised, they were just as instantly dashed. It was only group chat from the girls.

Well chicks, hope you've got your dancing shoes on! See you soon! ☺ *x Sarah x*

At that point I should have been putting the feelers out; laying the groundwork for the disaster to come. Clever excuses should have dawned on me, things like: *Aw girls, I'm gutted, not feeling well. Must have eaten something dodgy. I'm sure it'll be alright but giving you a heads up. Not feeling great right now x*

I could have written that but somehow denial prevented me. Surely Liam would phone any moment. He would be chirpy and say something like: *All good babe. Just jumping in the shower. Be over at eight.*

But there was nothing. *Nada.* By seven o'clock I was sitting on my bed, phoning the bastard on repeat. My hair sat piled on my head in a perfectly coiffed do, the make-up was applied to perfection, but I was getting tipsier as time ran on. One glass became two. Two rolled into three.

Restless and irritable, I spent the time scrolling social media, which reinforced my bad mood. Instagram photos of perfect couples and family gatherings highlighted just how pathetic my life was; sitting here in my dressing gown, waiting for a night-out that wasn't going to happen.

A little voice inside me murmured: *Go anyway! Go without him! You've bought the outfit, now hit the town! You can go on the pull. Screw him!*

That voice was feisty and confident although I was feeling anything but. I didn't want to flirt with anyone else. That's the thing about being in love. When you're smitten, you don't want to play the field. The need to attract attention from other men just doesn't exist. You want only one guy. Nobody else will do.

Damn it! I was hopelessly, pathetically head over heels about Liam and I couldn't stop. A surgeon couldn't reach into my mind or soul or inject me with even a hint of common sense. It was a brain transplant I actually needed; a mindset which makes me for fall for emotionally stable and available men; the type of guy who would put me first. I had to face the facts; I was stuck with this one. I should have walked away ages ago. Instead, I fell for him and now it's too late.

By eleven o'clock, I was wasted. Totally and completely out of it. I'd peeled off my dressing gown and fumbled into my pyjamas. My make-up was still on, inevitably smudged around the eyes and my lipstick had worn off.

A myriad of worried texts sat on my cell-phone. All from the girls. None from Liam. My friends wrote sympathetic stuff like: *Aww babe! I'm so sorry you're sick!* ☹ *Hope you feel better soon!* ☺ and *What a bummer to miss out on tonight! Hope to see you soon chick! xx*

They were being nice to my face but the cynic inside me imagined they were saying different things to each other. They might now be clinking their glasses and coming up with alternative theories. *Surprise, surprise, the night the mystery man is supposed to turn up, she pulls a sickie. Always knew he was a figment of her imagination.*

Suddenly the phone lit up like the Blackpool illuminations. The screen said: *Liam calling.* Holy fuck. My blood was boiling over as I clicked 'accept'.

"Where the hell are you?" I blazed. Any pretence of playing it cool was well out the window.

"Mia, babe, please don't swear. I have Emma in the car with me and you're on loudspeaker."

Indignation rose up. I pictured the little girl sitting next to him. What in God's name was he doing with her when he should be with me?

"Bloody hell Liam! We were supposed to meet up hours ago!" I thundered crazily.

"Yeah, look, I've only just had a chance to put

my phone on the charger in the car. I've been out and about all day and..."

"Liam!" I spat out at him. The next words seethed between gritted teeth. "You should have found a charger somewhere hours ago and phoned me. Do you have any idea how much money I've spent on this bloody night?"

"Told you, I'm sorry babe. I really am. Look, I can't talk at the moment. I'll leave Emma home and then I'll come round, okay?" He was trying everything to placate me with his usual charm.

"No." I shouted defiantly. "Don't you dare hang up on me Liam! If you hang up, it's over. I've waited ages for you to call. You're not going to fob me off now just because she's in the car."

I heard him sigh. "Babe, I shouldn't be talking on the phone when I'm driving. It was just a quick call to say I'm on my way. I'll explain what happened when I get there."

"No, you listen to me Liam. I am fucking sick of you. Sick of it, do you hear me? You are treating me like absolute shit!" My voice grew more and more hysterical. All the previous hours of pent-up emotion had come to a head. "You're treating me like an absolute cunt! Yes, that's right, you heard the word. Cunt! Did you hear that Emma? Did your precious little ears hear that? Your father is an absolute cunt!"

There's nothing worse than a woman scorned. When the red mist comes down, she's like a wounded animal. Capable of saying and doing anything. I look back on that conversation with shame. How could I have even thought of saying that to a six-year-old child? I'm disgusted with myself. My only excuse is that booze and anger don't mix.

Your father is an absolute cunt! That was when I heard the noise. First a screeching sound, then an almighty crash. Followed by a resolute thud and the background clatter of tinkling metal. I swear I heard the little girl shout out just before it happened. The innocent child screaming. Liam moaning. Then nothing. *Silence.*

That silence was the worst part of all.

"Liam? Liam?" I pleaded; my voice frantic with worry. "What the fuck was that noise?"

The phone went dead. I stared at the device in shock, my mouth hanging open. What the hell has just happened?

Liam crashed the car, that's what fucking happened. And it was all my fault. If I hadn't been shouting and screaming like a banshee, he wouldn't have been distracted. The car wouldn't have swerved, and they wouldn't have crashed.

But now the little girl is dead. *And I'm the one to blame.*

CHAPTER THIRTY
Mia (Now)

"M ISS SMITH?" A well-dressed woman arrives in the waiting room. She's carrying a buff file. The other patient looks up, grabs her bag and stands.

"I'm Doctor Sanders," the woman says. "Please come this way."

As the girl follows her out, my stomach begins to churn. It's really happening; I'll be called soon. I'll have to go through and start the ball rolling. There are butterflies in my stomach and I'm in two minds about everything.

On the one hand, I don't have the sort of money a single parent needs to raise a child. There'll be no help from Liam; he's under lock and key with another woman's baby on the way. The circumstances are hardly ideal.

On the other hand, a part of me wants to keep this baby. It's not just the usual guilt that I should be feeling. It's just that I don't see why Zoe should win. Why does she get to be mamma bear while I have to hide away in the closet? It's not fair that I have to play second fiddle; stay out of sight and pretend I don't exist. How many years do I have to blend discreetly into the background just to keep that bitch happy?

Liam had already banned me from phoning him on his normal cell-phone. He got me a pay-as-you-go device and dials me up when the coast is clear. If my name was to flash up on his normal screen, it would cause problems with *her*.

Liam portrays Zoe as some sort of psycho-bitch. A jealous woman still in love with him who won't let go. He says that aggravating her wouldn't be worth the hassle. He claims it's easier to have a quiet life. That's why he gave me a burner phone; a device solely for our own use. It keeps me anonymous; in the background just where he wants me.

He managed to compartmentalise his life with precision. Around Zoe, he played the doting dad and did odd jobs at home to help her out. Around me, he came out to play, unleashing his mischievous side. He's the party animal and I'm the sex toy.

Will I really go quietly in the night? Terminate his child and walk away? The loser in this triangle. And Zoe? She'll proudly show off her baby and her partner. The winner takes it all.

"Mia Matthews?" Clipboard lady snapped me out of my reverie.

"Oh, yes, that's me." Mildly flustered, I pick up my coat and bag.

"I'm Doctor Sanders," she reaches out her hand and shakes mine. "Please come this way."

I follow her down the corridor and into her office. There's a huge mahogany desk in the middle of the room. She sits at one side and motions for me to sit at the other.

"Mia, we know why you're here but there's a few questions I need to ask you first." The doctor picks up a pen and shuffles some papers on her desk. She rattles through the easy stuff about height, weight and age. Already my head is screaming: *I'm not sure I want to do this!*

She talks about two possible procedures. One is an internal process where a suction device is used to induce the abortion. The second is a medical termination, where a pill is inserted inside the vagina on a tampon. The tablet causes the lining to break down, bleeding to occur and the pregnancy to pass.

I close my eyes and grip my fingers together. When I open them again, Doctor Sanders is looking at me sympathetically.

"Are you sure you want to do this Mia?" she says, in a hushed tone.

I pause, then shake my head slowly. "No, I'm not absolutely sure."

She tilts her head to one side. "What are your reasons for wanting it in the first place?"

I suck in some air. How is it possible to explain this? "Well," I make a stuttering start. "The father of the child is in prison…"

The doctor's eyes flicker with understanding. "I see."

"… and then I found out there's another woman who is also pregnant to him." I stalled at this point realising how tacky and dreadful it sounds. Dr Sanders takes off her glasses and holds them in front of her. "That's a difficult situation," she sympathises.

I feel tears stinging the corner of my eyes. They squeeze out and run down my cheeks. How could I have fallen for a womaniser like Liam? How could I be so stupid?

But I do know why I fell for him. He was exciting and fun to be with; edgy, sexy and passionate. He lit me up like no-one else could. Before him I felt empty and bored but when he came along, he made me feel alive.

I pick up one of the leaflets sitting on the doctor's desk and open it. I expect to see a picture of a foetus inside a womb but it's much more discreet. There's a photo of a nurse smiling empathetically at a young woman, just the way Doctor Sanders is smiling at me now.

I shake my head slowly. "I'm not sure if I can do it," I stutter. "In fact, I know I can't."

Doctor Sanders nods. "That's okay, Mia."

"I'm sorry for wasting your time," the tears are now falling rapidly. I snatch my bag and get up to flee the office.

The doctor pushes back her chair and stands. "It's okay." She repeats, sounding authoritative but calming. "This happens all the time. It's normal."

I nod and wipe more tears away. I find I'm hurrying out of the office as fast as my legs can carry me. I rush down the hallway and straight past the receptionist. She looks up at me with concern as I whizz by. I push open the exit doors and gulp in the fresh air, but as soon as I jump out of the frying pan, I step into the fire.

A small crowd has gathered outside the clinic.

They're holding placards which say things like: *Abortion is murder* and *Everyone has the right to life.*

I try to ignore them as I walk on, but I notice one particular woman. She has a young daughter next to her. The little girl looks about six years old. She's also holding a mini placard. I guess she has no idea what this is all about but she's doing what she's told. The sign says: *Thank you for not killing me.*

I draw in a sharp intake of breath. Oh my God! The little girl smiles at me. All at once, everything flashes before my eyes. *The car accident. Liam saying something I didn't like. Me screaming down the phone. The sound of Emma's cries. The din of the impact. The sight of her white coffin.*

I hear a sob and realise it's me. Walking quickly on, I hear one of the women mutter under her breath. "Serves her right! No wonder she's crying. *Murderer!*"

I stop dead in my tracks. *Murderer? That's me alright.*

Emma's death is down to me.

CHAPTER THIRTY-ONE

Mia

I CUP MY belly and look at my reflection. I'm definitely showing. The little bean is growing well. Even my boobs look bigger; full and plump. I gently massage oil over the bump. I'm not going to get stretch marks, at least not if I can help it. I'm starving though; hungry all the time. I'm trying to be careful, resisting the urge to succumb to every craving. Better to eat healthy and be mindful. Women who go on about "eating for two" are just kidding themselves.

Zoe tells herself she's eating for two. I know she does because I've been snooping on her socials. She's on the lot: *Facebook, Twitter, Instagram, Pinterest.* She doesn't even change her settings to private.

She never stops posting and especially loves Pinterest. Always pinning cute pictures; babies wearing frilly pink dresses, new-borns smiling and infants with tiny tipsy toes. And of course, the nursery photos showing the dinky décor. Fluffy clouds on the wallpaper and woolly white sheep dangling from the ceiling. Pink candy-coloured walls and the cuddly teddy bear posing in the cot is an extra saccharine touch. A white lace canopy flows down both sides of the crib.

Pink walls and frilly dresses? Everything pink! She must have had her scan too and knows the gender. My heart stops in my chest. I can't breathe. So, Liam's having two baby girls.

A panicky feeling spreads through my body. My fingertips go cold and my heart hammers in my chest. I stand up and start pacing around the apartment. Hurrying into the kitchen, I flick on the kettle and then march into the bathroom, fidgeting with my hair. Needing to talk to somebody, I race into the bedroom and pick up the phone from its charger. It's impossible to bottle this up any longer, but who can I confide in?

I'm shaking with nervous energy as the revelation dawns on me; Liam's going to have two little girls. My little one's going to have a half-sister the same age. It's wrong. Wrong, wrong, wrong!

I can't allow it to happen.

How long am I going to play second fiddle to Miss Perfect? Why do I only exist in her shadow? The girl who has to keep her lips buttoned all the time. Forever lurking in the background. Never the leading lady, always the supporting role.

That bitch gets to go public about the baby she's expecting. She can tell the world about her relationship with Liam. Meanwhile I cower on the side-lines and he acts as if I'm not around. As far as his friends and family are concerned, my little one doesn't exist.

How far removed it is from the time he moved out of Zoe's house. They'd had a blazing row about him drinking too much. Liam moved straight in with Gaz. The first night he stayed there, they threw a party and Liam invited me. We had a ball that evening; drink, music, chatting and laughing. Gaz produced the gear and skinned up. We smoked and passed the joints around. I sat next to Liam, my hand resting on his leg. He put his arm around me and it was so relaxing. More than that, I was overtaken by a warm inner glow; he had finally walked out on her.

She was history. Now Liam and I could be an item; mix with friends and tell the world how much we loved each other. He didn't have to hide his actions from her anymore. Zoe could like it or lump it.

I was wrong. My little fantasy didn't last long. The bubble burst less than a week later, when we were lying in bed together on a Sunday morning. We lazily debated whether to go out for brunch or order food in when Liam's cell-phone buzzed.

"Shit," he muttered, as he picked it up. Looking at the screen, he rolled his eyes, "It's Zoe."

"Don't answer it," I pleaded immediately.

But he had already hit the accept button and I heard the words, "Hey Zoe."

I didn't like the way he said it or the softness in his tone, the compassion. It sounded like love.

I frowned and tutted. Then Liam did something I'll never forget. He looked at me, raised a finger to his lips and gave me the "hush" signal.

My eyes widened. Why were we still playing this game? He expected me to slither quietly into a hole while he had a cosy chat with the main woman? Why did I have to cow-tow to a bitch like her? I was being filed back into the miscella-neous folder; *The invisible woman.*

"Yeah, no, that's fine, I can do that." I heard him say. "Yeah, yeah, about twelve? Yeah, no worries."

My heart sank. Our lazy Sunday plans were ruined. The brunch idea was out the window.

"What's happening?" I asked, when he hung up, trying to hide the disappointment in my voice.

"It's Emma. She wants to go swimming today and Zoe wants me to take her."

I nodded, "Oh right. So, no brunch then?" I was still trying to play it cool. It was all about the mind games.

He looked at me, a casual grin on his face. "Sorry babe, not today." He snuggled back under the covers next to me and whispered in my ear. "Still a bit of time to play though." His breath was hot and his hands were tingling over my skin.

"Oh, is that a fact?" I teased, my legs parting with pleasure. *Keep playing it cool*, I said to myself, *I'm the dream girlfriend after all. Someone who goes with the flow.*

"Yeah, that's a fact. I love to face up to facts..." he joked but his voice was sultry and sexy. He kissed me, his hands travelling up my body. *Face up to facts, oh, the irony.*

✧   ✧   ✧

THE KETTLE FLICKS. The water bubbles furiously and steam billows up in a cloud.

That was then, this is now. I'm not exactly

sure when the game playing stopped. I got tired of playing it cool. I was no longer a dream girl; I had morphed into a nag.

"Why don't we get a place together?" I had suggested one night. He'd been complaining about Gaz; how he stank out the bathroom and never washed himself properly. He never bought any food but always helped himself to Liam's.

Liam was reluctant. "I don't know babe. I don't think you'd want me under your feet."

I wish he'd been honest. Why didn't he just say: *I don't think I'd want to be under your feet.* He should have worded it correctly.

"You'd love it," I protested. "I'd move out of Amy's. We could get a place together. It'd be great."

Liam shook his head slowly. "I don't know babe. Working and living together? We might pull each other's hair out." He gave me that charming grin; the one that showed he still loved me.

I downturned my lips, putting on a sad puppy dog expression. I was trying to be jokey about his response rather than give the game away by showing complete dejection.

"Hey," he fanned his arms out in a conciliatory gesture: "You know the saying. If it ain't broke, don't fix it. We're happy this way, aren't we? Why change it?" He gently teased a strand of hair off my face.

"Yeah, of course we are," I downplayed it.

"Well then," he surmised. "Let's just keep it the way it is. We don't want to spoil a good thing."

A good thing.

Now I look back on this with hindsight; as usual he just wanted to have his cake and eat it.

He could turn up at Zoe's and act the doting dad, but still have time to see me. Bunk down with Gaz and have the space to do his own thing. The best of both worlds. Liam liked to compartmentalise his life; go back to her place and play super-dad, then meet me for sex, drugs and rock n' roll. What's that saying about the perfect woman? A cook in the kitchen and a whore between the sheets. Liam has both. Guess which one I am?

I POUR HOT water into a cup. My good time days are over. I have a protruding belly, expanding boobs and a baby cooking inside. What happens when the sex kitten becomes the housewife? What's that other saying? Two's company but three's a crowd.

There isn't room for Zoe anymore. She's had her day. I've played second fiddle long enough. The constant shadow in the corner. Now it's my turn – she'll have to go. But how?

I sit at my computer and look through her Facebook; her smug selfies and those bragging comments: *Baby glow or just make up?* My insides seethe. Baby news! Why does she get to go public whilst I have to keep schtum?

Well, not anymore, I need a plan of action. I don't know how or when, but I have to get rid of her. It's high time that she is out of the equation. Like all good drama students: *Exit stage left.*

An unfortunate fall off a railway platform? Stepping out in front of a car too quickly? Or what about a touch of fatal food poisoning? A friendly lunch date, something dropped into her dish when she's not looking, an unexpected heart attack? *Accidents do happen.*

Zoe's Pinterest might be crammed with beautiful baby pics and stylish nursery images.

But my search engine is full of imaginative ways to kill.

CHAPTER THIRTY-TWO

Zoe

EADING STRAIGHT FOR the fridge, I pull open the door and light floods all over the kitchen. A continuously peckish feeling lies in the pit of my stomach. As if I need to remind myself, I'm eating for two. Rummaging through the food on the shelves, I'm looking for something – but what? I can't make up my mind. Taking a block of cheese from the top shelf and a tub of spread, I bustle about the countertop, popping bread in the toaster and filling the kettle.

It's when I pass the window that I get that strange vibe again; the feeling that someone is watching me. I lean over the sink and peer into the back yard. Reaching for the cord, I start to close the venetian blinds. As I do so, a black shadowy figure appears silhouetted against the rear garden wall. Oh God, there's somebody there! Whoever it is, they move deftly, slipping past a tree and somehow vanishing.

I hastily twist the blinds shut and dash over to check the lock on the back door. My heart hammers in my chest. I was right – there is someone watching me! Who on earth could it be?

Paranoia and anxiety swamp my brain. What if Liam has arranged for someone to attack me? Is he planning some sort of revenge? He's angry about the court case and the jail sentence, and somehow his tortured mind has put it all down to me. Would he think of having me dealt with?

The minute the thought comes into my head, I dismiss the idea. Liam's not angry at me anymore. He told me as much. The stupid bastard feels guilty and responsible for Emma's death, but he's not a murderer. I do believe him when he says he's going to use prison time to get clean. I know he's looking forward to the birth of our new baby, for goodness sake! How could I even think such a thing?

I'll never forgive him for Emma and I can't trust him ever again, but at the same time, he's the father of my unborn child. He has rights and he'll be allowed to have contact, so I can't kick him out of my life completely. *And I don't want to do that anyway.*

Somehow, I've got round to accepting that it was all a terrible accident; manslaughter, not murder. Even if it's not a friend of Liam's stalking me, someone is definitely out there.

Just at that moment, the landline buzzes to life. The noise makes me jump. I rush into the living room and grab the handset: "Hello?" I ask anxiously.

There's nothing. No answer.

"Hello? Who is this?" I repeat, my voice laced with increasing fear.

Still nothing.

There must be someone on the other end; it hasn't clicked off yet. I can hear breathing, but other than that, no words; just deathly agonising silence.

I slam the phone down in terror, my heart racing and thumping. Before I know it, my fingers have tapped out 999 and I'm phoning the police.

"Emergency, which service?"

"Police. Quickly please."

I can hardly believe I'm doing this. Have I really just asked for the cops? There's a bleep on the end of the line while they're connecting me. Then another voice: "Please state your location and describe your emergency."

"There's someone outside my flat, I'm being watched! I've just had a creepy phone-call; it was a heavy breather!"

I can feel my cheeks burn with shame, aware of how pathetic I sound. They're taking urgent calls about stabbings and burglaries. Yet here I am, wasting their time because someone phoned me and didn't speak? How dangerous can that be?

"Okay, we'll send someone around right away ma'am. I know it's difficult but try to keep calm. Now, if you can just let us have your name and address..."

"Look, I'm sorry for wasting your time," I stammer and hang up, my face blushing. I'm overcome with embarrassment.

The next twenty minutes are spent pacing the room and watching the telephone, anxious in case the heavy breather phones back. Needing to confide in somebody, I pick up the receiver and dial my mother. She listens to the dramatic tale.

"I'll come over right away," she says, hanging

up quickly before I can persuade her not to.

In no time, she's sitting next to me on the sofa as I continue to spew it out. I mention the stalker and the heavy breathing session.

"That's awful pet, you poor thing," she soothes, patting my hand in sympathy. But after a while, she asks, "Zoe, how sure are you there was actually someone out there?"

"For god's sake mum! Are you saying I've imagined all this?"

"Zoe dear," she repeats, her voice calm but firm. "Didn't that counsellor say something about PTSD?"

"Do you mean the *Post-Traumatic Stress Disorder* thing?" I say hesitantly, as the realisation dawns on me. Come to think of it, the therapist had said something on that subject; about how Emma's death could trigger some sort of reaction. He told me how a bereavement can affect people in different ways; that it's common to experience paranoia and anxiety after a traumatic event.

"I guess so." I mumble reluctantly. "But I'm convinced I'm being watched. I saw someone outside. I really did, mum!"

She rests her hand on mine: "You've been through so much dear." That patronising tone again.

"Yeah, I have," I sigh with resignation. I'm beginning to realise that there's no point trying to convince her.

"What has Liam said about the baby?" she changes the subject quickly.

"He's looking forward to it." I throw back

defensively. "Says he'll do what he can to help."

"That's all well and good but you can't rely on him. He won't be out for at least five years." She sounds exasperated. In her own sneaky way, she steers the conversation to yet another topic: "You might meet somebody else. Someone new."

I roll my eyes and look down at my ever-expanding bump in elasticated pyjamas. "Yeah right," I argue. "Who's going to want me, looking like this?"

"Don't be so hard on yourself Zoe. You're pregnant; you're allowed to put on baby weight." She reasons. "I'm talking about down the line. You might find Mister Right in a couple of years' time. Liam won't always be in the picture and you need a man who is steady and reliable."

"A couple of years!" I screech. "That's ages away!"

"Yes, dear but it'll be sooner than the day Liam gets out of prison, won't it?"

I should have known she'd state the obvious.

"You're right," I admit hesitantly.

If truth be told, I can't imagine being with anyone else but Liam. My first love. The guy who's etched on my brain. I planned we'd grow old together. I always had a crazy, romantic belief that no matter what life threw at us, we'd always be side by side; work things out like a perfect couple does.

Silly, but the idea is still there, deep down inside.

✧　✧　✧

"YOU MIGHT CHANGE your opinion…" the psychoanalyst says, as if reading my mind. "…about Liam, I mean." He's sitting in a suave leather chair, legs crossed. He throws a plaintive gaze over the top of his half-moon spectacles.

I shake my head decisively. "I doubt it."

"You're probably harbouring repressed anger towards him," he continues. "You need to feel that anger, expunge it and then let go."

"I don't see the point in being angry any-more." I'm fidgeting as I speak. "Surely it would be better to forgive him and move on?"

"Why would you want to forgive him?" the therapist asks. "Why should you?"

I ponder these words in the quiet stillness of his office. Sunlight filters through the blinds. A green leafy plant sprawls from a pot in the corner. I'm trying to get a jumble of thoughts into some semblance of order.

"What good would it do to keep being angry? Especially when I have another baby on the way? Won't it just make me miserable?"

The counsellor sits with his fingertips leaning on each other, making a tent of his hands. He props his chin on his hands, considering my statement in depth.

"When did somebody say you're not allowed to be angry?" he poses the question suddenly and then adds, "Were you ashamed of feeling angry?"

My brain's working overtime, raking through childhood memories. "I see what you're getting at." A light comes on somewhere in my mind. "My dad… he wouldn't have allowed anger. You would have been ordered to sit down and shut up. Told to be seen and not heard."

The therapist nods triumphantly. "And why do you think that was?" He tilts his head to one side.

I shrug. "Dunno. A superstitious thing, I guess. His old-fashioned upbringing: Don't let the sun go down while you're angry. Something like that, I think."

He smiles: "So, you've been stuffing it down perhaps? Hiding it away somewhere? With the help of alcohol? Or tablets? Or maybe even food?"

I look up in realisation. "I'm not eating much but I've probably had a few drinks too many."

"Maybe we should consider ways of releasing that anger physically, but at the same time, adopting healthier methods?"

I gaze at him quizzically. "Like how?"

He gesticulates with open palms. "Bash a cushion. Go into a field in the middle of nowhere and scream your head off? Run on the spot until you drop!"

"I think I get it." I reply, starting to under-stand. "Let the anger come up and out."

✧ ✧ ✧

IT'S THE DAY after and I'm standing in the kitchen. I have a sudden urge to grab a cup and smash it onto the floor. Opening the cupboard door, I retrieve a mug and hold it up. Before I know it, I've flung it across the kitchen tiles. I'm shocked by the impact; the sound of the ceramic smashing onto the floor tiles and disintegrating into smithereens. Millions of little pieces exploding around my feet.

The counsellor was right; it's deeply satisfying, but short lived. That split second of release vanishes all too quickly. Craving more, I pick up a saucer and fling it down recklessly. Then another. And another.

Now I'm standing in the middle of my own kitchen, surrounded by a billion shards of crockery, wondering what's going on in my head. I feel exhilarated, exhausted and spent, all in one go. I now survey the havoc I've wreaked. I'm buzzing but I'm the sucker who has to clean it up.

With dustpan and brush in hand, I crouch down and start sweeping up the debris. It's impossible to get everything out of the crevices. Weeks later, I'm sure I will still find tiny fragments stuck in nooks and crannies.

"Why don't you try thumping cushions instead," the therapist advises at the next session with a smile. "That's a softer and safer way to get rid of anger."

Smashing up cups and plates is one thing; little did I know, a new target would turn up just around the corner.

✧   ✧   ✧

SHORTLY AFTER THE cup incident, I bump into Mia. She's standing in the baby section and when I see her cradling her baby bump, I want to smack her. All that anger has risen to the surface. I want to reach across and wipe the smug smile off her face.

"Zoe!" Her saccharine grin widens. "We meet again!"

"Oh hi," I'm still distracted by thoughts of slapping her.

"It's Mia," she prompts, as though I didn't know. "Liam's friend."

"Yeah, I remember." I try to feign disinterest.

We're standing there, in the middle of the kids' department. I'm clutching a pink baby grow. She looks at it: "Congratulations," she beams insincerely. "Expecting a baby girl, are we?"

I'm flummoxed. Isn't it a bit forward to come out with a question like that? "Well," I replied. "Actually, I am."

Her face lights up enthusiastically. "Me too."

I'm surprised but I cobble up a pleasant response. "You are? When are you due?"

"April. I'm so excited," she grins. "And nervous. Shitting myself in fact."

She's being so friendly; so forward, almost in my face.

"Oh, me too," I agree reluctantly. "Even though I've done this before, I'm still nervous."

"Maybe that's why. Because you know what to expect." She lets out a slightly anxious laugh.

I chuckle. "Ha! Well, maybe!"

She looks at her watch. "Hey, I really fancy getting a coffee and taking the weight off my feet. Don't suppose you wanna join me, do you? I'd love to bend your ear about the baby stuff. My friends are so bored with me. They can't get into it at all."

I shift on my feet. Going for coffee with Liam's work mate? Seems strange, but then again, she's being so friendly and she's a mother-to-be, like me.

"Why not?" I manage to force a smile. It seems she's twisted my arm and swept me along with her pushy offer.

"Great!" a huge grin creeps over her perfectly made-up face. "What about Antonio's? They do these amazing chocolate desserts?"

The thought of chocolate cake dripping with ice-cream and sauce sways me.

"Good idea," I agree.

She links arms with me as we walk off. It seems strange, such an intimate gesture. I can't remember the last time a woman linked arms with me as we walk. I feel a little perplexed and slightly overwhelmed by her attention. We're cruising along the pavement, arm in arm; like two best friends on a perfect day out.

As we stroll, Mia turns to me and says: "Remember, you're eating for two. *And the chocolate desserts are to die for.*"

CHAPTER THIRTY-THREE
Mia

OUR ARMS ARE entwined as we drop into step together. I'm acting like her new best friend. We look like two chummy chicks, soon to be yummy mummies. She's buying into the fact we have so much in common with tons to discuss but all the while, my brain is working overtime.

"Hey, have you bought all the baby clothes you need now?" I chirp, already knowing the answer before she mouths it.

"Pretty much," she smiles smugly. She's waddling along in that attention-getting way. Her left hand holding her belly. She might as well carry a placard saying, *Look at me, everyone, I'm pregnant. Can't you see my bump? I'm going to be a mummy.*

Meanwhile, I keep my bump covered. I'm wearing a swing coat which falls gracefully over my curve. I've applied make-up and styled my hair. Just because I'm expecting, doesn't mean I let myself go; not like Zoe.

She's pulled on an old pair of leggings and a baggy jumper. She doesn't bother with make-up and has barely ran a brush through her hair. I spot our reflection in a shop window and notice that we couldn't look more different.

"I'm sure my mother will buy more stuff after the birth, but I've bought plenty just in case." she rattles on in that smarmy, self-satisfied tone.

"What about Emma's clothes?" I blurt out deliberately. I can't help it. Then I stop dramatically. I make a faux apologetic expression. "Oh, I'm so sorry, I shouldn't have mentioned her name."

Zoe casts her eyes downwards, trying not to cry. "It's okay," she whispers. "I actually like people mentioning Emma's name. It keeps her alive in our minds, you know?" She dishes up a sweet smile to show she's not annoyed. Damn it! I was hoping to unnerve her.

"I bought new clothes for this little one," she prattles on monotonously. "It doesn't seem right for her to wear hand-me-downs." She looks at her belly and rubs it affectionately.

"Yes, quite." I'm distracted because we've reached our destination. I usher her inside *Antonio's*. "Hey, why don't you grab a seat and I'll get the coffees."

At this suggestion, she seems to be caught off guard: "Oh, are you sure? Here, take some money." She reaches for her purse but I wave the idea away as though swatting a fly.

"No, no, it's on me, I invited you." I have my own reasons for getting the order myself. It's part of the plan.

"Oh, well, if you're sure..." she smiles as she waddles towards a window seat.

I can see why Liam stuck with her for so long. She's the epitome of niceness. A complete walkover. It makes me want to vomit. I bet he takes advantage of her all the time. When she gives an inch, he probably takes a mile.

I join the queue and set a tray on the rollers. I check out the vast selection of cakes and cookies. Maybe a traybake would go nicely with her poisoned coffee? Will I actually have the nerve to put my plan into action; to spike her coffee when no-one is looking?

I have the stuff in my pocket; a phial filled with diamorphine. It's small, but I'm assured by Big Al that this amount would blow anybody away. Apparently, it's clear and tasteless as well. All I have to do is tip enough of it into her Americano.

But it's working up the nerve, that's the thing. The queue is long, people are standing on either side of me. Someone could easily notice what I'm doing. I'll wait until we're at the table. Perhaps if she goes off to the Ladies, I could do the drop then.

"That'll be twelve pounds fifty," the girl behind the till chirps politely. I tap my card on the little machine and carry the tray carefully towards Zoe. She looks up and smiles as I approach.

"Oh, thanks so much," she grins. "That looks delicious."

She's right, it does look amazing; a chunk of chocolate cake slathered in fresh cream and a piping cup of coffee. The latter free of the additive still hiding in my bag.

"Doesn't it just," I agree cheerfully. "Get stuck in!"

We eat in companiable silence for a while, before I ask, "So, you and Liam?" I put on a teasing, over-familiar expression and ask, "Can you remember the night of conception?" I smile to show her I'm a girly-girl; a friendly confidante.

She gives a half laugh. "I can actually!" She sips her coffee to gain a little thinking time. Then she volunteers: "It was one Saturday. We were on and off like a light switch at the time. More off, to be honest. But occasionally, he would turn up and we lapsed back into old times, just like that." She clicked her fingers, as though this crap was romantic. I could tell he'd obviously been using her.

"Go on, do spill the beans," I egg her on with a giggle, taking another bite of chocolate cake and acting like the biggest best friend on the planet.

She holds her fork mid-air and has a faraway look on her face. She's taking herself back to that night. "Well, he had hung out with us one Saturday. I wanted to take Emma swimming and I really hoped Liam would join us. I'm not a big fan of the water but he is. He's great at larking about in the pool. He can splash around with her for ages. They're like two big kids. I was happy to sit in the café, have a coffee and a bit of thinking time."

A dagger of jealous pain has just been plunged into my heart. I can easily picture the scene of domestic bliss; Liam and his lovely little daughter cavorting and laughing; the perfect mum sitting there with that oh-so-fucking smug smile watching them. When that was going on, I was probably at home, getting dolled up to see the bastard, for one of the many nights on the town that didn't happen.

She continues to whitter on. "Liam had moved out at that time. He was living with his mate Gaz for a while, having a bit of space, but he came home with us that day just to please Emma. She kept going on about having a Chinese takeaway and watching *X-factor*." Zoe shrugs happily. "And he agreed." She spews it out effortlessly, this cosy reconciliation. *Mr & Mrs Perfect!*

On she drones, "He was going through one of those trying-to-stay-sober phases; attending meetings, keeping his nose clean, doing the right thing. So, I think he was glad to have an excuse to stay away from the sort of friends he met in the pub. The party types."

I hold my breath to keep calm. I nod, indicating that I want her to continue with this shit, but my fingertips are going cold with jealousy and my heart pounds like a drum. All those times I had dolled myself up to the nines! Getting ready to paint the town red with Liam. In actual fact, he was lying on Zoe's couch watching crap on TV and playing happy families.

"We ordered in a Chinese, watched TV and just relaxed. You know? It was so nice."

"And then?" I prompt impatiently, urging her to get on with this pointless diatribe. I wish I could swipe that sugary smile off her face.

"I told him he could stay the night if he wanted. There was no point in going back to his apartment. It'd be full of party goers taking drugs."

The chocolate cake was now sticking in my windpipe; *full of party-goers and me*. There I was, probably tarted up in a short skirt and high heels; a bombshell looking like a million dollars. Meanwhile he must have been cosying up with her, in her baggy jammies and woolly socks, having just scoffed a chicken Chow Mein and fried rice.

"So that's how it came about," she pasted on that self-satisfied smirk. "He stayed the night and we cuddled up. It just happened. I guess we know the right buttons to press. Like it was meant to be." She looks like the cat who got all the cream.

"Excuse me," I interrupt, abruptly. "My bladder is suddenly about to burst; you know how it is."

"Oh, of course, I do. Run for it," she says, sweetly.

I make a bee-line for the bathroom. I'm dying to get away from her. I can't listen to this schmuck anymore; a smarmy, delusional, over-romanticised load of crap. He had simply used her for a shag, that's the bottom line; gotten his leg over while I was waiting for him like a spare part.

In the loo, I try to pull myself together. I need to psych myself up for the task ahead. This is all part of the plan, I remind myself; to get friendly with her and pick my moment. Although I'm having second thoughts; there's a lot of people around. I realise I'm starting to bottle it, after all it's not an easy thing to do. I wonder how quickly the stuff will take effect? How far can I leg it before the paramedics turn up?

Perhaps I should suggest a day out together instead? Maybe a train journey? A trip where she could accidentally fall off a platform. Or a quiet restaurant with a better chance of dropping the stuff into her coffee?

I return from the Ladies, all smiles again.

"Wow, that's better," I grin. "I honestly thought I was going to pee myself."

"Oh, I know too well," she laughs heartily.

"So, you were saying," I resume eye contact, trying to pick up the threads where we left off: "Didn't he use protection or anything?"

"Well, I was on the pill at the time."

I raise my eyebrows. *Why she's on the pill if they aren't together?*

She quickly comes up with an explanation: "I was on the pill to regulate my hormones. It's more a PMT thing."

So, she was being a grumpy cow every month and he still kept going back to her.

"I dunno. We all know the pill's not one hundred per cent full-proof," she shrugs. "I mean, I did have a touch of food poisoning around that time so maybe it cancelled itself out." She gazes into the distance like she's only considered this possibility for the first time.

I fake an exaggerated smile. "Still, it all worked out okay in the end, didn't it?" I lied. "I mean, now you have this little one on the way?"

She smiles back warmly, "Yes," she affirms, "Yes, I do." She gives her bump that annoying cradling motion, as if it won't stay put without her help. She waves her hand in the air and adds: "Anyway, enough about me, do tell me about your man? How long have you been together?"

I try to avoid an acrid sneer. "Well, it's complicated," I stutter.

She nods and smiles. Her ears prick up as though she has all the time in the world to listen. I look at my watch. "Oh dear, I didn't realise the time. I've got to head on." Her face flickers into a hint of disappointment.

"But I tell you what," I take the chance to throw it in. "Why don't we make a whole day of it next time? Let's take a trip to Bangor on the train? I know some great shops there – fab for baby clothes and nursery gear. Reasonable prices too!"

Her face lights up. "Ooh! I'd love that! And the lunch will definitely be on me next time!"

I look at her, my face softening. If it wasn't for Liam, I would probably like her, in a parallel universe.

And yet here I am, planning how to get rid of her.

CHAPTER THIRTY-FOUR

Mia

I KEEP SNOOPING on Zoe's socials, I can't help it. Spying online is like unravelling one thread of a jumper. Before you know it, the whole garment falls apart. One click, and I'm hooked; like an alcoholic whose first drink always ends up in a blackout.

Facebook first; all the gloating status updates about her pregnancy. Reports on her food cravings come in as regular as clockwork. Today she's salivating for peanut butter and pears on stilton. Comments flood in: *Go for it, babe, at least you're getting the fruit in!*

Clicking on her Instagram next; she's posted her baby bump with her hand protectively draped over it. *Lovely photo babe*, a friend smarms. *Can't wait to meet the little one.* There are pictures of the nursery – cream wallpaper with soft blue clouds and the pink crib with stars dangling from above. By now, she's arranged a whole army of teddies propped up pretentiously inside it. *So adorable!* A friend gushes.

I scroll further. This time, way back into her past. Pictures of her university days. The bitch is standing next to Liam, beaming with happiness. They're posing together in a huge group, all grinning at the camera; looking young, trendy and full of themselves.

The green-eyed monster grips me again; it swallows me up with jealousy and resentment. A snide voice on my shoulder is saying: *Look at all their history. He'll never leave her. They're childhood sweethearts. He's going back to her after prison. You'll only ever be the bit on the side.*

She's the one he's going to marry; it's the stability she gives him. Zoe's the girl who'll walk up the aisle, and stand outside the church arm-in-arm with her catch for the group photos, grinning like a Cheshire cat. The star of the wedding album. I can see their hands clasped on a knife, slicing into the cake.

Meanwhile, he'll be sending money to me in secret. I'll be the one he visits on the sly; the girl he manages to keep hidden in a parallel world.

Why does he think he can do this? Because I've gone along with it since day one – that's why. I pretended to be a dream girl. I played mind games, thinking I was being cool, when all the while, I was just being a walkover.

Take those first few weeks together. We were never together in any real sense – it was never official. We didn't make it known to the other bar staff. Some of them suspected we were an item, but we never confirmed it.

Liam kept saying, "Let's not tell the others about this. They'll accuse me of favouritism. If I tell one of them to do something, they'll wonder why I haven't asked you. They'll say it's because we're a thing."

I looked at him, a teasing smile on my lips. I took a long drag of my cigarette and said, "Are you saying we're a thing?"

He reached over to kiss me. Then he whispered: "You can play with my thing anytime!"

Typical, he was always using sex to body-swerve real issues.

I gave a soft chuckle. I pretended to be chilled on the subject when really, I wanted to ask: *Are we a thing? Would it really be so bad if people thought you were favouring me over them?*

But none of that stuff was in the rulebook. Rule one says you play it cool. It was like a game of tennis – hitting the ball the back and forth. If I strike too many balls into his court, they merely roll up against the fence on his side. He had to have time to return a shot; let him come back to me. I wanted to know if he would do the running sometimes; that it wasn't always me chasing him.

I would stare at my mobile for ages, willing it to ring. It didn't ring and he didn't text, but neither did I. Rule two is: don't make the first move.

Eventually, he did get in touch. His texts came late at night. The cell-phone would light up and his name would appear on the screen. I'd open the text to read a few simple words: *Hey, you up? x*

I'd wait at least ten minutes before replying; couldn't give him the idea I was eyeballing the phone like watching paint dry.

"*Yeah, I'm up x*" I mirrored his short, three worded text. It doesn't do to write a long reply.

"Could do with a cuddle x" He made it sound like he was looking for comfort, that he needed someone to hug, not that he was just after a shag.

"Yeah, sure x"

And that would be that. I'd buzz around like a fly; shaving my legs, preening myself and quickly applying make-up. When he rang the door-bell, I deliberately took forever to stroll to the door and open it with a flourish. I oozed out an ever so confident "Hi".

I didn't ask questions; didn't mention Zoe or Emma at all. I refrained from saying things like: 'where is this going,' and 'what are we doing?' I was too smart for that. After all, I was the dream girl.

Well, where did being the dream girl get me? It got me to being second best. The bit-part player. Second fiddle to Zoe. She was the leading lady while I sat in the wings, awaiting my turn. When it suited him, I got called out to play, but only in secret.

ZOE IS GOING *shopping*. The latest Facebook status update shows her posing in Castle Court shopping centre for more baby clothes. I perk up; this is my moment. Perhaps I could 'accidentally on purpose' bump into her and suggest a quick drink. Maybe I could drop a shot of diamorphine or two into the glass; hopefully do some damage. It's time I toppled Zoe from the number one spot for once and for all!

I bump into her outside "Peek-a-Boo".

"Hey Zoe!" I beam, my face lighting up with all the thespian skills I can muster.

"Mia! Hi!" she smiles back. "Fancy meeting you here!"

I throw a glance towards the store. "Well, great minds think alike; I was gonna do a spot of baby shopping too."

Zoe holds up her bag: "Got a few little goodies," she chirps.

"Ooh, let's see!" I coo.

She pulls out a pink Babygro which has the cutest little fur trim around the ankles and wristbands.

"Aww, adorable," I say.

"Isn't it! It only cost me five quid in the sale."

"Fancy a quick drink?" I ask. "Take the weight off your feet?"

She considers this for a moment. "Oh, I don't know," she says. "Won't we have everyone staring at us? Two pregnant ladies drinking alcohol."

I wave my hand in the air dismissively. "It's only one. They can't begrudge us that."

She doesn't need persuading. "Oh, alright then, just the one."

We waddle towards Billy's Cave; a bar where probably no-one would care if we were snorting lines of coke off the tables. We settle into comfy chairs next to a fireside with two half pints of lager.

"So, how's things?" I begin. "Any word from Liam?"

She seems shocked by my question but regains composure quickly. "Yes, just last night actually. He phoned me. He's so excited about the baby."

"Is he?" I say, wryly.

"Yeah! He gets so excited when I tell him about the baby stuff and things for the nursery."

"Right," I remain deadpan. "Isn't it going to be hard, seeing he's in prison an' all?"

She's seems a little put out by the mention of prison but takes a sip of her beer before replying: "No, not really. I mean, I still have his emotional support. And I know that when he eventually gets out, he'll be the best dad in the world."

I'm having trouble swallowing my beer after that one. How naïve can she be? I can't help stirring the pot: "But has it always been plain sailing between you two? Didn't you say you two were on and off like a yoyo?" I just love winding her up and I don't give a damn if she doesn't like it.

In actual fact, what I'm dying to do is tell her what's really going on.

She sighs. "Yeah, we've had our moments but he's my childhood sweetheart. We fell in love quite young and I think we were meant to be together. Sometimes he's resisted being in a relationship. He likes to feel independent; you know? But he keeps coming back. Like a boomerang." She gives a little chuckle and takes another sip from her glass.

"He chased after me something chronic, you know," she prattles on. "When we were in Uni, he kept hounding me for dates. I wasn't sure about him. I didn't really fancy him at first, to be honest. But he persisted, asking me out all the time, making sure his crowd of friends were always in the same nightclub as my lot." She lets out a little laugh at the memory.

I give her a restrained smile and turn my eyes to the flames dancing in the grate.

"Anyway," she says, "enough about me, tell me about your man. I haven't heard anything about him yet."

I look at my empty glass. "We'll need another round for that," I caution sarcastically. "Shall we head on to another bar? If we bar hop, no-one will know that we're on our second drink."

She returns a conspiratorial smile: "Yeah, go on then."

In the next bar, I'll do it, I tell myself. I'll drop the drug into her drink. She'll get woozy and sleepy. I'll pop another one in for good measure, then I'll call an ambulance. I'll tell the paramedics I don't know what's happened. I'll say that I bumped into her and she asked me to join her for just one drink. You could tell there was something wrong with her, I'll say. She'd been drinking more than she let on. I'm pretty sure she's on tablets as well. You ought to know that this poor woman Zoe's just lost a child and the partner's in jail for it. I'll make sure to tell them she's got depression or something.

For added effect, I can even plant the empty phial into her handbag while we're waiting for the ambulance. Just as long as I use gloves or a hankie. I'm smart enough not to leave fingerprints.

Later on, they'll discover that the drugs were too much for her heart. And by that time, she'll have already passed away. Everyone will talk about a tragic overdose. A beautiful woman lost to suicide. Such a waste of a young life. She had so much ahead of her, but they'll think: is it any wonder in these circumstances, given all that's happened to her?

After that, she'll be gone; out of the equation, out of Liam's life and out of mine too.

It will just be me, Liam and the baby. Our baby. Our own little family. The way things are meant to be.

CHAPTER THIRTY-FIVE

Simon

A T THE RESTAURANT, we are led to a booth at the back. Candles flicker in wax encrusted bottles. A pianist tinkles in the background, the music creating a relaxing ambience.

"Shall we have a bottle of that Bordeaux?" I ask Laura, when the waitress arrives.

She nods her head in assent. I set aside the wine list and we turn our attention to the main menu.

It seems an age since we've been out like this. She's usually sitting in her pyjamas on a Saturday night, curled up in front of the TV, glued to reality shows and munching crisps. Tonight, she's wearing a red dress and her hair is piled up on top of her head. She looks the part alright; a world away from her normal pyjama attire.

There's an awkwardness between us as we attempt to discuss the menu. Our chit-chat would normally involve day to day stuff – the next PTA meeting, money for a school trip, and Caitlin's grades in a recent exam. The therapist warned us against talking about the kids. Instead, she emphasized the need to engage with each other. That's the official line but it's harder that I thought. It's a struggle just getting the conversation off the ground.

Just at that moment, the waitress returns to take our food order. What a relief! The girl is all high ponytail and good cheer.

I smile back at her and give my order. She's jokey and friendly and I'm enjoying the light chat with her. Yet I can't help but notice Laura shooting daggers at me. Surely, she doesn't have it in her crazy head that I'm flirting with the staff?

As the waitress trots off, I lift my glass towards Laura. "Cheers," I say, trying to improve the atmosphere.

"Cheers," she repeats, reluctantly.

We take a sip and the volume goes back to mute. I can't talk about the kids and I dare not mention work. I'm struggling to dream up a new topic. "Are there hobbies you'd like to do? What about starting the painting again?" God! I'm scraping the bottom of the barrel!

"Yeah, maybe...." She sounds bored. Her phone beeps. She forages through her bag and pulls the mobile out. "Sorry, I meant to put this on silent," she apologises. She nevertheless unlocks the device and reads the text that's just come in.

"Who is it?" I can't help but wonder if it's that guy. Is he the one texting her?

"Oh, it's just one of the school mums," she clicks off and flings the phone into her handbag.

There is silence again. I'm thinking of the other bloke. She's probably pre-occupied with his message, but it's not right for me to judge her. I've done the same thing with Kerry.

The evening drags on and we finally fall back on the subject of the kids, ignoring the counsellor's previous advice. It's better than being one of those couples who sit at restaurant tables with nothing to say.

After the meal, I notice a woman at the bar. Not bad looking. I realise it's that girl Zoe Waller. The one who used to be shacked up with Liam Fitzpatrick; it was that recent manslaughter case. The poor woman, her daughter died in that car accident. She's with another girl and they both look like they've had a few. I thought I recognised the other one for a moment but I can't place her. I excuse myself and tell Laura I need the bathroom. On my way, I make a point of walking past Zoe to say hello. I don't want it to look like I'm avoiding her.

"Hello Zoe."

She looks up. Her voice is slurred. "Oh hey Detective…" She's obviously forgotten my name.

"Are you okay?" I ask. It's not just that she's drunk. It looks like she's been taking something as well.

"I… fine…!" she slurs. "I…. fine…. I here with my friend…." She breaks off, as though she's forgotten her friend's name. The other girl looks as me with a wry smile. It dawns on me she's not bad looking either. Two hotties out on the town looking for a man.

"Mia," the friend interrupts, offering up her name with a gorgeous smile.

"I'm worried about Zoe," I motion to Mia. "I think we need to make sure she gets home safely.

She doesn't look in good shape. I don't think she should drink anymore considering what she's been through."

Zoe giggles and nudges Mia: "He's a cop, he's minding me."

"I'm just concerned for you Zoe." I repeat.

"I bumped into her in Castle Court," Mia explains. "We went for one drink but one led to another and now we're...."

Zoe giggles again but loses her balance and slides off the bar stool. Mia gasps and clasps her hand to her mouth. I automatically reach out to catch Zoe.

"Right, that's it," I declare, propping Zoe back on to the stool. "We're making sure you get home." I turn to Mia and say: "Look after her, will you? Make sure she's doesn't fall. I'll be back in two seconds..."

Mia nods deferentially, her eyes widened with shock. "Of course, no problem..."

"I just have to let my wife know what's happening." I interrupt as I move away hastily. I approach Laura with a look of determination and dread: "Laura," I flop down opposite her. "I'm worried about that woman at the bar. She was involved in the Fitzpatrick case. She's the one who lost her daughter. I think she's off her head. It looks like she's taken something. I think we should make sure she gets home safely."

Laura sighs. "Simon, it's not your responsibility to get her home. She's got a friend with her. Can't you phone one of the other officers on duty?"

"Yes, I'm going to do that now." I assure her. "I'm calling up a patrol car." I fish out my cellphone and ring the incident desk.

Whilst waiting to be transferred, I notice Laura has retrieved her mobile. I bet she's texting lover-boy; she's typing her reply with a smile on her lips.

CHAPTER THIRTY-SIX
Zoe

"HEY ZOE, JUST getting back to you about that Bangor trip? What about tomorrow morning? Mia x"

I look at Mia's text and my heart sinks. I really don't fancy traipsing around shops or lugging heavy bags onto trains; I feel too bloated for that. Perhaps I can entice her to the comfort of my own home instead.

My finger hovers over the reply button. How can I word this? I owe her a coffee and a bite to eat and it is my turn after all.

I type out a reply: *Sorry Mia, Feeling too exhausted to go to Bangor. Why not pop round here at twelve tomorrow and I'll throw lunch together? It's my shout x*

I hit the send button and await her reply. I'm worried that the sound of a "thrown together" lunch would put her off and she'll decide to go shopping with someone else, but my phone beeps with an immediate response.

"That'd be great! What's your address x"

I text back the address and postcode. I'll nip to the shops and buy something. I can hash up a salad and some warm ciabatta bread.

✧   ✧   ✧

IT'S THE FOLLOWING morning and I'm fussing around cleaning the apartment and go to the bother of getting dressed properly. Why should I care so much about what Liam's colleague thinks of me? But I do.

I set the kitchen table with cutlery and napkins and even stick a few flowers in a vase.

Mia arrives; all smiles. She looks spectacular as always. She's what everyone says about pregnant women; that they glow. With Mia, it's certainly true. Not in my case though; I'm just fat and frumpy.

"Come in! Come in!" I open the front door and stand back, giving her space to stroll inside.

"Oh, thank you!" she grins, putting one foot over the threshold. "Nice place," she observes, as she starts rubbernecking from the off.

"You think?" I ask, doubtfully. My flat is only a basic apartment. I assume she's just being polite.

"Yeah," she comments thoughtfully, as she walks around looking at all the photos on the walls.

"You and Liam?" she points at one in particular.

"Yep! A long time ago. We were a lot younger then!"

Liam looks fresh faced in the frame. I was slim and, dare I say it, a lot more attractive than I feel today.

"Lovely pic," she seems fixated. "You two have been together for quite some time?"

"Yeah, too long!" I joke. "Here, let me take your coat."

She shrugs it off her shoulders. Underneath, she's wearing a maternity dress that hugs her bump and outlines her gorgeously slim figure.

"Wow, I love the outfit." Suddenly I'm feeling very underdressed in my maternity jeans and flouncing top.

"Oh, thanks," she grins. "Treated myself to at least one nice bit of maternity gear."

"Come on through." I motion her to follow me into the kitchen.

She's still all eyes, looking around everywhere. She starts taking in the images stuck to the fridge door.

"More pics of you and Liam!" she gushes in a somewhat amused tone.

I follow her line of vision. It's the snapshot of us at Alton Towers. I was wearing Minnie Mouse ears for a laugh and Liam is standing behind me, his arms around my waist, grinning for the camera.

"Yeah, that was a great day," my voice is wistful.

"Some change to where he is now," she gives me a sympathetic look.

Her comment stings but I try not to react.

"Yeah, it sure is." I usher her to sit at the kitchen table. "Have a seat."

"This is lovely," she coos. She takes in the vase of flowers and the tabletop adorned with cutlery and a huge bowl of salad in the centre.

"Oh, it's nothing," I brush off her compliment. Surely, she couldn't find this meagre fare so lovely. She's just being overly polite and perhaps a touch insincere.

"I brought us a little something!" she suddenly gets back up from her chair and heads over to her bag. She produces a bottle of bubbly with a mischievous grin. "I'm sure one won't hurt us! They all say the occasional glass of wine during pregnancy is okay."

She doesn't need to convince me. I happily forage into the cupboard for glasses.

"Lovely jubbly!" I joke. She pops the bottle open effortlessly and I enjoy the comforting glug-glug-glug of the fizzy liquid splashing into the flutes.

"To babies," she clinks her glass with mine.

"To babies," I echo.

We tuck into the salad, forking mountains of lettuce and tomato onto our plates and tearing chunks of bread off the loaf in the centre.

"So," I begin. "Tell me a bit more about your man, then. You didn't really tell me much about him."

"Hmmph!" she makes a sound as she chews and considers my question.

"Well," she begins, "bit of a similar situation to you…"

I raise my eyebrows. "Oh yeah? Why's that?"

"Well, he's not really around much and I don't really have the financial support…"

"Oh, I'm sorry…" my mouth down-turns in sympathy.

She waves her hand away. "It's fine, it is what

it is…"

"I'm lucky with Liam…" I tell her, wanting to defend him.

She looks at me wide-eyed. "You are?"

"Yeah, I mean, I know he's locked up but he's so supportive emotionally. He's really excited about our baby coming. I know that when he gets out, he'll be a huge help." I smile contentedly, cradling my bump.

Mia knocks back another large mouthful of wine. "Isn't that a long time to wait though? Why would things be any better when he gets out?" she asks.

"I just feel it," I shrug. "He's getting clean and going to meetings, making the best of it inside. He's using the time to stay sober."

Mia nods but her eyes belie her. "I dunno Zoe, do they ever change, really?"

"I think so," I say adamantly. "Liam always tells me about people from the meetings, the ones that turn their lives around. They get a completely new lifestyle; prison is the wake-up call he needs."

She takes another swig. "Hmm," she sighs distractedly. She lifts the bottle and tops her glass up. "Fuck it, one more won't hurt," she laughs, and she tops mine up too.

"Zoe…" she begins, suddenly sounding very serious. "What did Liam tell you about that night? The night of the accident?"

I look at her blankly, not sure what she's getting at.

"Erm…" I root through my memories, trying to recall what Liam had told me. "He said that he popped in to the bar that night. Someone spiked his drink. He felt woozy when he was driving…" I break off, seeing the look of disbelief in Mia's eyes.

She shakes her head sadly.

"What? Did you see him come into the bar that night? Did someone spike his drink?"

She shrugs her shoulders. "I don't know," she answers simply. "I wasn't working a shift. Liam was off that day and so was I. Usually we're on the same rota together." A smug smile spreads across her face.

As I glance at her, I feel that the atmosphere has somehow changed. Why do I suddenly feel intimidated? Why is the air thick with tension all of a sudden? And what gives her the right to question me about that night?

"Did he mention a phone-call?" Mia asks, her tone heavy and serious.

"A phone call?" I repeat. I rack my brains. "Yeah, he might have said something about a phone call. Why?" My voice is shaky and my heart is hammering; my fingertips have gone cold.

A heavy silence follows and finally she says: "That was me. I phoned him."

She stares straight at me, her eyes defiant.

"You. Why?" I stammer.

"We had an argument on the phone." Now she's sounding silky smooth in the quiet tension of the moment.

"You were the phone-call?" I echo. My mind is all over the place. "You're the reason he got distracted…" My voice shakes. "You're the reason Emma's...."

"No," she asserts flatly. "It's not my fault. He's the one who was driving like a lunatic."

I push my chair back and take a large breath, trying to dispel a rising panic attack that begins to overwhelm my body.

"But..." I persist. "He said someone was screaming at him. Why were you screaming? Why were you so angry?"

Mia's eyes are piercing me but her expression is calm and deathly still. "He was supposed to be meeting me that night, Zoe. He had been seeing me all along. He is the father of my child too."

A veil of silence descends. The air between us is electric. Even though she confirms my worst fear, there's still that buffer of shock. Liam had been stringing along the pair of us, all this time. Hearing her say it is like a bullet between the eyes.

"No!" I shout. "No, no, no, no, no!" I stand up and pace across the kitchen. "No, you're lying!"

"I'm not, Zoe," she stands up and walks calmly towards me. "Your baby is going to have a sister and that sister is in here," she places her hands on her belly. Like she's taunting me.

"No! You lying bitch!" I bellow. All the rage and fury of the previous months has exploded inside me. "No!"

How right they are when they say there's nothing like a woman scorned. I'm not prepared for this; an unseen force takes over my body. It's as if a spirit enters my head and begins to acts with anger and venom. I don't recognise myself.

Suddenly, I'm hitting her, slapping her hard across the face. Her hair is whiplashing sideways as she tries to dodge me. Then she starts slapping me back. A bitch-fest of hate playing out on my kitchen floor. All the anger and deceit that we've both endured boils to a crescendo.

But I don't expect her to reach for a knife. I didn't think she would zone in on the colourful knife-block. It sits next to the kettle; a collection of green, yellow and red blades. Her hand snakes out, but instead of whipping toward me, it darts sideways, and there, in her hand is my kitchen knife. Somehow, she has grabbed it without me noticing and, the next thing, she's holding it up to my neck.

The air catches in my windpipe as I stand there defenceless, watching those hate-filled eyes and feeling the sharp tip of the blade closing in on my throat.

My breathing is short and sharp. "Please, no," I beg. Her hand trembles; the cold metal quivering on my neck. "Please don't do this, Mia," I whisper. "You can have him. Take the bastard. He was yours anyway."

You can tell any lie at all, if you're grovelling for your life and adrenaline is coursing through you. "He's only using me," I plead. "I'm like his mother. You're his lover."

Her eyes flicker in recognition, as though this statement rings true with her. At the very least, I know it's something she wants to believe. I can sense her hand slightly loosening its grip on the knife.

"You're right," she murmurs. "That's the way it is."

Her breathing slows as she steps back and allows the knife to fall down by her side. It clatters to the tiles. The sudden rage has left her system. It's as if she's suddenly aware of what she's just done.

She steps back and exhales loudly. "My god, I don't know what came over me just then."

"That's okay Mia," I say softly. I need to calm her down; to prevent another brainstorm. I kick the knife across the floor out of sight. I step towards her slowly, scared that any sudden movement will make her flare up again. Thankfully, she slumps down placidly onto the chair.

"Fuck!" she exclaims and starts sobbing softly. She puts her elbows on the table and cups her face in her hands. Now I have her exactly where I want her. Just as I'd planned it.

In one quick, fluid movement, I swipe the largest knife from the block, the one I had prepared for easy access. Before she has any time to think twice, I put my left hand under her chin, pulling her head up. I'm like a demon possessed and fired with adrenaline. I press the serrated edge of the blade against her throat.

"You bitch" I seethe. "You've had this coming to you for a long time."

CHAPTER THIRTY-SEVEN

Zoe

"ZOE, NO PLEASE," Mia begs. "Please don't do this."

The tables have turned. The knife is in my hand; the sharp metal blade lined across her neck.

"Oh, you can dish it out, but you can't take it, is that it?" My voice has taken on a mimicking sneer. It's like there's somebody else inside me; somebody that even I don't recognise.

"I'm sorry, I'm sorry," Mia tries to wriggle in the chair but I've pinned her against it with the weight of my body.

"Please put the knife down!" she begs again.

"And why should I?" I press the blade even harder against her skin. She sucks in a sharp intake of breath. I'm grasping her jaw so tight, she's barely able to wheeze.

"After everything you've done to us?" I hiss. "If you hadn't phoned Liam that night, he wouldn't have had the accident." I squeeze the razor-sharp edge against the skin of her slender neck. "If there'd been no accident, Emma would be alive!" I press the knife even harder. I'm buzzing with adrenaline. Her skin breaks easily and a stream of blood trickles down her neck. She's quivering now, trembling with fear. Tears well up in her eyes.

She's knows it's the end.

"And if you hadn't been fucking Liam behind my back, you wouldn't be in this position." The glinting tongue of metal slices deeper. Her scream dissipates into a whoosh of air as the knife slices her windpipe. Blood is now gushing down her neck like a river; a steady stream of glistening red. Her body flops onto the table. As I draw the knife through flesh, blood starts pumping out with every heartbeat.

It's like I'm outside of myself, as though my body has floated up to the ceiling and I'm watching the scene unfold beneath me. Mia is slumped over the table, her head swimming in a puddle of blood. I'm the one standing in shock, knife in hand. Blood has spurted everywhere. It has licked along the walls and spots have even flecked the ceiling. It's as if a carefree artist has flung an open can of red paint onto a blank canvas, creating a delightful array of patterns.

The spatter has even reached the fridge door. A spume of pillar box red has sprayed the photo of Liam and me. Spots of blood are dotted along my Minnie Mouse ears and I can see Liam smiling behind me through a mist of wet blood.

I stand there panting, realising what I've just done. I'm in the middle of a bloodbath.

This is what people must mean about being in a blackout. A sudden surge of anger and then – bam! It's all over. All the fury has left me and now I'm standing here, feeling incredibly calm. No more fight left in me. I'm exhausted, spent.

I suppose I'd better dial 999. I hear the word "Police." I realise it's me speaking. I'm on automatic, devoid of feeling. "There's been an accident. There's a woman lying dead in the middle of my kitchen." I keep my eyes on the photo of Liam and me.

I've done this for you Liam. To protect us.

Mia took Emma, she's not going to take me. It's self-defence.

"Yes, I did it. I killed her." My voice sounds too calm. The woman on the other end of the phone is trained to remain composed but I can tell she's shocked.

"You say you killed her madam?" she repeats.

"Yes, of course." I confirm. "I had to. It was self-defence. She's already killed my first child."

I imagine that they'll play this recording back. They'll use it in one of those true crime documentaries on TV one day. Maybe they'll call me the *Pregnant Knife Lady.*

"She killed your first child?" 999 lady parrots back.

"Yes, that's right," I respond serenely. "I was protecting myself and the baby. I'm pregnant."

Suddenly, I feel tired. I pull out a chair and sit down. I reach across to my wine glass. Might as well have a sip.

It doesn't take long for the police to turn up. I can hear the sirens and see the flashing blue lights swirling around my kitchen as cars pull up outside. They surge in, full of energy. They start asking questions and the paramedics are fussing around Mia. Suddenly the apartment is full of noise and drama. A green stretcher and a squad of uniforms. I sit calmly, answering each question one by one.

"Yes, I did it."

"It was self-defence."

"She killed my first child."

"She pulled the knife on me first."

I look over at the photo of me and Liam. We'll both be in prison now.

Together, forever.

Wasn't that what we promised each other? In sickness and in health. For richer, for poorer.

Till death do us part.

CHAPTER THIRTY-EIGHT

Kerry

STANDING OUTSIDE THE office on the third floor, I tap the glass and wait patiently for Dr McKay to rise from his desk and open the door. Who'd have thought I'd be back here again so quickly. He greets me with a kindly smile.

"Sergeant Lawlor," his voice is soft and reverent. "We meet again."

"Yes," I acknowledge politely. "I have my colleague with me this time," I motion needlessly to Simon standing next to me.

"Good to meet you sir," Simon stretches out his hand confidently. "I'm Detective Chief Inspector Simon Peters."

The doctor smiles warmly and nods his head in a demure, professional fashion. "Please come in." He ushers us towards the two chairs which are positioned opposite his desk.

As we settle ourselves down, I take a glance around his office. The sun is streaming through the windows casting a beam of light on a plant in the corner. A few fusty-looking hard backed books are lined along the book shelf behind him. There is a calmness and serenity about this space. It's a world away from the noise and din of our detective's den.

He locates a dog-eared folder from his filing cabinet and flicks it open. "So, the Matthews murder case. It's undoubtedly linked to the Liam Fitzpatrick manslaughter file?" He launches straight in, wasting no time as usual.

"Yes, that's right," Simon interjects. "It's now become the Zoe Waller and Mia Matthews incident. It's officially a related case."

Dr McKay nods and puts on his spectacles. "Yes, I've had a few sessions with Zoe Waller since your initial phone call." He shakes his head sadly. "I've made an assessment on her in relation to the incident."

"Thank you, doctor," I say eagerly. "We're keen to have your opinion. The problem we're having is this: initially, there seemed to be no doubt what had happened – Mia Matthews was murdered. However, the accused, Zoe Waller, is convinced it was self-defence."

Simon interrupts at this point. "That's not what the crime scene suggests though. The evidence tells us that it was a pre-planned murder. That's why we need your assessment. Can we charge Zoe Waller with murder? Or was it diminished responsibility due to mental illness or self-defence?"

At this point, I can't help cutting in, "It's quite clear from the crime scene that Zoe Waller attacked Matthews from behind with a large serrated kitchen knife. Matthews was trapped in the chair, seated, while Zoe was pinning her against the table from behind, knife in hand. There was an incision to the windpipe and the

deceased bled to death in about sixty seconds."
I'm leaning on the edge of the desk, gesticulating
gently as I speak. I'm aware I probably come
across as rather animated but I'm dying to get to
the bottom of this.

Simon nods in agreement and continues de-
picting the incident, "There was another knife on
the scene though, which bore the fingerprints of
both women. It was lying out of range of the
blood spatter on the kitchen floor. It could have
been part of the action but that's unlikely. It was
used to cut some bread that was on the table."

"Yes, I understand the ladies were having a
little lunch party just before the event." Dr McKay
had obviously read the file in detail prior to our
meeting.

"And there's another loose end." I add intently. "The deceased, Mia Matthews, had a sealed
phial of diamorphine in her handbag. This must
have been illegal use. She had no prescription for
it and there was no medical reason for possessing
it. In fact, she was pregnant too, so there would
certainly be huge risks if she was using. Perhaps
she had procured it from a dealer for someone
else. Maybe she was planning to transport it to
Liam Fitzpatrick in prison."

"What sort of quantity are we talking about
here?" Dr McKay butts in courteously.

"Fifty milligrams, enough to do damage,"
Simon advises.

"Yes," I agree. "Although the phial was sealed
and there's no direct link with the possession of
Matthews' drug and the actions of Zoe Waller."

Dr McKay leans back in his chair and rests his head in his hand, deep in thought. "I'm just wondering about the mental condition of Mia. Up to now, we've only appraised the mental state of Zoe but Mia's state of mind may also be relevant. We know that she had a burner phone in her bag and the only person who took calls was Liam."

"How would that affect your point of view?" Simon interjects.

"You mentioned that she was pregnant as well. I read on file that Liam Fitzpatrick is the father in both cases. It seems Mia was living a secret life and carrying Liam's baby; a man committed to another woman – Zoe. An obvious link to motive perhaps?"

"Yes, we think that's motive taken care of," Simon agrees. "Both girls were eighteen to twenty weeks pregnant to the same man. The evidence tells us that Mia Matthews was an innocent victim taken by surprise. Zoe Waller appears to have attacked and killed Matthews while the latter was seated and defenceless. This was intentional homicide by Waller."

I signal agreement. "Zoe must have used considerable strength to execute this crime so efficiently. It's just that, with her state of mind, we don't know to what extent it was intentional or deliberate. We checked the cell phones of both women. It's clear that Zoe Waller invited Matthews to the premises."

Simon bobs his head. "Therefore, the degree of intent is open to question. Was it pre-planned prior to the invitation or just an off the cuff reaction following an argument?"

The psychiatrist clears his throat and clasps his hands together. "I've interviewed Zoe Waller several times since she was arrested. It's clear she has a very serious case of post-traumatic stress disorder. Not surprising really. Her six-year-old daughter died at the hands of her partner and she's now a pregnant woman with her other half in prison. She already had some anxiety problems before Emma was killed. That event only served to trigger the mental illness."

"Sounds like a full murder charge wouldn't stick, then," Simon surmises.

"Are we looking at diminished responsibility?" I probe.

The doctor looks down at his file again, as though carefully considering his response. "The depth of her disorder was obviously worsened when she found out that Mia was also pregnant to Liam. The girls were obviously rivals."

He gets up from his chair and walks to the window, glancing out at the view as he thinks aloud. "A person gripped by a psychotic disorder is highly motivated and draws on an inner strength. Arranging for the victim to be seated in that position and having a knife to hand would have been plain-sailing for someone in her state of mind. The only question is whether she planned the whole thing beforehand or was it merely spontaneous? In the latter case, something in their conversation may have triggered the event and the end of Mia Matthews' life. Perhaps that was the point Mia announced her pregnancy?"

"There's another little issue that the forensics pointed out," Simon adds. "Some of the victim's hair had been tugged out at the roots. An indication that there was a fight beforehand."

"Or perhaps Zoe pulled Mia's head up by the hair before she grabbed her jaw, setting her up for the cut," the doctor poses. "Either way, I have to tell you that Zoe Waller is very seriously mentally ill and has been ever since the Ravenhill car accident."

"So, you think she's able to plead diminished responsibility?" I press again.

He holds his palms upwards in consideration. "What I think is that she's not fit for trial. Right now, she's living on a different planet. In a world where she's in the midst of happy families with Liam Fitzpatrick, their new baby on the way, she floats in and out of a life where sometimes Emma is still alive and sometimes not. The irony is that maybe Mia Matthews was having problems as well. Perhaps that's why she was carrying the diamorphine."

I rest my head in my hands in contemplation. "There is one big difference; Mia Matthews ended up dead by Zoe Waller's hand. That's the difference between them."

CHAPTER THIRTY-NINE
Zoe (then)

I SAT IN the swimming pool café nursing a cappuccino and watching Liam and Emma in the pool. The smell of chlorine was actually comforting. It was our happy place, where Emma and Liam bonded; no distracting parties or drugs, just good, clean fun.

A siren started up and an excited cheer rose among the kids. They knew what that sound meant; the wave machine had been turned on. Soon they would all be bobbing about and laughing frantically.

That's when I spotted her; the woman to my side. She had dark sunglasses propped on her head and a paperback in her hand. I could actually feel her presence before I noticed her; I sensed she was watching me.

I stared over and she smiled.

"They love those waves, don't they?" I ventured.

"Yes, they do," she agreed, curtly.

"Which one's yours?" I asked.

She didn't reply immediately. She seemed thrown by my question. "Oh, not sure you can see him." She pointed towards a group of children. "I think he keeps dodging under the waves."

"Oh right."

It seemed she was discouraging conversation; should I continue this small talk or leave her alone? As if reading my thoughts, she snapped her book shut and stood up.

"Have a good day," she quipped tersely.

"I will!" I was full of the joys of spring. I knew I was going to have a good day, Liam was clean and sober, doing his meetings and back on track. We would go home, have a takeaway and cuddle up on the sofa watching a movie; just a perfect day.

But I couldn't get that woman out of my head. Something didn't gel; there was something odd about her, something distinctly unnerving.

I half expected to bump into her outside the changing rooms, to see her hand-in-hand with her little boy. I wondered if her child would chat to Emma; a new friend.

But she just vanished.

Looking back, I knew it was Mia, with a wig on, stalking us. I'd had that awful sense that she was watching all the time. Liam maintained it was paranoia. He said I just needed to speak to the doctor and get him to up my medication, but I was adamant. Maybe that's the first time the plan came into my mind.

If I wouldn't go to the GP, Liam said I should at least talk to a counsellor, to off-load this permanent paranoia. But I didn't want to talk about my recent behaviour; it was my own little stalking secret. There were nights I drove slowly past Liam's work, crawling along the kerb at a snail's pace. I parked the car in such a way that I could watch what was going on in the pub without anyone being able to see me. Emma sat quietly in the back seat, my accomplice on a detective mission.

I saw him chatting away to one of the bar maids; her head tilting back, a laugh escaping from her throat. I recognised her face. It was definitely Mia; the girl from the swimming pool, minus the wig. Now, her glossy hair was billowing down her back like something out of a shampoo commercial. He used to make me laugh like that. A long time ago.

That old, ugly emotion rose in my chest; the green-eyed monster – a jealous, envious rage. There was a desire to seek revenge, to destroy her. But my revenge would come slowly; over time; with plenty of preparation. A recipe of time, patience and a brightly coloured knife-block.

Liam was living with Gaz at the time but when we arrived home from the pool, we persuaded him to stay for a while. I phoned for a Chinese takeaway and Emma curled up next to him on the sofa.

"It's on the way!" I announced cheerily, hanging up.

"Great! Switch on the TV and I'll warm the plates!" Liam enthused.

The three of us sat on the sofa, trays on our laps, tucking into the sweet and sour Cantonese.

"Dee-lish!" Liam cheered triumphantly.

"Fab-u-lous daddy!" Emma giggled happily.

My heart soared. It was just the three of us. A

happy family. The way it should be.

Deep down inside, I believed this was the way it was always going to be. Liam and I would grow old and grey together. Like those romantic films where the couple always end up in each other's arms in the final scene.

Shacked up with Gaz, I knew he'd move back home eventually. He'd soon party himself out, get bored and come back to the fold. That was certain.

Later, I crept upstairs to the bathroom, passing Emma's room. Liam sat on the edge of the bed reading to Emma, while she was tucked up, her eyes drooping shut. My heart melted.

That's why I chose to do it; the thing I did next.

I went into the bedroom and opened my bedside drawer. I lifted out the packet of condoms inside. Sliding one out of the pack, I took a pin in the other hand. I deftly pricked the condom as many times as I dared. Then set the package back.

When Liam came downstairs a while later, I held up my glass to him and smiled. "You don't mind me having a drink, do you?"

"Of course not." He slumped down beside me on the couch." The difference between us is you can take one glass and leave it. If I have just one, the bottle would be down my neck in ten minutes. I don't fancy a hangover tomorrow."

I looked at him with admiration. "You're doing so well, Liam. I'm proud of you."

At that moment, he looked at me the way he used to, giving me that seductive smile and curling an arm around me.

I nuzzled in to him and whispered, "If you're too tired to head back to Gaz's, you can stay here if you want."

Later, as we lay in bed, I put my little plan into action. My leg draped over his. I had gone to bed naked; my taut breasts and warm thighs rubbed against him. We both knew which buttons to press, and we pressed them.

"What about a condom?" he groaned. He was now impatient, dying to plunge into me.

I leaned aside and opened the bedside drawer. I retrieved the prepared condom. I mumbled about how hard he was while I slipped it sensuously over his penis. Our bodies locked together.

I always believed things would turn out for the best. I knew he'd come home eventually, that we'd always be a couple. If not before, definitely when our second child came along. I could picture Liam and Emma playing happily with our new baby.

I thought back to those early days, when Liam chased me. Picked me out from all the other girls. We were destined to be together, forever.

Nobody would ever come between us.

THE END

Printed in Great Britain
by Amazon